Dew in the Morning

Dew in the Morning

Shimmer Chinodya

Published by
Weaver Press, Box A1922, Avondale, Harare. 2019
<www.weaverpresszimbabwe.com>

First published by Mambo Press, Gweru, 1982.
Reprinted 2001
This second edition, Weaver Press, 2019

© Photograph of Shimmer Chinodya, Weaver Press,
Typeset by Weaver Press
Cover Design: Weaver Press
Printed by Rocking Rat, Harare.
Distributed in South Africa by Jacana Media.

ISBN 978-1-77922-351-7 (p/b)
ISBN 978-1-77922-352-4 (e-pub)

Shimmer Chinodya (1957) was born in Gweru, the second child in a large, happy family. He studied English Literature and Education at the University of Zimbabwe. After a spell teaching and with curriculum development, he earned an MA in Creative Writing the Iowa Writers' Workshop (USA).

His first novel, *Dew in the Morning* was followed by *Farai's Girls* (1984), *Child of War* (under the pen name B. Chirasha, 1986), *Harvest of Thorns* (1989), *Can We Talk and other stories* (1998), *Tale of Tamari* (2004), *Chairman of Fools* (2005), *Strife* (2006), *Tindo's Quest* (2011), *Chioniso and other stories* (2012) and *Harvest of Thorns Classic: A Play* (2016). His work appears in numerous anthologies. Chinodya has also written educational texts and manuals, and radio and film scripts, including one for the feature film, *Everyone's Child (1996)*. He has won many awards, including the Commonwealth Writers Prize (Africa Region) for *Harvest of Thorns*, a Caine Prize shortlist for *Can we Talk* and the NOMA award for Publishing in Africa for *Strife*. He has also won awards from ZIWU, ZBPA and NAMA, and has received many fellowships abroad. From 1995-97, he was Distinguished Dana Professor in Creative Writing and African Literature at the University of St Lawrence in upstate New York.

1

Jairos

We arrived just before sunset, and by the time we had finished unpacking the lorry it had grown dark and the dew was already falling on the grass. That night the moonlight fell on the village huts and the leaves, and the metal of the lorry gleamed in the night. All the things had been brought down from the back of the lorry and lay in a confused heap.

I could hear my father talking in low tones to the village headman and somewhere in the night an owl hooted. At last we went to sleep. We simply threw mattresses and blankets on the ground and lay down, with the big yellow moon above us.

We woke up to a fine blue morning. The doves were cooing and somewhere in the forest strange birds were heralding the morning:

"Alu – Alu
Oro Wani
Alu
Oro Wani
Alu"

Very soon we were running about, finding pleasure in twigs, leaves, grass and fruit and hacking away at the undergrowth like wood-starved animals with our shiny little axes.

We finally managed to make a rough wooden sledge, on which we took turns to sit and push each other over the sand. Having gone quite far along the path and needing water to drink, we asked a small boy we saw to direct us to the village pump. The boy touched his rubber catapult and fingered his fine long bark whip and stared at us.

"We want some water," said Yona. "Where is the village pump?"

"You left it behind you," said the boy in a dialect slightly different from ours, but pleasant to listen to.

"Is it far?" asked Jo.

"No," said the boy, cracking his whip loudly on the sand. "You can come with me to our huts if you want water."

We followed the boy across the clearing towards the closest of three squat huts. Inside the hut a young woman sat dozing in the afternoon heat. She had thick dark knots of plaited hair and had taken off her blouse. A little baby-boy nestled in her arms, barely shielding his mother's breasts. The hut was small and black with the smoke of a thousand fires. The roof was low, black like the walls, and from it dangled axes, cooking sticks, strips of oxhide and some strange objects. The smell of cowdung rose from the newly polished mud-floor, where a three-legged pot lay on its side, cakes of dry sadza matted on its insides. There were a few dirty plates in disorder on top of a built-in earth shelf, a wooden mortar and a grinding stone. The boy handed us water in a gourd, and while we were drinking, the baby pushed his head into his mother's belly and butted her like a calf. She protested, pushing her nipple into his mouth. He did not suck. He plucked his mouth away from her and yelled, leaving a ring of moisture round her nipple.

"A! A!" she protested again, slapping the boy on the tummy. Then, turning to us, "Hello. Are you the new family?"

"Yes," replied Yona. "How do you do?"

"Thank you for the water," I said, as we stood to go.

"No need to thank me," laughed the woman, her white teeth flashing. "Now, what can you eat? Give them some *mazhanje* from under the granary, Tani."

"Thank you," said Yona, "but we have to go."

"What! You won't have mazhanje? Perhaps you people from the towns don't eat fruit. Why? Why? Perhaps your mother does not want you to eat in people's houses. All right then."

I would have liked to have the fruit, but Yona had already declined, so we had to go. The dwarf hut with its smoke-blackened walls, warm smoky smell and half dressed occupants gave me a strange sense of freedom. When we got outside Jo started talking to the boy and asked him for his whip. "But do you have cattle?" asked the boy, giving him the whip, however.

"We don't herd cattle in town."

"So you live in the town?"

"Yes. We come here only during school-holidays."

"You go to school," he grimaced. "Teachers beat people."

"Not if you do your best."

"I think they would break my body."

"Are you going after your cattle now?"

"Yes. I might lose them and they might go off and eat somebody's mealies and then I'd be in trouble."

"Have you ever lost them?"

"Only once. They ate an old man's crops. The old man hid in a bush. He caught me and whipped me."

"Oh."

"Hyenas might eat the cattle too."

"Do hyenas eat people?"

"Only drunk old men with too much mucus in their noses. Hyenas love mucus."

🔥 🔥 🔥

Before he left for the town father found a man to build our huts and instructed the village headman to give us a temporary piece of land to farm.

After four days the huts were finished and we moved into them. We helped mother build a long bench of beaten clay round the inside of the hut and an earthen shelf for the pots and plates. We cleared a square patch round the huts and planted flowers in neat rows. Village women frequently stopped to admire our flowers on their way to the water-pump.

Jairos, the village headman, came frequently to see us. He was a thin man in his fifties. His head was small and round and bald, the only hair on his face being his twisted moustache. He wore khaki clothes normally worn by people in the Civil Service and these were going brown with too little washing. He spoke so avidly about everything that whoever listened to him had to stay clear of the globules of saliva that shot from his mouth. When he smiled, he exposed a fine set of teeth stained grey with four decades of tobacco. He had been introduced to money and gin early on, and, having taken a great liking to these things, would do anything to obtain them. There was a funny atmosphere about him – something of the dreamy optimism which believed that things would come out well in the end no matter how bad they got. He seemed quite lazy too: he would get a little boy to scratch his arm for him if he could. A few days after our arrival he had asked me to build a framework for his fowl-run for the small fee of a coin. Mother had laughingly stopped me from displaying any of my expertise. Jairos further had an irremediable habit of confusing our names and no matter how hard we tried to set him right, he continued to make the mistakes until we gave up and were compelled to turn up, all three of us, when he called one of us.

He was very fond of tea and sugar and bread and margarine. Unfortunately, he could not afford regular provisions of these himself, so he made himself our regular guest at meal-times. He would put as many as twelve spoons of sugar in one cup of tea and when sadza and meat were placed in front of him he ate all the meat first.

Eventually he grew bold enough to serve himself from the meatpot. One day he brought a young girl with him. He proceeded to occupy an empty chair and rolled himself a cigarette while the girl sat cross-legged on the floor.

"Maziziva," he said to my mother, "I have promised so often to show you my daughter. Unfortunately, her mother has kept her busy most of the time. My conscience has been nagging me until today I finally decided to bring her over. Well, here she is."

"What is your name, girl?" mother asked with a smile as she put some food in front of Jairos.

"Her name is Lucia," Jairos announced. "You can call her Lulu."

Lulu declined to eat, it being bad manners to eat in strangers'

4

homes on the first visit. She had a smooth light skin, long dark hair and narrow features.

"But I thought your oldest girl was married," said mother, puzzled.

"My oldest girl with my first wife – yes," explained Jairos, munching away at a bone. "My first wife died long back, of pneumonia, if you want to know."

"Does Lulu go to school?"

" Not yet. She will go as soon as I get the money."

"But when will that be? The years will not be waiting. How old is she?"

"Let's see,'" said Jairos, putting his spoon away for a while to ponder. Then, with a fresh burst of confidence, "How old are you, Lulu? What! You don't know how old you are! Come on, tell Masiziva your age."

"But you don't know yourself. Headman Jairos," teased mother, "perhaps she is not your daughter."

"O yes, she is," Jairos protested. "Can't you see that she is so much like me? All her features came from me. Only her toes came from her mother. I don't have big toes like that!"

"You still haven't told us when she was born," persisted mother.

"O yes. I remember. She was born when the road from the town reached this village. The mealies were tasselling…"

"That doesn't tell us what year it was."

"O Masiziva," he said, throwing the bone down abandoningly in mocked exasperation. "You are such a scrutiniser."

He finished eating and I held up a dish of water for him to wash his hands. When he saw me collecting the dishes to wash outside he looked alarmed.

"What, Masiziva! You make your boys wash the dishes!"

"What can I do, Headman Jairos? My girls are still too young."

"Well, then get a girl to do the washing up. Come on, Lulu, my girl. Help Godi wash Masiziva's dishes."

In the end Lulu helped me to wash the dishes, outside the kitchen. We worked quietly, until Jairos came out and went away with her.

I met Lulu again at the pump a few days later and she agreed to go picking *mazhanje* with me.

"The forest is dangerous," sang Jo, when I ran back home to fetch an empty flour bag.

"A man got lost there for a week," sang Yona.

"Godi and Lulu have become fast friends already, smiled mother.

"We won't get lost, mother. Lulu knows the forest like her mother's hut."

"All right, bring us back some fruit."

We found a lot of fruit in the forest just outside the village. The fruit lay thickly under the tree, like brown eggs waiting to be picked up, and it pained me to think that a lot of it would rot on the ground uncollected. Lulu knew the delicious trees and we filled our containers from them. We eventually came to a shallow clear stream. It was a shady place, with branches of trees from opposite banks entwining above the stream. I could see small fish darting on the sand at the bottom of the stream.

Lulu took off her dress and waded in. I followed slowly. I couldn't swim, so I gulped and gasped and choked, paddling madly like a dog, with the water thundering all round me while she wrung her hands in laughter. My stomach was soon full of water. After the swim we lay on the grass drying in the sun, like two wet fish, and soon fell asleep. When I woke up Lulu was putting on her clothes. The sun was low in the sky and the birds were flying home to roost. I put on my clothes, too. We took our fruit and made our way home hurriedly.

〰〰〰

As soon as Jairos got us a small plot of land we started planting our crops. Matudu, the man who built our huts, came to plough our field with his fine pair of oxen. We followed behind the plough, dropping the seeds into neat brown furrows and savouring the smell of the oxen and newly turned earth. The seeds soon germinated, small and tender in the dew. We rose early in the blue-grey dawn to the shouts of the ploughboys and the bustle of yoking the oxen. We walked across the glistening green, dew-laden grass to the fields. While the sun steadily ascended the sky, getting hotter, we sweated in the fields. Our backs ached and the hot sand burnt our feet, and the hoe handles cut blisters on our hands. We drank *maheu*, worked again, then went home for a late breakfast. As we went home tiredly at noon we usually met herdboys bringing home the cows to be milked.

We usually returned to the field late in the afternoon, when it became cool, to put in a few more hours of work. After supper we read for an hour or two in the lamplight before going to bed. The nights were short it seemed, just when we were settling into the comfortable sleep of the early hours, dawn sent mother, hoe in hand, rapping on our door.

To break this routine of work and rest, we decided to go fishing on Thursdays and Sundays. We sat on the bank of the stream pushing the slimy, wriggling worms onto the hooks so that blood burst out and the worms dangled hopelessly, to a drowned death as we threw the lines into the water. For hours we sat watching our corks for any promising ripples. But the fish did not bite. We would whip the lines out of the water only to find the worms still dangling from the hooks without the slightest nibble taken from them.

By sunset, long after the worms had withered and broken into threads, we had still caught nothing. The frogs started croaking from the reeds.

"Go –

Go –

Go –

Go home.

Go home. You've – caught – no – fish

No – fish –"

We collected our things and hurried home in the dusk. Sunset had come suddenly upon us. There was no moon and the darkness fell quickly, so that we strained our eyes to see the path. We found mother waiting for us anxiously at the village-pump.

"What are you doing at the stream after sunset? Don't you know you can drown? And walking in the darkness too – don't you know there are snakes and hyenas here? I'll have to stop you from going to the river if you continue like this. How much have you caught anyway?"

Twice more we failed to catch any fish. Each time we went to he river in high spirits, mother having convinced us that it was the best weather for fishing. All day we sat quietly, watching the water, hoping. A dirty old man in rags often fished beside us. We watched him enviously while he hooked fish after fish from the stream. In the end we felt that the stream was favouring the old man because he was old and ragged and poor. Eventually, he asked us to show him one of our lines. He took my line between his long, uncut fingernails, and as I knelt in front of him I saw his ribs showing through his chest. He adjusted my cork and gave me back the line.

Feverishly, I pushed a fresh worm onto the hook and threw the line into the water. Almost immediately, the cork darted forward.

"Pull," said the old man.

I felt the weight on the hook and whipped the line out of the water. The fish broke out of the water and flew towards me, its silver skin shining in the sun. It was only a small fish, but big enough to make us wild with joy. Jo rushed to where it flapped on the grass. He lifted it between his finger and thumb and danced with joy, while the old man's face broke into a pink, toothless smile.

Yona and Jo adjusted their hooks too and we caught a lot of fish. We went home with a heavy tin and were heroes that evening. Mother could not believe we had caught them. She thought that the old man had given them to us.

🌺🌺🌺

On the evening when we had returned late from the stream, mother had warned about the presence of snakes and hyenas, and we soon got our first experience of these animals.

Among the snakes, our biggest visitor was spotted by mother while she was clearing a patch of ground in front of our huts for sweet potatoes. She screamed, hurled down her hoe and bolted out of the grass, stumbling in her gum-boots.

A Man happened to be passing by, and, hearing her scream, came hurriedly towards us. He took one peep in the grass, shook his head and let out a long, low whistle. He cursed and spat at the snake as if to disarm it, and then picked up a long, thick stick. As he inched forward in the grass I took one step forward.

I felt my whole body shaking. I wanted to hide my fingers. The snake was cool black with a rough skin matted with grey scales that glimmered in the sun. It was as thick as a child's leg and inside its small, terrible head its beady yellow eyes twinkled menacingly, too small for its body. Behind its head ran a mane of erect spikes. It looked to me like some long ugly black fish which had slithered out of a murky pond; on seeing it I was quite ready to believe that creatures such as dragons existed.

I was beginning to think it was dead, when it made a slight movement with its back, as if poising itself for a strike. The ugly head opened, and out shot its tongue. But the man was too quick for it. His stick came down again and again on the frantic wriggling in the grass, with a sound like wood hitting rubber till at last, squeaking like a giant mouse, the snake rolled into bloodless death.

After burning the snake with grass and paraffin, and washing his hands of the event, the man went away in heavy silence.

That same morning when we had scarcely recovered from the shock of the snake, Lulu came running breathlessly to tell us that hyenas had attacked and killed one of her father's cows which was about to calve.

The attack had occurred deep in the forest, under the great, shadowy trees. We saw the mutilated remains of the cow from afar. Its huge belly had been torn open and was almost empty. The intestines and liver and other parts had been removed and the ribs jutted out like a wooden framework.

The big balls of the eyes were open, the pink nose half buried in the earth. As we stood back out of the way of the gusts that blew from the carcass, I tried to imagine the bellowing that had emitted from the frothy mouth as its belly was pierced and the liquid calf torn out of its womb by sharp carnivorous teeth. I tried to envisage the vain kicking of the legs as the bright red blood gushed out of the torn flesh and spilled onto the thirsty hot sand.

They chopped the remains into sizeable chunks and threw them into the cart, hides and all. They chattered frivolously as they went away, accepting the loss and now thinking of the meat.

"There is half a cartload of meat," Jairos explained to my mother after the salvage. "You can have a lot of it if you want. In this village we don't charge anything for meat like that. What, you won't have any of it, eh?"

◊◊◊

Mother was packing our trunks, and had to stop this to make Jairos a cup of tea.

"So who will look after your crops while you are away in town, Masiziva?"

"I am only taking the boys to school. I will come back in a week."

"Bring some old newspapers for my tobacco when you come back. And tell your father to buy me two bottles of gin."

On the morning of our departure the sky was clear and everything took its normal course, as if we were a negligible part of the village. But somehow the trees seemed taller and greener, the dew glossier on the grass, and I knew nostalgia was descending on us even before we left the village.

Lulu came with us to the bus stop, admiring our clothes. I did not think I looked my best. My trousers fell into generous folds below my knees and swept the ground. I frequently took off my shoes to shake the sand out of them. My white shirt blew into a balloon behind my back. I wanted to tell Lulu that my best clothes had been left in town.

We got to the bus terminus and eventually the battered old yellow bus arrived. In the flurry of carrying things into the bus and the crisis of finding a seat I forgot to wave goodbye to Lulu.

◊◊◊

"It's a virgin land," father kept explaining to the many townsfolk who came to ask about our new country home. "It's a young land with lots of wide-open spaces and good soil."

"I hear there are donkeys and no cattle in your home area," taunted a next-door boy, licking an ice cream.

"That's not true," I said, "there are lots of cattle and sheep and goats as well."

"I hear there are tsetse flies, too."

"Not any more. The tsetse teams pushed the insects down to the great valley."

"But it's quite a bushy place, isn't it, with no roads and only a few scruffy huts?"

"There are still a lot of bushy areas of course, but. . ."

"And you have to walk miles to get your water."

"Not at all. The village pump is only two hundred paces from our compound."

"That's still very far, if one wants to have a decent bath. What are your houses like?"

"They are not exactly houses. They are huts, made of poles and grass."

"And those accounts of the snake and the hyenas the teacher read to us from your composition. Are they true?"

"Yes."

"And the villagers collected the remains of the cow and ate them?"

"Yes."

"And you ate the meat too?"

"No, only the Headman and his family ate the meat."

"I don't believe you. There are no butcheries there and you couldn't afford to leave it alone. You probably ate it too."

He didn't finish the sentence. I hit him hard on the mouth and he threw the ice-cream away, howling loudly, fingering his swelling lips. I felt my anger subsiding quickly into remorse and even fear. Eventually his mother came out to take him away. Exaggerating the degree of his injury, I felt like a murderer. Of course he did not die, and when he recovered and we became friends again I wondered how I could have felt any remorse towards him after the unforgivable insults.

"And will you be going to savage land this April?" teased the boy again towards the end of the term. I did not hit him. When I replied in the affirmative he asked me playfully to bring him some nuts.

2

Madora

April holidays in the country are fun. Everywhere there is a sense of ripeness. The grass, at one time short and sprouting out of the black-burnt plains of October, is then fully grown. The trees seem to dance in a khaki sea of it. Many varieties of fruit ripen, too. The village paths are littered with dry maize leaves, nutshells and sticks of sugar-cane. In the fields, the hard work and sweat of December show their fruit. The mealies are tall and ripe, the fields strewn with round white pumpkins and watermelons. It is hard to believe that these crops were planted by men. The view from the window of the bus is pleasant. The wavy sea of grass threatens to spill over the road. A village occasionally spins past and the crouching compound huts appear threatened by the green mealies surrounding them, and revolve out of view. We arrived at noon, when everyone was out in the fields working. We took off our shoes, glad at last to get rid of them, left our things in a heap near the kitchen and set off to the field. The girls saw us first and ran up to meet us. Mother simply laughed and raised her arms in joy.

"We were expecting you tomorrow," said mother, putting aside the groundnuts and shaking the soil from her bosom. She had gained weight. Her arms were a little broader, the sun had given her skin a darker tan.

"You should all put on weight," she said, giving us boiled pumpkins, "you worked hard last summer."

Yona and I exchanged knowing winks. The girls went off to fetch

12

green cobs and very soon the cobs were sputtering on the fire. We ate quite a lot, and capped it all with sweet melons, digging into their soft red flesh with our fingers.

We worked till sunset, picking nuts and talking. Then we went home, feeling tired and happy and needing rest. Presently the moon came out and the night burst into light — you could pick up a needle from the ground in the moon-light.

Mother read the letter from father and opened the parcels. We had all done well at school and father had asked her to bake a big cake for us.

"So who was doing the cooking?" she inquired.

"Godi and Yona cooked in turns," explained Jo, then added, breaking a solemn promise, "Sometimes they made poor sadza and father had to cook. Or we would have cokes and pies from the grocer's."

"O, my poor children! Mother is cruel, isn't she? To leave her husband and children alone. Never mind my children, we will make up for it. We will be happy this holiday."

We went out to play in the moonlight and while we were there Lulu came to join us. I decided to accompany her home afterwards. It was not far. The leaves gleamed in the moonlight, as if a coat of oil had been rubbed onto each leaf. The people were fast asleep in her compound. I left her on the border of the clearing, and turned back along the path feeling unafraid and happy. I felt like sleeping out of doors in the moonlight but I knew it would be very cold at midnight and the dew would soak me. In the morning, I noticed that part of the forest on one side of our compound had been destroyed. The trees had been felled; the great trunks sprawled on the ground, dry brown leaves clinging to the withered twigs and branches, yellow chips littering the perimeter of the tree-stumps. Only one huge tree remained in the middle of the scene – the sole survivor of the axe.

"There are people who want to come and live here," mother explained. "A retired policeman and his family."

"A retired policeman, mother?"

"Yes, so you had better behave yourselves, because he still has his handcuffs."

"When are they building the huts?"

"In June."

"But did they have to chop the trees down now?"

"Yes. So that they can burn them up before the beginning of the rainy season."

"Have you seen the family, mother?"

"Only the father. His name is Pendi. He came to talk to Headman Jairos."

"What is he like? He sounds like the kind of person who would give us trouble."

"No, Godi, you worry for nothing. It will be nice to have neighbours, newcomers too."

I did not think so. I wanted the forest all to ourselves. Perhaps I was selfish.

As soon as he caught wind of our arrival Jairos turned up to collect his old newspapers.

"Where's the gin?" he demanded.

"Father couldn't afford it," said Yona.

"Not afford one small bottle of gin for his headman. Jairos is disappointed and he might not get the big field I promised him."

He rolled himself a cigarette, crouched at the fire to light it, and sat back at the table blowing horizontal mushrooms of smoke into the hut.

"The chief tells me I can accommodate more Derukas," he told my mother by and by. "Very soon you will be having the Pendis as your neighbours. Pendi will be coming to build his huts in June. He's a real man, Pendi. A fine man. Last time he came to talk to me he brought me two full crates of bottled beer and two bottles of gin. Now that's a man I wouldn't mind taking into my village. I want this village to be full of people like Pendi so that we can have beer parties every night. I want this to be a big, happy village. There is plenty of land for everyone…"

❈ ❈ ❈

By May, after the harvesting work is over, the grass has achieved its maximum growth. There are acres and acres of it — yellow elephant grass. The tree-trunks are half buried in the yellow sea of grass. In the morning the grass is loaded heavily with shiny beads of dew, so that a man walking through the grass is thoroughly soaked to the waist.

Village women start cutting the grass. They work with sickles, cutting the yellow blades at the roots and laying them out in bundles. The sun gets warm and the women remove their blouses. The grass tickles them. They return home just before noon, carrying thick bundles of grass on their heads. The bundles are carefully stored away for later use. In the fields the working season is over. The maize stalks have been stripped of their cobs and stand lamely in the fields, bent by the wind or broken by the hooves of cattle. The weeds grow without disturbance, threatening to obliterate the dry maize stalks.

The fields have become grazing areas. The cattle are no longer looked after, they spend weeks on end browsing in the fields and eating the delicious dry maize stalks. The herdboys are now on holiday for about five months. Their only work is to assemble their herds once every three weeks to take them to the dip. The dip tank is about eight miles away. The boys wake up in the chilly dawn to open the kraals. The journey to the dip is a long hot run through the forest along cattle tracks clouded by swirling dust, the discordant tinkling of cattle bells, and the stink of cattle and the warm damp steaming cakes of cowdung. The boys are pouring with sweat and the cattle trotting lamely by the time they reach the dip tank.

The dip tank is not a big place. It stands in the middle of an open space denuded of its vegetation by the hooves of the cattle. It is covered by a low roof of zinc tiles, and tailed by a narrow wooden passage through which the reluctant cattle are driven into heavy, grey, metallic dip water.

The dip-man, a middle aged man in khaki, ticks off the cattle on the brown tickets.

While the cattle are taking their turns to plunge into the dip, the boys compete in cracking whips to see who can make the loudest noise. Some of the boys play paper-football, eating salted ground-nuts, chattering, laughing and quarrelling. They are all rather reluctant to go home when the dipping is over.

May gives way to June and the weather becomes cooler. The days are short and the crisp air numbs the fingers in the morning. The nights are long and the trees grunt and croak in the wind, complaining against the cold. Because the nights are long people don't go to bed early. They sit round the fire, pushing time in talk, telling stories and roasting groundnuts over the fire. There are more beer parties and more drums. The drums beat louder and the singing is more energetic. People can afford to go to bed late. This is also the time for courtships. The shy-eyed girls stand under the afternoon shade of the trees, unconsciously chewing grass stalks and twigs while the sweet-tongued young men pour out their hearts to them. These are long, lazy months.

September brings higher temperatures. Veld fires soil the blue skies with their smoke and there is the smell of burning in the air. The tall elephant grass is burnt down to the roots and the tree trunks are charred and blackened. The once flourishing plains of yellow grass are reduced to a flat black landscape.

October, the hottest month of the year, brings a metallic sun, that pours its hot rays onto the earth without mercy. The sand becomes impossibly hot under the naked feet. Rivers run low. The land aches for rain.

Rain comes in late October or early November, washing the soot off the trees, soaking the black plains and bathing the land. But rain does not come every year.

That year the rain did not come. The ground remained black from the burning in October. The tree trunks remained grey with the soot. The cattle roamed the plains and untilled fields, nibbling the meagre green-black shoots battling to come out of the ground. Day after day the villagers looked at the unpromising sky, shielding their eyes from the hot sun with their hands. It was the same story throughout the country — drought; no rains with Christmas only a week away. The rain was two months overdue.

Even in the towns people noticed the drought. The small vegetable gardens started wilting behind the houses. People sweated and resorted to iced drinks. At night the heat made them sweat in their beds. The streets were dirty and dusty with the dirt of months, stained with half

16

dried pools of oil and dog's urine. Black smoke oozed persistently out of the factory chimneys, defying the angry bright blue sky. There was no rain to wash down all the carbon and soot.

For us in the countryside it was a long hot holiday. We sat in the shade, waiting for the rain. Instead of the rain, *madora* came.

The *madora* are fat black edible caterpillars. They are about ten centimetres in length, dark green and segmented, with hairy little legs. They are full of a green juice which readily squirts out when they are squeezed slightly. When squeezed, boiled with salt and sun-dried they make a crisp, tasty relish.

The *madora* come once in several years but when they come they come in monstrous numbers, literally flooding the land. They are not as destructive as locusts because they eat only green tree foliage and their spell lasts only one or two weeks. Nobody is sure where they come from or what they really are. A villager may chance to see two or three of them on a leaf and three days later there will be thousands, millions, zillions of them in the trees and the bushes. Villagers flock out to collect them while they last.

That year they came like raindrops. They massed over the ground, flowed up into the trees and bushes in endless files and attacked the foliage, gobbling up the green leaves till one live tree in ten stood winter-naked, the ground under the eaten trees black with their droppings.

The *madora* had been sent to relieve the effects of the oncoming drought, people said. Women went into the forest in long files, balancing buckets on their heads, pushing torn blouses into place, babies strapped to their backs. Sometimes a few men went with them, carrying axes with which to fell the trees in which the *madora* lodged.

We loved *madora* but mother was afraid of the forest. She only allowed us to go after Lulu had promised to come with us. Lulu's mother was in the party. She was short, slim and light-skinned and walked briskly in front of the row. There was Lifi, the old woman whose mentally retarded daughter had strayed into our hut one night. She was a bent old woman with white hair, but in her prime she had been tall and beautiful. It was surprising that she still had the energy

17

to go on these long, exhausting trips. There were three other women I did not know. One was short, dark, and suckled a naked infant on her breast as she walked. The other was a frivolous, bright-eyed maiden. The third woman was a tall, bony girl with a torn blouse through which two round breasts showed, threatening to tear down the remainder of her blouse. There was also Lulu's budding cousin.

We went past the dwarf crouching huts and the thin howling puppies, and past the black scorched fields which should by now have been tilled. We crossed the river in which Lulu and I had bathed the year before, and climbed into the forest. The trees grew closely together, dwarfing the bushes. Here the sun filtered through the close cover of the trees and danced on the grass.

We spread out over the pathless forest. The *madora* hung heavily on the branches of the trees and the bushes. Everywhere the leaves had been eaten or half-eaten. The creatures hung from the twigs like thick shreds of black strings, crawling slightly. On the ground we frequently came across strings of *madora* crawling in long files, with their ends joined together.

Picking *madora* is like picking loose threads from a cloth. The black caterpillars come cleanly off the branches, putting up a stiff, ineffectual resistance. We plucked them off into our buckets till our fingers ran green with their juice. Lulu's mother and the old woman Lifi wandered away towards the left. The three other women turned away towards the right, leaving Lulu, her cousin and us to take the central direction. Lulu and I exchanged phrases now and then, and Jo occasionally joined our conversation. Perhaps he had changed his ideas about Lulu. Yona seemed to have taken a sudden interest in Lulu's tall, budding cousin and I was very much surprised at the temporary absence of his shyness.

The sun rose and we felt thirsty. We ate some berries and picked *madora* till our buckets were full. We sat down to wait for the others. Presently, Lulu's mother emerged from the bush, put her bucket down, groaning from its weight and threw herself on the grass near Lulu and her cousin.

There was no hurry to go home so we sat in the shade for about an hour, till Lulu's mother said rather worriedly, "Lifi has perhaps taken another direction home."

"She will find herself in Mbumbuzi Forest before she knows where she is," remarked Lulu jokingly. Mbumbuzi was the most remote part of the forest south of the village. Few people ever went there. We eventually went home without her. The other women had returned but Lifi had not come. Jairos came to tell us he was organising a search party to find her.

For three tense days the people in our village talked about Lifi. For three successive days the search party made excursions into the forest to search for her, beating their loud drums, only to return at sunset with the hopeless news that Lifi had not been found.

When Lifi appeared accompanied by two strangers, people were beginning to reluctantly believe that she could never be found and there was much rejoicing in the village. Lifi hugged her daughter and cried, thankful to be back home.

She explained later that while the search party was looking for her, Lifi was alone in the forest, searching for the others. She was tired, pressed down by the bucket carried on her head and scorched by the blazing sun.

The forest was thick, with the tall trees fighting a tropical battle for sunlight. Strange birds darted casually among the trees, calling in deep tones. The forest was on a gently rolling slope with no hills, rock boulders or crests to indicate direction. Lifi looked up and thought the sun was strangely out of place. All she could make out was the grim monotony of the forest.

In the latter part of the afternoon, in desperation, Lifi started walking towards the setting sun. Little did she know what this mistake would cost her. Had she remained where she was for a little longer she would have heard the drums of the party which had come to look for her. By the time the party appeared within hearing range of the place she had been resting, she was too far away to hear them.

She was still walking when the sun set. The forest showed not the slightest signs of thinning out. No familiar stream appeared. She sat against the trunk of a big tree and felt hungry for the first time that day. Anxiety had repressed her hunger and thirst.

She ate some half-ripe brown berries. The berries were fleshy but had a sweet, sickly taste. She wanted the water in them. By the time she finished her meagre supper the darkness had descended and the full bright yellow moon was coming out. She pulled her cloth over her head and tried to sleep.

Sleep did not come quickly. Where was her daughter, she asked herself worriedly. Perhaps she had lost herself on the village paths, and then no one would find her and she would sleep in the bushes and catch a cold from the dew. A snake might strike her. Lifi herself shivered at the thought of snakes. She gathered her cloth round her and peered into the bushes. The crickets cried and the bats flapped in the grey sky and far away an owl hooted. Not a frog croaked.

Eventually she fell into a deep dreamless sleep.

The birds were chirping and the sun shining when she woke up. The sun was warm and cheerful and she felt happy. She let the dew dry. Her *madora* were still alive in the bucket after the night and she started squeezing them.

After the dew dried she started walking again, this time towards the East. Had the other women gone home, she wondered, or had they been lost too? Why wasn't someone coming to look for her? Or didn't anyone care at all? She ululated frantically. Her voice crashed into the forest and died. No response came.

That night she slept under a tree again, feeling very hungry. The moon rose a little later. She was sitting with her head bent over her chest in contemplation when she sensed some movements close to her in the moonlight. She lifted her head in alarm and before she could think the sniffing buck had galloped away, crashing through the bushes in fright. Meat, she thought, but almost immediately rebuked herself for thinking of meat when she didn't even have a weapon. After all, the animal might easily have been a hyena instead of a buck.

She dreamt that the search party was passing a short distance ahead of her. She hailed them and ran to meet them. She tripped, fell, rose and fell again, shouting hysterically. The party did not seem to hear her. They disappeared into the forest, beating their drums.

At last morning came and Lifi woke up. She had been crying in her dream. She ate green berries and started walking again. She felt an urge to walk, as if she remained in one place hunger and thirst and despair would drive her insane. It would be better to die where human beings could find her before the vultures and hyenas came to finish her off. She limped on, tired, hot and constantly thirsty.

Towards sunset, the forest started thinning out. Lifi suddenly found herself entering a vast plain of grass. Right in front of her scattered in the grassy plain were cattle and two boys sat weaving cattle whips out of strips of bark.

Her mouth opened but no sound came out. She stumbled towards the boys holding out her hand as if to prevent the scene from melting into unreality. Her bucket fell from her head and clanked noisily onto a log. The green *madora* scattered everywhere. She hurried on.

The two boys raised their heads at the noise and looked with a mixture of surprise and dread at the thin unexpected woman. Lifi asked for milk. Her voice was cracked and dry. For days she had not talked to anyone. The two boys gave her milk and took her to their home. The people there gave her a proper meal and listened in amazed sympathy to her story. Old as she was, she had walked forty miles from her village with only the berries to eat; narrowly escaping the hyenas which roam the forests at night. After resting for two days, Lifi was accompanied by two men back to her village.

3

Rain-Maker

We did not go to pick *madora* again, after Lifi's ordeal, now that mother had enough reason to stop us. Instead, we started making preparations for Christmas.

The huts needed a fresh coating of red mud. We dug a circular hole; the earth was soft and moist and stoneless till we reached the fine, red virgin sandy clay four feet down where no pick or hoe had touched. It was hot down in the deep hole. We watered the red clay into a thin paste and smeared it over the walls with our hands. Soon the huts were looking neat and dazzling in their new coat of paint.

We weeded and swept the compound clearing, raising clouds of dust that made us cough. There was firewood to be chopped and brought home in the wheelbarrow; cupboards, tables and chairs to be polished; pots, plates and pans to be thoroughly scrubbed with Vim; and bread and cakes to be baked over the sand in the three-legged pot.

We made countless trips to the pump, each took a long hot bath and finally went to bed.

Late that night we stirred awake to find father standing with a light in the doorway, smiling at us. He threw a giant packet of sweets onto the blankets and said festively, "Merry Christmas."

It was a merry Christmas, though far different from the colourful town celebrations we were used to. We woke up early in the morning

22

wondering aloud if the trees and the cats and dogs knew it was Christmas at all.

Father sent us to call the village elders for a Christmas service under a tree. I went to Simon's compound.

The path I took was well trodden, with thorny bushes flanking it closely. I ran swiftly and broke into the clearing of Simon's homestead. The clearing was small. There were two small huts in the middle and three dogs glanced indifferently at me as I walked across the clearing to the smaller of the two huts.

Two huge drums of beer stood under the eaves of the huts. I crouched beside the doorway of the hut and said, "Good morning."

Simon's strong bass voice called me in. The ground smelled strongly of dirty water and urine. I went into the hut, bowing my head, and sat on the hard earthen bench near the door. Simon's wife sat near the fire, cutting up chicken. Simon himself sat on the bench two feet away, skinning what looked like a hare. His small boy helped him by holding the animal for him to cut. His daughter sat cross-legged near the fire, watching the chicken with interest.

I greeted them slowly, and then quickly told them why I had come. Simon puffed at his strong-smelling home-made cigarette and continued cutting the hare. There was no hurry. His wife unaffectedly brushed her faded blue dress, closing it round her legs, scratched her cracked foot and loaded the chicken into the pot, pressing it down with the lid.

"Did your father bring us gin and cigarettes for Christmas?" asked Simon, grinning to show a cracked grey tooth.

"My father doesn't smoke or drink," I smiled, "but he brought many things to eat."

"Where is the service?" asked Simon's wife, a short dark-skinned woman with surprisingly small limbs.

I told them.

"We will come," said Simon ceremoniously, and then addressed his wife jokingly, "You leave your chicken for a while, mother of my daughter, and come to the service."

"You go," she said, unmoved by his bass voiced humour. "I can't leave the pot alone here."

23

"Your mother is so fond of chicken, my son," Simon winked at me. "Never mind, I will come. When does your father want us?"

"He wants you now," I said as politely as I could.

Simon laid the gleaming pink, naked hare on its dark brown skin, wiped his fingers with a cloth and came with me. His small boy came with us, doggedly running in front of us.

There was quite a small gathering under the tree when we got there. The women sat on the mats chattering, my mother among them. A few blank-eyed men sat on the logs with their chins on their knees. Father sat on a chair in the middle of the group making the final check on his Bible reading.

We started off with a Christmas song, the girls singing the first part, mother humming the alto, we boys singing in tenor and father chiming in the bass. Father read the lesson and then gave an elaborate sermon. The congregation listened in easily disturbed attention. Women chatted freely, casually greeting each other, laughing. Jairos stumbled in late and looking around for a chair and finding none, submissively took his position on a log and sat down to listen to the sermon, nevertheless coughing and smoking freely to assert his importance.

The congregation watched father, nodding slightly, understanding very little and evidently thinking the Bible account of the birth of Jesus a superb folk-story.

At last the service was over and everybody rose to go, the women yawning and stretching their arms, obviously happy that it was over. Half the congregation came to our compound for breakfast, either upon my lather's lavish invitation or on their own. Bread and cakes and biscuits were brought out, and tea made in a bucket. There were not enough cups to go round so the children had to wait. Eventually we had our turn and a score or so of other children joined us in gulping down mountains of bread and oceans of tea. It was a heavy breakfast. Afterwards we fooled around eating sweets, kicking balloons and waiting for lunch.

Lunch was hot rice and chicken and there were only two elderly guests, the rest of the morning guests having flocked off to the township to spend the day there.

That night it was dark without any moon, but the beer parties continued. Everywhere we could hear people singing drunkenly in the darkness, paying no heed to the barking dogs or the dark night.

On Boxing Day we set about repairing the fence of barbed wire round our home. We replaced two worn poles with fresh ones, sweating and panting as we planted and pulled the wire into place. My father sometimes believed in work for its own sake, and he wanted to go back to town feeling he had done some work over the short holiday, even if work meant uprooting a thick pole and planting it half an inch further to the right! Consequently late that night, in spite of the pressing darkness and our fatigue, we were levelling off the slope of our clearing by shovelling the earth from the higher end of the clearing to the lower end, as if even one storm of gushing rain would allow the shovelled earth to remain in place!

On the next day he left for the town, taking with him a liberal package of sun-dried and salted *madora*. We accompanied him to the bus stop and left him after he was on the crowded bus. We trudged home to another hot afternoon. The rain had still not come.

♪ ♪ ♪

The sky remained blue, and the earth cracked with the heat. Everywhere, people talked about the lateness of the rain and the growing prospects of drought. The same story came from other parts of the country.

Then, one hot afternoon, it was reported that the rain-maker had come. We lay in the shade to avoid the afternoon heat, and saw people moving along the path going to Jairos' compound. Jairos himself came to tell us to attend the rain-making ceremony.

We went rather reluctantly, not believing it would work. There was quite a large gathering in the open space in front of Jairos' homestead. Groups of women and children crowded under the eaves of the two small huts for shade; the men sat with their knees up to their chins in the hot sun, sweating, holding slim knobkerries and axes and walking sticks.

In the centre of the gathering sat the rain-maker. She was dressed in black from head to toe: an elaborate headpiece of black feathers on her

25

head, black cloths binding her chest, abdomen and legs, black bangles – she even sat on a black mat. She was light-skinned, tall and slim, a thin-faced woman in her early thirties, alert eyes glancing easily and authoritatively over the gathering, hands folded humbly in her lap.

Jairos rose from among the men and wheeled towards the rain-maker. He stood above her, bowing his head as he bent down to say something to her. Simon shouted from the crowd, angrily advising Jairos to revise his manners and crouch as he talked to the rain-maker. There was silence. Jairos looked around him dubiously, then crouched on his heels. He brought out his tin of tobacco and began to make himself his usual wet cigarette. The rain-maker spoke to Jairos in subdued tones, unaffected by his bad manners. Then Jairos rose to say briefly that everybody was to go to the tree of the ancestors.

The crowd rose, muttering about why they should be moved, and formed a rough line. The rain-maker rose elaborately, taking her time. Somebody started singing and the crowd joined in, clapping to the rhythm. Then the rain-maker led the procession, Jairos close behind her. Women ululated, children sang praises and men grunted as the procession reached the tree of the ancestors and formed a ring.

The tree was in the forest some distance from the headman's compound. It was a tall *muhacha* tree, towering above the other trees. Its trunk was wide, its branches small and numerous, forming a leafy crown. The ground around the tree was grassy, without any bushes, showing that the area had been trodden on before, but a long time previously.

Close to the tree, on either side of it, were two graves. One was the grave of Jairos' grandfather and the other was of Jairos' father, who had been the previous headman. The two graves were now mere frames of wood enclosing the half-moon shaped mounds of earth. The wooden frameworks had almost collapsed, the slim poles were broken or rotten or eaten by ants. The heaps of sand had subsided with the passage of years and now the weeds grew thickly on them, sporting a greener hue than the surrounding grass. No one had bothered to repair the frames of the graves.

The crowd ringed in the area in between the two graves. The

singing continued for an hour, with drums of oxhide barking away the rhythm of the tunes. Expert dancers rose to sketch their steps, turning their feet jerkily over the grass.

Suddenly, the rain-maker's head shot forwards, burying her headpiece of feathers in the dust. Her body shook and jerked and shivered as if she was battling with death. The froth foamed and bubbled from her mouth. For a split second the singing stopped and all eyes were glued on her. Then the singing started again, slowly climbing to a climax.

Jairos and Simon grabbed the rain-maker by the arms and held her down. She kicked and her body writhed like a worm, her legs pedalling the air, head tossing from side to side, arms pulling away powerfully, her whole body thrown into impossible angles. Gasps of breath broke through her frothing mouth, her belly heaved quickly.

The black cloth around her belly broke free with the force of her body and fell loose onto the grass, exposing her chest and abdomen. Her breasts were full and brown like a girl's, the long black nipples upturned to the sky.

Jairos and Simon struggled with her and gradually calmed her. The singing stopped. She spoke in a thin voice, gasping like a drowning person. She spoke a strange language, her voice thin and loud, but meaningless to us. They held her closely and let her speak till she finished and fell on her side, dragging her nipples in the sand. She lay as if in sleep and they covered her with the black cloths. Eventually the rain-maker awoke from her trance and told them what needed to be done.

There were two strange birds to be caught and destroyed, and a dead woman's hut to be burnt. The two birds lodged within the trunk of a tree on the borders of our homestead. Simon went to fetch them and returned within half an hour, carrying an eagle-like bird in each hand. Jairos cut the birds up and burnt them over the blazing logs. The fat hissed and everywhere there was the sweet smell of burning meat. A hungry dog unadvisedly pounced on one of the fleshy fragments. Jairos saw it, cursed violently and hurled a blazing splinter at the dog. The scalding splinter caught the dog on the belly and the dog scuttled away, whimpering.

The hut to be destroyed stood alone on a cleared patch in the middle of the forest. It was an old deserted hut with rotten poles, which crumbled at the touch of a finger. Green shoots were budding from some of the younger poles, struggling to live. The grass roof was grey and broken with the sun and the rain. Half of the grass had slumped into the hut. The hut's occupant, an old singular woman with no known relative, had lived alone in the hut and died from a stroke of lightning.

Towards sunset, they set fire to the hut. The old grass caught fire quickly and the rotten poles blazed down to ash. And the thick black smoke rose up to the yellowing sky.

The rain came that night.

I woke up to the sound of it.

It was dark and the lightning flashed. Through the slit in the doorway I saw the slanting white rain and the still rain-soaked bushes and the pools of water on the sand.

It poured down steadily. Drops of rain trickled through the grass roof and dropped onto our blankets. I suddenly felt the chill, and the fear of the darkness and the lightning and the rain.

The rain continued for the next two days. It poured down from the grey sky without a break, till the ground lay under inches of it. The droplets trickled through the roof and fell on our damp, dull fire, causing more smoke. The frogs croaked.

Then on the third day the rain stopped. The sun broke suddenly through the grey clouds to shine on the flood. The trees moved again and the birds called.

For three thanksgiving days people were forbidden to do any work in the fields.

Then ploughing started. At four in the morning people woke up to harness the oxen where they stamped and clanked their bells in the muddy kraals. The morning was full of the sound of the shouts of the boys driving the cattle, the splitting cracks of the cattle whips slashing bare oxhide and the squeak of the plough wheels in the grass.

Matudu came to till our new plot of land. His fine pair of oxen worked from dawn to noon turning our field into one stretch of brown.

Everywhere, the black burnt fields gave way to brown and afterwards to green. The weeds sprouted with the crops again —demanding again the labour of the hoe and the free flow of sweat over black flesh in the strong blazing sunlight.

The rain came again and again and the crops grew. We had only half finished the weeding when the holidays ended but when we came back in April we were to return to the biggest harvest ever known.

4

Derukas

Elsewhere in the country it had not been such a good farming year. The rain had come in two lean spells lasting a few days each, insufficient for the proper germination of seeds. In the southern regions of the country, the drought had been acute. People had taken refuge from the blazing sun in the verandahs of white brick houses. It was a seemingly prosperous land of well built houses, flourishing self-service supermarkets and district councils. But then people could not eat brick houses and supermarkets and council buildings. Although people there used tractors and fertilisers, applying advice from local agricultural demonstrators, farming was bad. Because it was a densely populated region, fields were small and the soil old and overworked. Most of the trees had been cut down for wood and the land lay in aching nakedness, raped by the plough.

For seven successive years the weather had been harsh in this region. The Government had for long watched the area with a wary eye, resenting the erosion and wastage of land and lack of contribution to the economy. At last it was decided to move people from this region into the remote virgin lands in the north to give the southern region a chance to become green again. At first there was opposition to this plan by the villagers but eventually, after much persuasion, they agreed to destroy their huts and houses, to leave their deceased kin's graves and their fatherland and to move into the new land.

Other people decided on their own to move north. Some of

these people were misfits in their communities – alleged practisers of witchcraft, crop stealers or just sheer bad neighbours who moved into this new region to exchange their identity for a new one. The third group of newcomers were people like us, city dwellers who had decided to re-establish their links with the country. These were the seasonal migrants between town and country. Towards the end of July, during the middle of the cold dry season, when roads were negotiable, the movement from the south started. Families came in convoys of closely packed Government lorries, taking two or three days to complete the journey, so that passengers frequently camped out for the night.

The first, the bigger train of lorries, passed our village and rumbled on into the forests of the remote north. There, where some people still wore only pieces of cloth between their legs and girls went around bare-breasted, the newcomers were received with curiosity, reserve and suspicion.

Closer to our own village the slow trickle of newcomers like us had prepared the local people for the invasions. In the end, we got relatively few newcomers, only about half a lorry-load of passengers getting down to settle in our village. They were not an unusual lot, four or five families who spoke the lazy southerly accent. Jairos was of course interested in them, and at once gave them generous grants of land.

The newcomers were called Derukas, and they brought with them a distinctive Deruka life-style based on shrewd hard work. The ambition of every Deruka family was to build a good brick and zink house. Building was done in the dry winter season. All aspiring house-owners became builders at this time. Everywhere the earth was torn open into little quarries and men dug down in search of soft brown clay. At the pump boys could be seen pumping water into drums, and rolling the drums to the quarries where the clay was mixed and bricks moulded and laid out in neat rows to dry in the sun. Few builders, however, fired their bricks. Scarcity of rocks in this area of deep aeolian sand, the cost of bringing material from the town, and the shortage of building experts added to the problems. As a result an alarming proportion of the newly built houses began to crack only months after completion.

The Derukas were generally great farmers. They cleared huge fields and grew maize and groundnuts. A few started to grow sunflowers and cotton to sell to the Grain Board. They kept many cattle, grew vegetables in the vlei gardens, dug fish ponds by the river and raised chickens. Some of them sold vegetables, milk and eggs.

In contrast, the local people built their huts with grass and poles, seldom bothering to plaster the walls with mud. Passing by these huts at night, one could see sticks of firelight in the gaps between the poles. In daytime one saw few chickens, small kraals and small fields of maize and millet. Many of the local people seemed to live from one day to the next, eating their sadza, drinking their beer, and raising their children.

At that time there were about twenty homesteads in Jairos' village. Before the Pendis arrived the compound nearest to ours was Jairos', with nothing to distinguish its owner; two dwarf huts with low, smoke blackened roofs, one small granary that could hold no more than four bags of grain, and a few small chickens.

Further on was a bigger compound. It had seven or eight huts built dangerously close together. A single fire could burn down all the huts. It was a polygamist's compound, the only one in the village. His name was Ndoga and he had three wives. He was short, dark and ugly, with dirty black woolly hair. There were always grass seeds and bits of blanket wool in his hair. He had bulging, bloodshot eyes which looked as if they might fall over his flat nose to his feet. He wore khaki's which were greased with the sweat of years. But underneath his filth and ugliness he was a hardworking man. His granaries were always full and his sons brought buckets of warm white milk from the kraals at midday. For a polygamist, his wives were happy. He had thirteen industrious children and five lean hounds which accompanied him on buck hunting trips. Further up the slope were two compounds close together. The first of these was that of Jairos' brother, Simon. A short man with loose limbs, Simon had been given a name appropriate to his clumsy step. Yet he was more clear-headed than his brother Jairos. He drank far less and worked hard to feed his family.

Next to Simon was an old bachelor who lived alone in a single hut. He was a tough-drinking, dark man with a coarse deep voice that could make children cry when they heard him sing. His main pastime was drinking, and when he drank, he sang even more loudly.

Among the women was Lifi, the woman who had lost her way in the forest while picking *madora*. She was a bent little woman in her eighties and lived with her mentally retarded daughter who was going on for fifty. The old woman always followed her daughter to make sure that she did not lose her way. Frequently, the retarded woman would collect firewood to deliver round the compounds so that wherever she and her mother went they were given food and a place to sleep in.

The old woman looked back on her younger days with nostalgia.

"My husband was a tractor driver and foreman on a farm," she would recall slowly to my mother. "I used to have everything I wanted. When the owner of the farm killed a bull for the workers it was I who shared out the meat. I always had the liver and the tongue to myself. But then my husband died of a strange disease. Perhaps some of the jealous workers he supervised killed him. That was when I fell from comfort and luxury. Would you believe I was once an important person, my daughter? Not me, in this withered flesh and these rags. I was left alone in the world to look after my daughter."

A tear trickled down her cheek and fell unbrushed. At her age, crying seemed a natural thing to do.

"Old age is a worm that eats youth away, Masiziva. But you have got many years ahead of you and lots of healthy, happy children. You will live to a ripe old age like me. But you will be wealthy and happy."

"Won't you eat before you go?" mother pleaded with her. "The girls are putting the pot on the fire."

"I shall eat someday before I die. I have to follow my daughter now."

That night after supper we went to our hut to sleep and found Lifi's daughter lying half asleep in our hut. Mother wrapped her up in a blanket and took her to her hut. Lifi turned up early next morning to look for her and was greatly relieved to find her.

🦋🦋🦋

"They are great people I am bringing in," said Jairos with gleaming

33

eyes. "Rich people with great totem names. I want this village to be filled up by Derukas. I want beer parties going on every night in this village. I want all these thick forests to be chopped down to provide fields. I want my people to be happy and prosperous."

He looked very happy with himself.

" Have you got a fire burning?" he asked, and hissed with pleasure on seeing the fire. "My people, locals and Derukas alike, love me very much," he said happily, emptying his bulging pockets. Out of the pockets came four small, dry-looking fish, three eggs, a piece of onion and a shred of biltong. These all went onto the table, each item getting a brief explanation of its source: the fishes given by friendly boys at the river, the eggs given by a very generous housewife, the meat and the bulb of onion got from Simon' s wife, just saved from going into the cooking pot.

We gathered around him, laughing, as he surveyed his small treasures. He tossed the shred of biltong into the fire, where it smoked and blackened in the heat. He snatched it out of the fire with his fingers and threw it onto the table.

"Salt! " he cried, making swallowing movements. Shuvai got him the salt. He heaped about two teaspoons of it onto the meat and disposed of it in two quick bites.

"Water," he cried, munching. "Put it on the fire. Yes, in the kettle. Not too much! Bring it here." He put the eggs very carefully in the kettle and put it on the fire. The kettle must have been on the fire for just over a minute, the water only getting warm, when he jumped from his chair and crouched by the fire to look into the kettle.

Half a minute more of frantic blowing at the fire and the eggs were ready. I saw mother biting her upper lip to stop herself from laughing as Jairos half ate, half drank them straight from the shells.

He licked his fingers dry, whisked the fishes back into his pocket and rose to go, momentarily forgetting the onion.

"O," he remembered suddenly. "Plant this onion for me. Keep it well watered, you hear."

It was only a small bulb, one which wouldn't grow much.

"O yes," he remembered again. "You boys must go and repair the

34

fence of wood round my garden. You know where my garden is, in the vlei."

"No."

"Well, you can ask, it's the big one near the stream, with a big tree in one of its corners. You can't miss it. The goats broke down part of the fence. All you have to do is put in a few logs. It shouldn't take you thirty minutes."

"He is going too far now," protested mother, after Jairos had left. "Doesn't he know we have got a great deal of our own work to do? Just because he is the village headman he thinks he can make us slave for him. The regional chief himself has no right to give such orders."

In the end, mother decided that we would have to go and repair Jairos' garden, otherwise we might seem to be disobedient children.

When we went to the vlei to have a look, however, we found nothing growing in the garden.

There was no proper fence at all; only one end of the plot was fenced. But this was poorly done; stakes of fragile wood had been piled into a rough wall which collapsed from a slight push. It was no longer a question of repairing, but building the fence. We went home feeling depressed, wondering how mother could have decided to make us do the work. Fortunately we were spared the effort.

In the vlei carpeted with lush yellow grass, there was a mouse hunting party. The boys were burning the grass, so that the mice scuttled into the open, where they could be beaten to death, sliced open and roasted over the fire. When we saw it, the fire was threatening to run out of control.

We were not surprised to learn the next morning that half the vlei had been burnt black by the fire. Jairos himself came fuming with anger to tell us about it.

"They dare to burn the vlei without my permission! They destroyed my garden, the headman's garden!"

A few of the gardens had been destroyed by the fire. Jairos's had been completely destroyed. The fire came to us as a blessing, since it would have been absurd for us to have to make the garden afresh.

"It's Makepesi's boys who did it."

"Who is Makepesi?" asked mother.

35

"You don't know him? He is the snake in this village."

"Is he the one who lived in the big city?"

"Yes. He thinks he is clever. Everybody in the village fears him, except me. They think he is a gangster. His father was a renowned medicine man in his time, and people think Makepesi got his pretty young wife by a charm. Now that's nonsense which only fools believe. His charms will not work on me. This very morning I am going to order him to pay a fine of a goat. His boys can't be allowed to fool around like that. I don't care what people have been saying about him. He threatened to kill me last December when I talked about giving part of his field to Charamba. Why am I not dead? Why didn't his charms finish me off? And why shouldn't I give his field away? He hasn't paid his taxes, and has committed many crimes against honest people of this village."

"Perhaps it was an accident, Headman Jairos."

"An accident, Masiziva! You don't know Makepesi. He is a real shrew, that man. He did it deliberately to spite me. I am not letting him get away with it this time. Not only am I fining him a goat, but I am going to give his field away to Charamba who needs it."

"But Makepesi is a dangerous man, Headman Jairos."

"Not at all. He wouldn't hurt a finger of mine."

5

Pendi

Although the Pendis had not made a second appearance for many months, Matudu had been building their huts.

One hot afternoon we were playing at Matudu's claypit, filing toy bricks out of hardened clay, when a battered looking Zephyr veered from the trees and ground to a halt twenty metres from the claypit. A man opened the door of the car and jumped out. He walked with a sprightly step towards the semi-finished huts where Matudu and his sons were fixing the roofs. He was a tall, slim man, light-skinned, with alert red eyes and forked moustache. He made his way carefully round the clay pit as if it were some infernal hole. He looked in a superior way to where we sat, mud-splattered, in our superficial dirt. He nodded vaguely at us, a slight grunt issuing from his throat.

Later a woman came out of the car, taking her time. Even from far we could see the easy comfortable features of a city woman - the vibrant skin of her body, lightened on the face by Ponds Vanishing Cream, the stockinged legs, the shiny dark wig. We even caught strong whiffs of her perfume as she passed us, followed by her children.

Mr Pendi was now talking to Matudu about the huts. The woman inspected the huts critically, taking care not to soil or scratch her stockings on the walls. She spoke quickly to her husband in sharp phrases, and even from the distance we could hear that she had not been satisfied by the huts.

Mr Pendi continued talking to Matudu, unaffected by his wife's sharp remarks. We took this opportunity to slip away quietly to our huts. Mother stood in the doorway of the kitchen, watching the visitors unobserved, brushing her dress in preparation for going over to make their acquaintance.

She went round at last, to shake hands with the visitors. There was the usual long talk between Mrs Pendi and mother, in the middle of which mother called us to introduce us one by one to the new family. I sensed a sharp change in Mrs Pendi's attitude to us when mother introduced us as her children – she smiled constantly and her voice sounded buttery.

That night a strong sweet oily smell of frying meat drifted from our neighbour's huts and we could hear frequent peals of laughter above the music of the gramophone. The noise went on into the night, long after we had gone to sleep.

As we lay in the darkness of our huts, I caught the smell of tobacco and heard the muffled sound of sandals on the sand. Later I heard Jairos' familiar laugh. He was paying his fourth visit on the Pendi's during their first twelve hours in the village.

The Pendis' huts were completed within two days. Mrs Pendi took off her stockings and pointed shoes and wig, and set to work giving the mud walls a tan of red and black, and sweeping the clearing to make it habitable. Mother went over to help her. They worked together like old acquaintances.

All the family possessions had not been brought on the Zephyr, so the next day Mr Pendi went back to town, by bus, to fetch the property. He came back three days later, in a hired lorry full of furniture and other things.

They unpacked the lorry at once. and we helped them. There were sofas, coffee tables and wardrobes, trunks, boxes, plates and pots — all sorts of household goods. Mrs Pendi kept explaining the history of each item, fingering the items possessively, at the same time complaining of the bruises and the scratch marks sustained on the lorry.

The Pendis had four children, the oldest being a girl of seven. The children came to play with us and were soon sharing about half of our meals, and mother didn't mind. But the meal-time visits continued with such precision that we began to have fears of playing host to four more little Jairoses. At last when the four visitors arrived for the umpteenth time mother told them to go and fetch cups and plates from their mother's kitchen since we did not have enough to go around. The kids raced home eagerly but their mother intercepted their return, obviously sensing the trick behind it all. For some time the meal-time visits decreased in number.

One evening I was busy bathing on the lawn just before supper. The evening was dark, but the light of the stars outlined everything fairly distinctly. I splashed myself quickly with the water, eager to get out of the darkness.

Suddenly I sensed a shadow standing close to me. For a moment I was shaken, and hurried to remove the stinging suds of soap out of my eyes. It was five-year-old Sam Pendi, paying us his evening visit. He gloated over me, naked and soapy in the zinc bath, waiting for me to finish so that we could go into the hut together.

I washed on, slightly irritated by the presence of the boy. Then the unmistakably jet of urine came splashing over my back. I smelt it, and felt its warmth. I turned and it splashed into my face. I thought I heard Sam giggling as he propelled the jet into my face.

I was blinded by anger. I jumped out of the zinc bath, overturning it and cutting my leg on its edge as I did so, but I never felt the pain. I gave the boy a clean hard slap which sent him reeling to the ground. The blow must have stopped his breath for a while. He stumbled to his feet and started a bold, deliberately loud crying. A wave of guilt numbed me as I dried myself and snatched my clothes on. Mother caught me hesitating at the door outside the kitchen.

"What happened?" she asked sternly: "Why is Sam crying?"

"I don't know," I croaked.

"Yes, you know. Why is he crying?"

The soap and the smoke stung my eyes. Mother went outside to talk to Sam, who was still crying. I saw orange tongues of light from Mrs Pendi's lamp as she came out of her hut. Eventually Sam stopped crying and went away with his mother. Moments later mother returned, looking very serious, and I felt like a brute.

39

"You beat the boy."

I kept quiet.

"You know I have always told you to be good to our neighbours."

"He urinated into my face, mother."

"Did he do that? Urinate in your face? But then you should not have beaten him."

"I was angry."

"But he is only a young boy," said Yona, Sam's best friend.

"Perhaps it was an accident."

"It wasn't an accident!" I shouted angrily. "He did it on purpose."

"You shouldn't have beaten him all the same," said mother and added, "Go and apologise."

I felt guilty and afraid of the dark. But there was no evading mother's orders so I crept out of the hut.

The moon was coming up now, gloating over the horizon. It was a big orange ball and clothed everything with its yellow light. The sand gleamed faintly. I felt less afraid in the moonlight, closed the steel gate behind me and walked quietly. There was no fence yet round the Pendis' homestead, so I went straight to the huts across the clearing.

In the moonlight the two huts were clearly outlined, the big four cornered hut with the slanting roof dwarfing the smaller round hut. I made for the smaller hut. It faced away from me, so that I could only see a small trapezium of red light coming from the doorway. I hesitated near the door, plucked up my courage and slipped into the hut.

They were having their supper. Mr and Mrs Pendi sat at the table and Mrs Pendi suckled the infant as she ate. Mr Pendi's fierce face was lit up by the oil lamp on the table, so that the shadows of his moustache looked like two huge barbs. He attacked a bony chunk of meat and I saw the fat dripping from his fingers. Sam and his sisters sat on the floor eating.

"Good evening," I muttered. I had not been noticed.

Mrs Pendi ducked her breast into the blouse when she saw me, plucking it out of the infant's mouth.

"Have some sadza," said Mr and Mrs Pendi together from the table.

"Thank you very much," I said tensely, "I have eaten."

40

"Then eat some more," said Mr Pendi, grinning at me.

"I came to apologise. I beat Sam."

"It's all right," said Mrs Pendi, smiling. "Sam is a very naughty boy." They didn't want to know why I had beaten him, I supposed.

"Have some sadza," said Mrs Pendi again, forcibly, as if I would be committing a crime if I went away without eating.

"I have to go now," I said, rising. In a moment I was out in the moonlight, hurrying home and feeling much better. Apologising had been easier than I had anticipated.

The Pendis aspired to being a progressive family. Their children were clever and bright-eyed. Sam was the second child, the first being a girl called Emma. Emma was sometimes a loose-tongued, vulgar and spoilt child. On one occasion when we were playing with them she had invited Jo to be her hide-and-seek partner, and Jo, obviously misunderstanding the invitation, had behaved in a priggish manner by flatly refusing and calling Emma names. She would complain loudly when her mother told her to wash the dishes or fetch water. Many times her mother beat her. She was a fast runner and ran away. But then Mrs Pendi was a runner too; she took her dress up in her hands and followed Emma like a bolt of lightning.

In spite of the child beating and the noise the Pendis were not bad neighbours. Occasionally Emma could be a surprisingly good child, washing her infant sister's napkins and voluntarily going to the pump to fetch water. Mrs Pendi was perhaps a little too talkative; railing endlessly about her children, her husband, her huts and fields, but she had warmth. She was sociable and very generous. She confided in my mother, laying her heart open to her, telling of her ambitions and aspirations, her hopes and fears.

One day Mrs Pendi came to our field to help us pick the nuts. We sat in the shade eating boiled mealies and she talked. She told us how she had gone to a boarding school and excelled in English and athletics; how she had always wanted to go to a sewing school but failed because of her family's poverty; how she had married Robson (Mr Pendi) because he was smart and intelligent; how she had suffered on delivering her first child, Emma; how Sam's birth had been much worse and almost fatal; how Robson had narrowly missed death while investigating a criminal case…

She had had two operations to deliver her first two children and was consequently a fragile woman. The housework was rather heavy for her condition so she got girls to help her.

The first of these girls was a tall dark strong southerner with round powerful arms and huge limbs. She had long, strong strides and took only two minutes to go to the pump and back. When the baby cried she sang and rocked her to sleep. She never complained when Mrs Pendi scolded her. Perhaps her heart cried.

She was a very hardworking girl, but she did not stay long. She was soon dismissed and replaced by Mary, Matudu's second girl. Mary was an easy-going beauty. When Mrs Pendi scolded her she smiled and answered back.

At that time the Pendis were building a brick and zinc house. An expert from the south had come to do the building, and Mr Jacobi's boy, Thomas, was to help the builder.

Thomas was a strong, laughing, singing boy. One of his favourite tunes had the refrain line: "Help! Get me some help!" He sang with so much emotion that you would think he genuinely needed help as he worked.

Mary had taken a fancy to Thomas and we often heard them talking. "I love you, Thomas," she would say very loudly as she straightened her back and put down the pot she was scrubbing. "I love you like a banana."

"If you love me like a banana, then eat me," Thomas would say.

"Truly, Thomas, I love you. I can't sleep nights because of you."

Thomas would burst out laughing, and the builder would join him. Sometimes he sang love songs to her, and she stopped to listen, but he always laughed in the end. This extravagant flirting would go on till Mrs Pendi stopped it by calling Mary in to do something.

Mr Pendi could be a violent man. He was a hardened drinker, often going out to drink and coming late in the evening, singing on his way home through the darkness. At beer parties he could be seen sitting on a chair in his dignified suit, while everybody else sat on the ground or on stools. Because he spent his money freely on beer he had a huge following of friends.

He had a gun, and sometimes he went out at night to hunt, so that we saw the bright beam of his powerful torch flashing boldly among the trees as he went out. When he returned we were asleep, and we never heard the bark of his gun. But he almost always brought a buck, and in the morning there would be meat and a buckskin and buck head.

Sometimes he gave us some of the meat. It was lean meat, and mother said it was so because the buck fed poorly.

He could be hard on his wife. We often heard them scolding away at each other, far into the night, while we lay in bed. Her voice loud and sharp, half-pleading and half-protesting; his, deep and firm and decisive.

In his wife's presence Mr Pendi was loud and harsh and even hard on Mary, their housegirl. But when he was alone with Mary he talked softly to her.

"Warm the water for me, Mary, my girl. I want it real warm today." He had been drinking all day and wanted a bath.

"Soap and towel, Mary."

"Yes."

"Make sure the water is warm, Mary."

"It is."

"Good girl. Now take the water to the bathroom."

Mary carried the water to the bathroom, a rectangular wall of grass open at the top.

"Mary!" called Mrs Pendi. Silence.

"Mary!" she called again, more loudly.

There was a moment of silence, and then Mary's voice came from the bathroom. "Mary. Where have you been? I called you two times and you did not answer. Where were you?"

"What's wrong?" said Mary.

"Stop asking me questions. I do the asking and you do the answering. I demand an answer. Where were you?"

43

Mary shook at the pointedness of her questions.

"You are a stupid girl, Mary," said Mrs Pendi, her voice rising. "I will tell you where you were. You were in the bathroom with my husband. You want to take my place, don't you? Tonight I will teach you to leave men to their proper women."

Something violent must have happened. We next heard Mary running away crying, her voice receding quickly, saying between sobs that she was sick and tired of it all and was going home; that she was sick of the bullying and slave-driving; that she was going away never to come back again, never to this troublesome place; she was going home to her mother.

If it was acting, it was excellent acting. Mr Pendi calmly finished his bath.

"What is all this noise I hear?" he demanded. "Why is Mary crying? Why has she gone away in the night?"

"Don't ask me," replied Mrs Pendi edgily. "You should know."

That pressed the red button.

"What's wrong?"

"What's wrong indeed! You think you can cheat me and get away with it! You think you can fool around with any dirty savage girl and get away with it? I am not blind, am I?"

"What!" he exclaimed, surprised by her pointedness.

"What were you doing out there in the bathroom with Mary?"

He laughed angrily.

"I said, what were you doing out there in the dark with Mary?" she continued relentlessly. "You think it's decent for a married man to behave as you did. With a woman — a girl — a housemaid, a dirty ignorant girl from two compounds away. And right in the bathroom ten paces from me and the children?"

There were tears in her voice. Loud as the voice might be, her trampled heart was crying out for the hundredth time. But her indignation was like a rubber stick hitting iron.

"I have always told you you are a troublesome woman," he said, evading the core of the matter. "You think I can stand all the empty accusations. You treat me like your own son, your own little boy. What would I do with a girl from two compounds away?"

"What did you do with Clara?"

"Just because she was away for a minute taking my water to the bathroom you think I was having a fine time with her?"

"What else could you be doing?"

"Watch out!" he shouted. He must have made movements to strike her, for she lowered her voice immediately.

"It was wrong of you to be with her."

"It is you who are wrong to accuse me."

"I will leave you to marry your Claras and your Marys and see what good housewives they will make you."

"You can leave tonight, if you want to."

"All you care for is your beer," she said. Things were getting dangerous now. "You don't care for me or for the children, You don't love us. You always come home late, and then I can't say one civil word to you. How do you expect me to react if you make passes at every girl with a bust in this village? How can I stand it?"

"You have a very wild kind of jealousy. Why are you not going away? I said you could pack and leave tonight. Why are you not packing?"

"You have no feelings. You married me only for convenience. You treat me as if I am only one of your Claras, your Petulas, your Marys."

She was crying loudly now and the children cried with her. He let her cry for a while and then eventually muttered her into silence. But the quarrel had not ended. We woke up to it. It must have been nearing midnight. I woke up with a start to the rapping of mother's bedroom door and to the crying of a girl.

I jumped out of the blankets and peeped through the doorway. The moon was bright outside.

Mother opened the door and came out. Emma crouched at her door, crying. Emma was naked. "What's wrong?" mother asked quickly.

"He's beating her," she cried.

"What?"

"Father is beating my mother. He will kill her if you do not come to stop the fight. He has been drinking. Please come and stop it Please! Please!"

From the Pendis hut we could hear a thudding sound as if a man was throwing logs on the floor. We heard muffled screams and suppressed yells, below the thud.

"Please!" cried Emma. The thudding sounds came faster. Emma had sometimes been a naughty and disobedient child but I admired her that night.

Mother stood on in confusion while the ruthless wife-beating continued.

"Go, mother," urged Yona timidly.

"I can't go," said mother mildly. "I'm also another man's wife. I cannot intervene. I am not a man."

She could not go then, even if she heard him beating her to death. He wouldn't kill her. He would come to his senses before he killed her.

It could not go on. It stopped with a final thud and a crack. I thought bones had been smashed to fragments on the floor.

"Go back to bed, boys," said mother. She took Emma's hand and led her away to the fence. Emma held the two strands of wire apart and stepped across. Mother stood at the fence for some minutes, listening. The handle of the lamp clinked on the glass and the yellow flame fluttered in the wind. There was a smell of paraffin in the silent night. Slowly mother came away from the fence. The wind tugged at her petticoat and threatened to blow out the lamp.

We went to sleep.

We woke up to a quiet morning. Mr Pendi was up and about, but we did not see his wife. Eventually he went away with his gun and while he was away mother went to see Mrs Pendi. Mr Pendi returned an hour or two later, with a dead buck on his shoulders.

There was the smell of roasting meat in the air, and a buckskin hung drying on the line. There was no talking and laughing yet. But Mr Pendi had gallantly apologised.

6

Cheru

We had never held much for housegirls, being a close-knit family, and somehow the incident in the Pendis' home had made us hostile to the idea of housegirls. Many of the Deruka families who employed local girls in their household had nothing but complaints against them; it was alleged that either the girls' affairs meddled with their work or even endangered the reputation of their employers, or the girls were dismissed after being caught carting off quantities of this or that to their own homes, or simply absconding from work on the claim that they were mistreated.

When mother was advised by the doctor not to do any heavy work because she suffered from severe pains in the legs, we found ourselves with no option but to get a housegirl to do the cooking and the housework. The prospect of living with an outsider in our home, for the very first time, naturally made us anxious.

The news of our wanting a girl spread quickly around the village. We found a woman waiting for us with her daughter when we came from the fields. The girl was dark, with long hair and good white teeth. Her eyes were large and wide apart, giving her face a serene look. She was fourteen or fifteen but was already a young woman, sitting in cross-legged silence even after her mother had left.

I want you to feel at home here, Cheru," mother said to her. "I want to treat you as my own child and I want you to regard me as your mother. My boys will treat you like their own sister. I want us to live nicely together. I won't drive you like a slave, after all you are only a girl, and are helping me. But you will work well, right?"

Cheru's large black and white eyes remained fixed on the floor for some time, only looking up to give mother a polite glance.

"Your work," explained mother, "will be to cook, to wash the dishes and to help in the fields whenever you can. I will show you how to do your work."

Cheru washed the dishes with the girls, Shuvai explaining to her in her calm dignified way the use of Vim and the dishcloths. Mother prepared the supper explaining elaborately how much salt she wanted put in the meat, how she wanted sadza to be allowed to simmer on the fire before mealie-meal was added and how she wanted the cooking sticks and pots to be washed immediately to discourage the flies.

In the morning we went with Cheru to harvest the mealies. We worked quietly for a while. Her dress was torn under the armpits, showing thick dark sweaty curls of hair. She evidently wore nothing under her blouse, as her nipples stuck out like marbles in her thin blouse. Her legs were strong and curved inwards slightly. She stood knee deep in the grass, softly plucking the mealie-cobs from the stalks. There were grass seeds in her hair. Thin dark streams of hair ran down her face, past her ears. She had slim strong arms but her nails needed cutting.

A locust jumped from the grass and fluttered away desperately, landing near her feet. She crouched quickly and quietly. Her cupping hand darted forwards and snatched the locust from the grass. In a second she was pulling the insect's legs out.

"Put it in your pocket." She gave the locust to Yona.

"Can you eat it?" asked Yona and Cheru nodded.

"Don't you eat locusts?" she asked. Her lips were dry, but her pink tongue was glistening wet inside, half shut in by the bright while teeth.

" We eat only certain types," explained Yona.

" People say that it you eat this sort you will have bad eyes," said Jo.

"Gossip," said Cheru, smiling. "My mother and I have been eating this sort since I was a toddler but we can still see well. My mother and I used to catch enough locusts to fill a small pot."

We caught *madora*," I said.

48

"We caught *madora* too," she said. "We used to fill buckets with the creatures and then we would have relish for months. Sometimes my father came with us. He brought an axe to chop the trees and we picked the *madora* from the branches."

She was free and bright, talking.

"My father was a violent man. He used to fight with my mother and my sister and I ran out to sleep in the bushes. He chased her around with a spear. He had the spirit of a dead man inside him and no one could drive the spirit out. Wherever the drums were beating, he was there. If there were no drums beating in the neighbourhood, then he walked miles in the night to get the drums. Everybody knew him. His spirit made him drink like a bull and quarrel with people. But he worked hard in the fields and we cried very much when he died."

"Your father died?"

"He died in a fight with another man. I was like Tendai when he died, but I still remember him. He had been drinking heavily with his friends when they started quarrelling. They stabbed him with a knife and there was dry blood all around him when we discovered him lying dead the next morning. He bled like a slaughtered ox."

"Did the police come into the fight and find his murderers?"

"No. No one called the police. We just buried him. My father had been wronged but he got his revenge. Two weeks after we buried him the man who stabbed him died of a very strange disease."

"Your dead father had the power to kill his living enemy?"

"You don't know my father. He was the strongest medicine man in our village. At that time we lived about two days' walk from here. Many people came to my father with their problems, while he was living, and he cured them all. He knew the medicines to keep ghosts and witches away from the compounds. We never saw any ghosts near our compound."

"Have you ever seen a ghost?"

"Only once. I will never forget it. I was coming from my uncle's compound with my mother at night. The path went between two graves and an old homestead. The homestead had been abandoned. We first smelt a strange smell, a smell like rotten sacks. Suddenly, we saw it. It was right in front of us. It was very tall and very dark and had its head in the sky. We fell down in fear and closed our eyes. I couldn't speak. It went away into the trees."

"A tall dark ghost! But people say that ghosts are like fires, and that they shine like lamps."

"Yes, there are all types of ghosts. There are tall dark ones which are really the spirits of dead people. They appear at the graves, usually near abandoned homesteads. The ghosts that shine like fires can be seen anywhere at night, especially by those people with medicines to keep the ghosts away. There are also the ghosts kept by witches. They are like very small men and they have very small feet. You can tell that the little men have been in your compound if you see the small footprints. The witches send them to beat people. Sometimes they even beat a man to death."

"How do the witches get their little man?"

"If you find a stickhole spun into the mound of a grave only two days after the burial, then you will know that the witches have raised the spirit of the dead person and turned it into one of their little men."

Perhaps her smiling eyes were only telling established untruths. "You said you were living in another village. Why did you leave it?'

"It turned into a bad place. People were dying like ants. Every night before we went to bed we emptied our water buckets and threw away any food left from the supper. We feared poisoning. There were too many graves and too many corpse-eaters in the village. Many of the graves were dug up and the bodies removed. A child once reported that his mother stored children's hands and legs in a big three-legged pot. My sister died and my mother decided to leave the village."

"Is there anybody living in the village now?"

"No. Everybody left. Few people even go there now, especially at night. They are afraid of seeing the strange fires."

The sun had gone down. It was getting towards winter now and the darkness fell quickly.

As we walked among the dark trees, going home, I saw an imaginary tall dark giant striding across the path ahead of us, dragging his chilly atmosphere of death and rottenness about him. The fireflies suddenly chilled me as they flashed in the grass.

Perhaps the spirit of Cheru's dead father protected us, for we got home safely in the darkness.

Cheru's mother was at home when we arrived.

She was very much like her daughter, with a large wide face and a smooth dark complexion. But instead of being white and well placed, her teeth were small and brown from drinking too much. Her face had many razor slashes where the medicine man had cut to put herbs into her bloodstream. Her dress was torn, exposing her polished-looking black shoulders.

Cheru gave her mother a short greeting and sat cross-legged near the door of the hut.

Cheru's mother talked about the weather, the rain, the scarcity of relish and about *madora*.

"Please keep a keen eye on Cheru," she said by and by. "Don't let her play with boys. I don't want to see her coming home with twins in her belly. But I don't mind if she plays with your sons.

They are all too young to harm her, and besides they are good boys, are they not?"

"She will be all right," laughed mother. "She is old enough to realise the dangers of being free with boys. As for my boys, you can rest assured they will treat her as their own sisters."

"You are a good woman, Masiziva. You are better than all the new-comers. You are kind. You know some of the new families won't give poor people like us a grain of salt if we ask for it?"

"Perhaps you want some salt." Mother guessed from the hint. She said to Tendai, "Give her a cup of salt."

"Get her a bucket of nuts for peanut butter, boys," said mother again.

Cheru's mother clapped her hands in gratitude.

"Oh thank you, Masiziva. You know the trouble of your fellow villagers. Now I will have enough peanut butter for months. You are very kind, Masiziva."

"I was thinking," continued mother, "of sewing a few clothes for Cheru. A working girl should wear good clothes to show that she is working. "

"You're a good woman, Masiziva. You know even if you don't give Cheru her pay for two months I won't worry because I know she is safe in your care. Be good, Cheru."

She put her bucket of nuts on her head and took the cup of salt carefully in her free hand. She went home in the darkness, the gate tinkling behind her.

❀ ❀ ❀

Cheru was a willing worker but a little too childish. She was only fourteen.

She loved little Rita, and when Rita cried she took her into the bushes on her back, and sang her to sleep.

"Keep quiet Ri Ri Ri Rita,
Hush Rita, baby of the mother. . . ."

When she went to the pump and met her friends she played and talked for hours, sometimes hurrying home at sunset to wash the afternoon dishes for supper. Her dirty dishes dried in the sun and there were lumps of mealie meal in her sadza.

But mother was invariably patient with her. We loved Cheru when she talked but felt uneasy when she spent hours at the waterpump and burnt the meat.

Cheru was a free girl. Even on nights when the moon was full, she would bath with the girls on the lawn and we saw her womanish figure clearly outlined in the moonlight. Once I found her singing and dancing alone behind the hut, wheeling her hips. She stopped dancing, uneasily.

But generally she was a shy girl. Her friend was Mary, the girl who worked for the Pendis. Mary was about sixteen, but behaved even more childishly than Cheru. Cheru's friends sometimes came from the village and played till the young moon threw long shadows as it sank. They sang and danced and giggled, obviously inviting us to join them. Once or twice we went to join them; on most of the occasions we stayed in the hut like a pack of prudes, giving a half-deaf ear to the girlish screams outside as we pretended to be reading.

One day we went to the river to fish and at about midday a group of girls came to the river to swim. There were about eight girls, all talking

52

and laughing as they came down to the bank.

They came to a dead stop as they came down and saw us. Cheru was there, her black eyes looking down on us.

"There are boys fishing here," said one of the girls, needlessly.

"No use swimming here," said another girl and they turned back and went away, their skirts dancing above our heads.

When we arrived home just after dark we met Cheru at the gate, going to the pump.

"No wonder she is always late in preparing supper, after playing the whole day," muttered Yona: When we went in with the fish, mother was holding the basin of sugar and saying, "This basin was full of sugar after breakfast. . . ."

She took the fish to scrape them, and just when she was putting the basin of sugar away Cheru came in suddenly, with the bucket of water on her head. She loomed in the doorway like a woman from the night, with droplets of water on her eye lids. She wasn't afraid of the dark.

❊ ❊ ❊

After about three weeks Cheru fell ill. She could not move, and spent the day lying lethargically on a blanket near the fire.

"What's wrong with you?" mother asked her.

"Nothing."

"Do you feel any pains?"

"Nothing."

"Perhaps we ought to take you to the clinic?"

"No, I will be all right."

"Has this happened to you before?"

"Yes."

"Well, I suppose your mother ought to know about it."

Her mother came and took her home but returned that evening to explain.

"It's nothing, Masiziva," she said, "she will be all right."

"But don't you think you ought to take her to the clinic?"

"They wouldn't be able to help her."

"And you have no idea what her problem is?"

"It's nothing to worry about, Masiziva."

"It's just that she seemed a healthy girl and then yesterday morning she woke up and couldn't move. Naturally I'd be worried."

"There is no need to. Of course it's not your fault! I know you too well even to suspect that."

"But please, Mai Cheru, just to relieve my thoughts…"

"Well, if you are so worried," said Mai Cheru with a sigh, looking sadly into the fire, "It's like this… Cheru has been suffering from a strange illness. It's not an illness, actually. The thing is, the spirit of her dead aunt wants to possess her. It affects her mind and her body. That's why she is so quiet. I was half-reluctant to let her work lot you, but she insisted. Now you know."

"Is that what makes her ill?"

"Yes."

" You are sure, Mai Cheru?"

"Of course. Other things have happened in our family since Cheru's father died and we have paid many a visit to spirit mediums. Every time we have been told that it's Cheru's aunt who has been causing these happenings because she has something to say to us."

"And unless you allow this aunt to possess her, Cheru will not he well?"

"No, she won't. Unless we brew some beer and meet her wishes there can be no rest."

"Poor Cheru. Such a young girl, and so quiet too."

"It's nothing to be frightened about," laughed Mai Cheru, her eyes sparkling in the firelight as she crossed one leg over the other. "It's not an evil spirit or something like that. It's just that Cheru's aunt wants to get in touch with us, to let us know that she is looking to our problems and what she feels and thinks.

"You know people out there in the world of the dead see things better than we living people do. She wants to help us but she can only do so if she gets somebody to act as her mouth-piece."

"And Cheru is to be that mouth-piece?"

"Yes."

"And is she going to remain her normal self?"

"Why, yes, of course, except when the spirit possesses her, and that happens not too often, maybe once or twice a year."

"I suppose, if that will help her to get better you had better do it."

"Yes, Masiziva. What can we do? We people with a black skin cannot escape from our customs. We have actually started brewing beer today, and we will have the possession ceremony this Saturday. There will be many people, and lots of food. Meat, stamped mealies, beer, *maheu*, dancing and drums. You can let your boys come to see how it is done, so that they can know about it and be able to write it in their books at school."

"Well…"

"Perhaps your church does not allow you to take part in such festivities?"

"Not quite…"

"Or perhaps your husband?"

"To tell you the truth, Mai Cheru, my husband and I know very little about these customs. Not that we hold them in contempt, far from that, partly because we have lived in town for a long time."

"And you never hold beer parties to honour your dead?"

"Not as far as I can remember. I know back home my people did a few things. But generally we believed that the dead should be allowed to rest in peace."

"You probably have good ancestors, Masiziva. Your ancestors are lying still in their graves and don't believe in causing any inconvenience. But they are looking after you very well, Masiziva, or you wouldn't be alive."

"What would eat me?"

"It's such a world of evil, Masiziva, that somebody has to be watching every step you make. This dark night outside our huts holds every kind of evil you can imagine. You've been living with us for quite a few years now, but have you buried any of your children? Yet you hear of a death here, a death there, everyday. Not ordinary deaths caused by ordinary diseases, but most unusual ones. We have seen people die of swollen stomachs, of a swollen toe, or from strokes of lightning that descend from a bright blue winter sky. And you don't believe there's evil? You still don't believe that you have strong ancestors looking after you?"

"You're very right there, Mai Cheru. Our deceased parents do look after us. It's only that we don't speak enough to them. You wouldn't believe what my father said to me on his deathbed."

"What did he say?"

"He asked me to remove a speck in his eye. I couldn't find that speck, but he promised me a good life."

" You see now, Masiziva. The dead are alive. A person just doesn't die and vanish out of existence. The human soul is too strong to do that."

"Yes."

"Well, I have to go now, Masiziva. I am sorry Cheru has had to leave so suddenly."

"No, its all right. I can see it's urgent."

"We will have to work fast. The worst we can do is to disappoint the dead."

She stood up to go and then mother said, "If there is anything you need ... O yes, Cheru hadn't taken her pay for this month."

"But it's only half way through the month, Masiziva."

"It's all right. It isn't her fault that she has had to leave work."

"Oh thank you. It's nice of you."

"She can always come back to work if she gets better and feels like doing so."

"I will tell her that. I have to go now or I wouldn't stop thanking you. Good night."

"Goodnight and good luck."

"Do you believe in ancestral spirits, mother?" we asked quietly after Cheru's mother had gone.

"Everybody does."

"Then why is it that you don't pay much attention to them?"

"Perhaps we don't need to. Unless they show up themselves first."

"What about ghosts and witchdoctors and things like that?"

"That's another thing," she laughed.

"Some people believe in planting odd things around their homes to keep evil away."

"Yes. But one doesn't have to touch a herb unless one has to."

"And you think there are evil people in this village, mother?"

"That's anybody's guess. As Mai Cheru said, every man is capable of being a devil. But I would say this is a safe village, compared to other ones I have known."

"What happened in the other villages you have known?"

"Come on, you had better stop asking too many questions, or you will be afraid to go to your hut in the dark! "

♥♥♥

On that Sunday the drums boomed all night in Mai Cheru's compound. In the middle of the night, when the half moon was climbing to the zenith, we heard Cheru's voice screaming at a very high pitch as the mysterious spirit possessed her body. She raced into the forest, gasping out indistinguishable totem sounds among the excited and gratified shouts of the crowd who ran after her, listening to the messages from the world of the dead. When we saw Cheru again she was fetching water at the village pump. She looked very normal, and greeted us. But she did not come back to work for us.

It was only then that I realised the mysterious promise she had become while she was with us; she whom we had been at first so anxious about, with her chilling night stories and quiet dark eyes and flowering womanhood.

7

Beer-party

"Another chicken stolen!" exclaimed Jairos, on hearing of the theft, "What, and another batch of eggs gone!"

We by then owned about a hundred healthy chickens. Our hens laid scores of eggs every morning, in the bushes, on rooftops, in cardboard boxes. Admiring our chickens, Jairos had eventually proposed to bring three of his own hens to our pen, ostensibly so that his hens could adopt our breed of chickens. Just after he brought his hens over, our stock started diminishing.

Naturally, on learning of the disappearing eggs, Jairos got worried, since his own hens were in danger. He brought some roots one day and mixed them with chicken droppings, setting fire to the mixture.

"The thief will come to confess that he stole the eggs," he said laughingly as he performed his small ritual. "The stolen eggs will cackle in his stomach till his health and conscience will urge him inevitably to come and confess."

I imagined Jairos had brought the nearest roots he could find and had improvised the ritual. If it worked at all it was not impossible that Jairos himself would suffer the inconvenience of chickens cackling in his stomach.

"Oh yes," said Jairos again, brushing his hands of the ash and bits of herb, "The thief will come to beg forgiveness."

A few moments later:

"Masiziva, there is a simple custom in this village that I hadn't told you about. It is a simple custom observed in this village that every Deruka family should brew beer for the village on at least one Christmas. We call it thanksgiving beer. Just to show the village elders you are thankful they accepted you into the community, you see? You haven't brewed that beer yet, and I don't see why it can't happen this Christmas."

"But I can't brew beer," said mother anxiously.

"You will have to get someone to do it for you, Masiziva. I know you are disappointed somebody has been stealing your chickens and eggs but that's to be expected in any village, and that shouldn't stop you from showing your gratitude towards the village elders."

"It will be a noisy Christmas," complained Yona, after Jairos had gone. "People will be making an open beerhall of our homestead."

"And urinating behind the huts," remarked Jo.

"I doubt if it is the true custom of this village to make newcomers brew beer," laughed mother. "I don't really trust him. Anyway, I will have to get someone to brew the beer for me."

She got Simon's wife, Mampofu. Mampofu brought two huge drums and we went to fetch wood for the fire. Soon a big fire was blazing, Mampofu stirring mealie-meal into the drum of bubbling, boiling water. Late that night the thin porridge was still bubbling even after she had removed the fire, and covered the drum with zinc sheets for the night. The brewing continued for the next four days. Mumera was added to the thin porridge, the porridge boiled again, diluted and left to ferment.

On the day before Christmas, three women came to help Mampofu to sieve the beer. They squeezed the thick brew with their hands, talking, gesticulating, turning to blow their noses on the ground and rubbing their slimy fingers on the sleeves of their old dresses.

Villagers trickled in to taste the beer. They sat near the grain hut, chattering, scolding, arguing over the small white mug, and demanding more beer, while Mampofu the brewer, authoritatively refused to refill the mug. It was good beer, very good beer, they said.

After supper we left for the bus stop to meet father. The night was dark, without a moon yet. A few dark clouds dappled the orizon on the east and the south. The stars shone down on the earth, and in the starlight we groped our way towards the bus stop.

The path was narrow. Already the dew was falling. We could feel it on the grass, soaking our tennis shoes.

We went down into the valley and the night chill of the valley hit us, numbing our mouths, chin and fingers. Here the ground was damp and trembled at the tread of our feet. Even in the starlight we could see the faint yellow gloss of the grass and the green-black of the tall dark reeds. The frogs croaked desperately in the murk and the fireflies flicked their lights on and off in the reeds like little torches. We left the valley and its orchestra of frogs and went up the bank into the safe, warm darkness of the trees.

Our path ran into a big compound. We came upon it suddenly. The two huts loomed suddenly in front of us, the warm homely smell of smoke and sadza drifting out of the glowing doorways. We could hear the chink of pots and plates inside and knew the people had finished supper and the girls were washing the plates. We turned and went past the kraals. We saw the dark forms of the cattle, shiny black eyes glaring at us as we went past in the darkness, full of smell of the cowdung.

We broke out of the trees onto the dust road. The dust road ran like a long dark groove between the two flanks of trees, huge and desolate.

We sat under a tree in the midst of the silent night and waited. Silent, Holy night, I remembered, and the shepherds waiting. But all was not calm and bright. Dark clouds were rolling over the horizon and ploughing up to the zenith. The sky swelled with the darkness. The wind swept in from the south, loading our faces with dust, and flapping our clothes away from us. Overhead the terrified clouds scrambled and scattered and crashed.

Then the wind stopped suddenly and the rain came down on us, thundering in from the trees. We crouched hard against the tree trunks, away from the rain. The earth steamed and smoked as the dust hit our nostrils. A whip of lightning cracked overhead and the earth trembled as the echoes shook the dark, rain-sodden forests. The rain drove round against us and for some minutes we were exposed to it. It left us shivering and soaking as it melted away. The spent clouds rolled down to the horizon and fell in languid heap, exposing a crisp half moon. We shivered.

We heard the bus miles before it appeared. It chugged and rattled and rumbled through the forests and the earth trembled under our feet. Its thick beams of light cut the damp night sky, teasing the forests. The lights hit us and we saw the bus going down into the dip of the valley. It scrambled up to us. We saw its interior lights and smelt its heat and its petrol. It stopped right beside us and the conductor jumped out and ran up the steps to the roof. Two men followed him out of the bus, one tall man in a hat and an overcoat, and the other short and fat, wearing a thick coat. We turned to the tall man excitedly.

"Haa! Hallo boys. You came in all this darkness and the rain to meet me. It must have rained enough to sweep a hut away. What! You are all soaked and as wet as fish. I didn't expect you here at all. You are grown-up boys now, aren't you, no longer afraid of the dark."

The things were brought down from the bus. The conductor banged on the side of the bus and jumped in. The bus hurried away, leaving us standing in the cool crisp moonlight.

"This is Mr Jacobi," said father, introducing the short, fat man. Mr Jacobi shook our hands. His hand was huge and fat and soft. He had brought only a crate of beer and an oil lamp for Christmas.

Yona and I took the two heavy boxes and we went back along the path between the dark trees. Mr Jacobi came with us, carrying his crate determinedly on his shoulders, and the lamp in his hand, having refused to let Jo help him.

"I will light the lamp so that we can see the way," he said, stopping.

"But it's all right," protested father. "There is enough moonlight."

Mr Jacobi lit the lamp. The flame jumped, throwing its yellow light on the wet grass and the sand. We went off again.

"Mr Jacobi lives up on the slope," father explained. "He has built himself a good brick and zinc house, the first one in the village."

"You know Petros?" said Mr Jacobi briefly.

"The tall boy with big gumboots," said Yona.

"The one who shoots birds with a gun," I added.

"Yes," replied Mr Jacobi. "That's my son."

"I see," we said.

"Have you finished the weeding?" asked father.

"Not yet."

"The rain disturbed you?"

"Not very much, the virgin soil is very hard to weed."

"Oh, yes, very hard. But it is a good soil, this. It drains very easily. You can go weeding immediately after a storm, don't you think, Mr Jacobi?"

"A very good soil," nodded Mr Jacobi.

"A good soil and a good land," said father.

"I like this village because people brew beer," said Mr Jacobi.

"Has your wife brewed beer for Christmas?"

"I don't know," said father. "The boys know better."

"Jairos asked mother to brew the Thank-You beer for the village," Yona explained. "The beer was strained today."

"He insisted!" exclaimed father, bemused.

"Is it good beer?" pursued Mr Jacobi.

"Everybody who has tasted it says it is good beer," said Jo.

We went into the forest and passed the huts we had earlier run into. The huts were more distinct now, and a dog bayed weakly at us from under the grain bin.

"I have never seen such stupid villagers," said Mr Jacobi, stopping. "Do you see what this is?"

"What?"

"This earth mound here. It is an old grave. Three paces from the path and five paces from the hut. I wonder how people can ever live so near a grave."

We had not noticed the grave on our journey to the bus stop. I supposed we must have passed close to it in the darkness.

"These people like to live with ghosts," continued Mr Jacobi. "Otherwise how can they have their graves so close to their huts? In the South where I come from graves were placed in the forests, away from the homesteads."

"But this is not the south any more," said father. "The people. here are not as superstitious."

"You think so? I don't think so. I think they are stupid not to send their children to school. Look at the way they build their huts – a confusion of grass and poles – and their huts are built so close together that one little fire will burn down a whole compound. And the way they grow their crops – weeds and plants and bushes compete for the soil."

"They still have a lot to learn."

"And there is that headman, Jairos," he was laughing now, loud fat laughter which I thought could be heard for miles. "That idiot, that imbecile, Jairos. Not one little idea of administration in his head. Giving people's fields away for money is all he knows about. And asking for tobacco and gin. They should set up a council here to run things properly. Jairos! My son would run this village better than he does."

"No," protested father. "Councils are bad. They force people to do things they do not want. They intefere too much with the freedom of the villagers. They make you work and sweat doing silly projects, and make you pay money to build beerhalls. They force cattle into paddocks and force people to get a licence to cut grass or timber. No! Councils will turn the village into a town."

We crossed the stream among the frogs and fireflies. It wasn't exciting any more, not with Mr Jacobi railing away about the village, and his lamp throwing bold yellow light which eclipsed the fireflies.

At the pump Mr Jacobi left us to take another path, and we went home. Mother came sleepily out of the hut, her face swollen with sleep, so that her head fell away when father rather too excitedly tried to put his mouth on hers. But we had to wait until we got to our sleeping hut before we could laugh about it!

✢✢✢

It turned out to be a very noisy Christmas as Yona had predicted. Very early that morning the beer drinkers assembled at our compound to drink our excellent brew. They had come at sunrise, with white grains stuck in the corners of their eyes, and white smudges of dry saliva on their cheeks. They sat in a ring, men and women alike, while the huge white mug was passed round for everyone to take a swig.

The attendance at father's Christmas service was bigger than the previous year's, and afterwards we had many guests for tea, although the beer party did much to dispel some potential guests.

After breakfast we left the noise of our compound to attend a wedding ceremony a mile away. There was already a huge gathering when we arrived. The wedding pair sat in an artificial shade of sacks. The bridegroom, newly barbered, was sweating slightly in his uncomfortable brown suit. The bride was a light-skinned sweet-looking beauty, cool in her spotless wedding dress. They were Southerners.

The crowd stood round them singing and clapping their hands. Now gifts were being given and a balding, loud old man climbed on a drum to announce the presents, shouting with as much vigour as if he wanted to spill his lungs out through the mouth. Pots, pans, mats, chickens, goats and even cattle and money were given to start the pair off in life.

The wedding was conducted in town fashion and the local villagers were impressed by the grandeur of it.

A few metres away a bull was being skinned for meat. The sweet oily smell of roasting meat hung in the air and Jairos could be seen actively helping himself at the fires. Women sweated at the roaring fires, cooking the food in huge black drums.

There was a big hustle when the food was brought out. There were large dishes of mealie rice, almost drowning under pools of fatty yellow soup and the chunks of meat. There was rice and chicken for the special guests. The children dashed for the meat, although there was enough of it to cause toothache afterwards. There was Mazoe and Coke and *maheu*, and, of course, beer. Buckets and buckets of thick, khaki coloured beer.

After eating, the singing and dancing was resumed with renewed vigour, with drums and gramophones and human voices mingling their noises simultaneously. Jairos rose, drunk to his nose, to give a speech on little other than money and beer and meat. He gave his speech with a patronising air but no one minded. In the end the bridegroom himself rose to jive to the gramophone, throwing off his coat and kicking his shoes away. There was much clapping for him and the people wanted the ceremony to go on.

The sun was setting when we left the wedding.

"Let us go to see the field," said father. I could see he was in one of his happy, extravagant moods. He had been to see the field in the morning, but he wanted to go again.

We went. We plodded along the sandy path in our Christmas trousers and shoes. We ended up taking our shoes off and walking barefoot on the warm sand.

We broke into the green expanse of our field. Here the work of the hoe, the labour of the hands, the ache of the back, the salty taste of sweat and the burning thirst had been transformed into living green. The mealies stood erect and tall, sporting a polished looking green-black blue. The lush, thick-stemmed groundnuts were flowering, pumpkin and melon tendrils meandering in the green. You felt like standing in the green for hours, admiring the even colour of it, as if you could actually see them growing and hear the crackling of their roots.

Down in the vlei the fireflies were burning and the chilly vlei air came up to us. It was time to go. We turned back along the path, among the tall dark trees and the crouching bushes where the birds roosted secretly, past the tree stumps where the buck galloped away, crashing into the trees as we approached.

The beer party was still going on in our compound. Men and women sat in broken half rings, chattering at the top of their voices.

Father went round telling the party to disperse. Eventually people clapped their hands in thanksgiving and left in staggering pairs and trios. Matudu came forward hiccupping to say that my father was the kindest and the wisest and the richest and the everythingest man to tell the party to disperse. I expected the beer to spill out of him at any minute.

As I stood in the doorway of the kitchen, watching the last drunkards staggering home, I heard little voices and stepped to look round at the back of the hut.

A female figure was sitting across a man's legs and even in the darkness I saw the movements and heard the gasping noises – I had walked onto them suddenly, without realising what I was doing. The movements and the voices did not stop. I went back quietly into the hut.

"Mrs Simon is an expert brewer," mother was saying over the pots of rice and chicken.

I wondered who they were out there doing it just behind our hut. They were probably very drunk and might stay there all night. But when I went out to check an hour later there was no sign of them.

₩₩₩

Boxing day was not an anti-climax. Father's buoyant mood kept us happy. Early in the morning he sent us to call headman Jairos. We found Jairos up already, drinking off last night's hangover. He came with us at once, first shutting his beer away. He ploughed the path with his car-tyre sandals, wetting his trousers to the knee in the dew. We found father at the field, chopping down a tree.

"Good morning," he greeted Jairos. "How are you?"

"Hangover!" complained Jairos, making himself a cigarette.

"How was your night?"

"We didn't sleep. We spent the night drinking."

"You drank more after the wedding and all those beer parties?"

"Yes, Munyu brought a pot of delicious beer from Goto village and we drank till the second cock crowed."

"You enjoyed yourself. How is your wife and your girl?"

"They are all right."

"And your crops?"

"Oh, they are well too, the mealies are tasselling now."

The crops were not well. In fact there were no crops in Jairos' field because he had not ploughed a single furrow since the rains began.

"I called you, headman Jairos," said father eventually, "because there's a piece of land I want to add to my field to make it straight."

"Yes."

"You see this edge here. The person who chopped down the trees left many bushes close to the edge. These will harm the crops."

"Yes," said Jairos pacing up and down. "I can see the corner is not straight."

"I need to grow more crops to sell," explained father. "My family is growing."

"Go ahead and chop down the trees," said Jairos, laughing.

"But you will give me ten dollars."

"Ten dollars!" smiled father.

"Yes. Ten dollars is not too much to pay the headman for moving him in the morning dew on Boxing Day. You will give me ten dollars and one hen and one bottle of gin."

8

Marufu's Cattle

Exactly a year later, a few days before Christmas, father wrote to say that he would not be coming home for Christmas.

"He says he can't afford to come," mother explained sombrely, folding his long letter. "He has more than enough expenses as it is – your school fees."

"Won't he come at all?" asked Tendai, touching the letter as if she could read.

"I don't think he will come at all," said mother gloomily. "He isn't sending us anything for Christmas either. No meat, no beans, no flour. We will just have to do the best we can on our own." She laughed bitterly, holding the letter out. "You can read the letter if you want."

Yona took the letter, read it quickly and passed it on to me. It was an elaborate one, written in father's clear bold galloping handwriting. It began by asking after everybody's health and the weather and the crops. Then followed a detailed account of all school-fees to be paid, the rent, the water charges and various other expenses. He had compiled a neat list of our school uniforms and school things. I knew it had taken him hours to compile and check the list to make sure it was accurate to the cent. The total was a formidable one. Then followed a long paragraph explaining why he could not come home or send anything for Christmas. My eyes hovered questioningly over the last paragraph, afraid to put the letter down.

On Christmas eve Mr Pendi came to say that he had seen father in town. There was no letter, no parcel.

Christmas came. The Pendis invited us to breakfast. There was a bucket of coffee and a dish of bread, scones, biscuits and cakes. We reciprocated by inviting the Pendis to lunch.

After midday it rained. The torrent poured down from the black sky. Rivulets of water cut the sandy surfaces of our compound, dragging the fine sand to the edge of the forest. After an hour the sun came out.

"Go out," mother chided us. "You stay-at-homes. You never go out as boys of your age do. You want to spend the whole day indoors seeing the turn of my cooking sticks."

It was enough to make us put our raincoats on and go out. The wet sand was swollen. The rain had wiped out all the footprints. Globules of rain hung everywhere on the leaves and the grass.

We passed a compound by the side of the road where a beer party was in full swing, with drums and gramophone playing simultaneously. A woman greeted us from the ring.

"Hello girls."

Yona replied with a thin girlish voice and we ran away laughing.

It was our raincoats which made us look like girls.

We met a man we knew and said, "Christmas Box!"

"Kisimisi, my children," he said, giving us a coin each.

In the township the two stores were closely packed with boys and girls jiving to the gramophone. There were girls with torn stockings and broken shoes stitched together for Christmas, barely concealing cracked feet and heavily oiled legs; boys with heads newly barbered and combed, boys with clean white shirts, balloon trousers and shining shoes, sweating in their thin ties borrowed from brothers and fathers for Christmas. We saw Cheru in the crowd, wearing a bright red dress and pointed high heel shoes. She was spinning her arms and swinging her hips. She stopped dancing when she saw us, her lips barely forming an indistinct greeting. She started dancing again, very slowly, inching into the crowd, out of view. We stood in the doorway, and then the rain came and we had to go in. The rain slashed the tin roof of the store, drowning the sound of the gramophone. The roof was leaking in one corner and girls pushed away from the dripping roof, laughing and falling.

We decided to go back home before another storm built up. Already the wild grey clouds were mumbling overhead. The storm broke on us when we were still half the way home. It closed on us, humming and pelting us. We arrived home after sunset, soaked to the skin. We stood round the fire enjoying its scalding heat.

"Did you come by the field to check for stray cattle?" asked mother. We had forgotten to do so. We could not have done it in the rain, anyway. But now stray cattle might be in our field, eating the mealies.

"We forgot."

"Then I will have to go myself and check. I know it's no use sitting here round the warm fire while the cattle eat my mealies." She put on her raincoat and gumboots and went out.

We couldn't leave her to go alone, though we were soaked to the skin and cold. We left the warmth of the fire and trotted after her. It was getting dark and the rain was slackening. The grass was heavy with the raindrops. My head hit a branch and the water showered down on me. I looked up angrily.

On the other side of the path the open fields gazed at us, their low crops eclipsed by the darkness. Everywhere there was the sound of raindrops falling from the leaves. From the vlei the frogs were blasting out their miserable music with alarming loudness.

We stood at the edge of our field scanning the dark for any movements. "I can smell them," said mother. "They were here a minute ago. Either they are still here somewhere in the field, or they have just left. There is nothing left in this field, I tell you. Nothing."

I was afraid of her voice alone. It was loud in the dark. She splashed into the flooded furrows and we followed her. A firefly jumped up in front of us, flicking its light on. Jo gripped my waist fearfully with both hands. I was frightened and angry.

"Let hold of me, you coward!" I shouted.

He let go quietly, and overtook me.

Mother strode on ahead. The great instinct of a farmer urged her on, driving her to defend her crops from animals even through the darkness and the rain. She came to a dead stop in the middle of the field.

"They have eaten everything here too. Good God in the heavens, they have eaten every shoot." We looked down in the darkness and saw nothing. We turned back and went home. I was surprised. My mother's strange mood touched me lightly. It was the old and the responsible who suffered most from such disasters.

In the broad daylight of the morning, the disaster was unbelievable. In every quarter of the field, the cattle had eaten the mealies. Almost every plant had been nibbled. The leaves had been ripped off leaving only the green sticks of stems.

There were hoof-prints everywhere and many plants had been trampled into the ground. The greatest damage had been done in the centre of the field where the mealies had been tallest. Here the shoots had been chewed to the roots. The cattle had converged onto the centre from everywhere.

"That is what comes out of worshipping Christmas," said mother in a strange new voice. "This is what people pay for staying at home and drinking tea while their crops stand in danger from roaming cattle. This is what I have to pay for my sweat and labours. Look at this! My God! There was a whole kraal of them here. I leave my town with its lights and its sofas and come out to the country to work, and this is what I get for my labours. I do not work for the bellies of my children. I work for the bellies of other people's cattle, don't I? I grow crops to fatten other people's cattle for the market. . ."

A woman came towards us from a path in the forest. Her dress was wet to the hips from the rain and the dew on the grass.

"Good morning, Masiziva," she said, stopping.

"A bad morning, Mai Mashoko. Look at this, Mai Mashoko. Surely these people want something from me. Do you think anyone could be so careless with their cattle, there was a whole herd here."

"I saw the cattle yesterday afternoon," said Mai Mashoko.

"Whose cattle were they?"

"Marufu's. You know him. He's a Deruka who lives in headman Matuvi's line. He has a big herd, a very big herd. I saw them in your field and drove the herd to his homestead. I said to Marufu's boys, 'Why do you let your cattle eat Masiziva's mealies?' The boys said they had been looking for the cattle, so I went to Marufu and said, 'Your

71

cattle ate Masiziva's mealies.' And you know what Marufu said? He said, 'Did the cattle eat your mealies, Mai Mashoko?' I said, 'No,' and he told me to go."

"Tell me, Mai Mashoko, did he say that?"

"He said it. Every word of it with his own mouth."

"He thinks my field is a grazing area for his cattle. I'll go and give him a piece of my mind."

"It won't have any effect on Marufu, Masiziva. Marufu will shut his door in your face and set his dogs on you. That man is a devil. You say there is Satan and the devil, but Satan is nothing compared to Marufu. You know what he did when his neighbour Gonai's son broke the leg of his goat by accident. But Gonai, that blessed man of peace, made up by giving not only a living goat, but a much bigger one, to Marufu. Marufu killed the injured goat and ate the meat with his family. And you think he is a man, Masiziva? He is a devil. If I were you I would not go to him."

"Then what do you think I should do, Mai Mashoko? I can't just keep quiet about it."

"Do anything, Masiziva, but don't go to Marufu. He cares more for the life of a goat than for the life of a boy. He will beat you. Go and see headman Jairos."

"You think Jairos will help?"

"He is the right man to approach. Put a fence of barbed wire round your field, Masiziva."

"Eh… Eh, Mai Mashoko, barbed wire costs money. And with this army of ours going to school there is absolutely no hope of buying barbed wire."

"But you are a clever woman, Masiziva. You grow groundnuts. You sew clothes. Sell your groundnuts and your clothes and buy wire."

"It was kind of you to drive the cattle out, Mai Mashoko. Thank you for your sympathy and advice."

"I couldn't leave the cattle in your field, Masiziva, unless I was a devil. I only wanted to give you advice. Not everyone in this village is a good person. I advise you because you are a good person. Not one day have I heard you open your mouth to slander anyone. But beware of devils like Marufu. Whatever you do, don't go to Marufu, Masiziva."

"The law of this land," said Jairos emphatically that night, "is that no man's animal should go into a person's field and eat his crops. No herdboy should ever lose sight of his cattle. Crops are vital to the life of every villager. All men know this."

Jairos sat at the table, looking down on mother.

"That is the law of this land, Masiziva, and ever since I became headman thirteen years ago this law has always been observed. The day the first rains fall and people put their ploughs to use, the herdboys gather their cattle and graze them in Mbumbuzi forest. Only after harvesting can the cattle be allowed anywhere near the fields. You have been wronged, Masiziva. But there is one question I want to ask you. Whose cattle have eaten your mealies?"

"Marufu's, " answered mother, unnecessarily.

"Now what is Marufu?"

"What do you mean?" asked mother puzzled.

"I mean, is Marufu a local or a Deruka?"

"He is a Deruka."

"Now you see the situation. Marufu is a Deruka and you are a Deruka. Now a Deruka man's cattle went to a Deruka woman's field and ate her mealies."

"What are you getting at?"

"You don't see my point, Masiziva. The Derukas are my guests and I don't aim to promote any quarrel between two of my guests."

"But this is not a quarrel, headman Jairos."

"How do you expect me to react, Masiziva? It is not Marufu who ate your mealies. Marufu's cattle ate your crops. Now do cattle think and reason like people?"

"No."

"No. They don't. Cattle will eat anything, regardless of whom it belongs to. Marufu's own cattle could go to Marufu's fields and eat Marufu's mealies…"

"Quite right."

"Your mealies were eaten by accident, of course. Do you agree?"

"Well… yes."

"Therefore we can't lay any charges on Marufu because it was an accident. One day you will own cattle too, Masiziva, and your cattle will eat Marufu's crops. How would you like him to lay charges against you?"

"I see your point, headman Jairos. My point in reporting this to you is so that you warn people to take greater care of their cattle. . . ."

"That I will do, Masiziva, that I will do. I have always emphasised the importance of crops." He finished eating and went away, and I knew he would never gather enough courage to speak to Marufu. He would break his promise, as he had broken numerous others before.

Here was a headman who spoke of prosperity, peace and progress. And yet made not one positive effort towards these standards. He spoke of good houses when his own compound consisted of only two huts, two unplastered huts with old grey roofs. He spoke of cotton, groundnuts and sunflowers when his own fields were reverting to bush. He spoke extravagantly of paddocks, irrigation schemes and booming townships when he neither had the strength nor determination to dig a single little ditch. He spoke of honesty and decency when he stole eggs and failed to hand in the taxes to the district office. The shocking state of his household spoke against him. Every three or four months he sold an ox, but he spent all the money on beer. He even sold the oxen which drew the plough, and his family were all disappointed. He never stopped long enough to think what he would use during the next ploughing season. His family had been so opposed to his selling the oxen that even young Kaya had refused to drive the oxen to the market. Eventually Jairos had driven the oxen to the market himself, swearing and cursing and driving with as much vigour as if the world might come to a stop before he could spend any of the money. He did not come home for three days after the sale of the oxen; he came home ragged and hungry to beg. Rumour spread round that he had spent the money on beer and gambling and buying a very expensive herb that was supposed to make him the most prosperous village headman in the country.

"You will just have to forgive and forget, Masiziva," he said. Mother forgave and forgot and January showers perhaps fell with a healing effect, because our nibbled mealies started budding again. But after

74

the disaster which had occurred that Christmas, we could never leave our crops to the fate of roaming cattle.

I was sitting reading in the shade one afternoon when I heard the grunting and sneezing of goats. The leader of the group, a huge he-goat with twisted horns and dirty grey skin stepped into the field and neatly uprooted two mealies and munched them. He looked at me with his bulging black eyes and I caught the stink of his body.

I picked up a thick piece of root and flung it at him in anger. The stick caught his hind leg with a snap. The goats jumped and scattered into the bush, the he-goat limping frantically behind them. I followed them, whipping them with a stick till my arm ached and the stick broke into pieces.

I saw a group of herdboys standing in the bushes watching me. They were all youngsters of eight or nine, and held their whips in their hands. I threw my stick down and softly went up to them. "Whose goats ate my mealies?" I demanded.

"We don't know," said two of the boys.

I grabbed a whip from one of the boys. The boys jumped and ran, crying even before I hit them. I lashed furiously at their legs. The last boy to run away was too slow. I grabbed his hand. He embraced me in fear. His face looked up at me, making little expectant crying noises. I pulled his arms away and pushed him off. Up went the whip and I cut him on his neck, shoulders, arms and legs. He cried silently, twisting the flesh of his face. He made no attempt to run away. I gave his legs one final slash and let him go. I watched him go away slowly. I was filled with satisfaction and a strange fear.

"A woman was here with her small boy just now," mother said to me gravely when I got home at sunset. "The mother said you beat him."

"Yes, I beat him. His goats ate the mealies. The goats come every day."

"You shouldn't have beaten him in the face. His face and shoulders were all ridged up with the whip marks. His eyes were red and bulging. Beat them on the legs next time. His mother was complaining that you beat only her boy when there was a group of boys. She says

75

you chose her boy."

"But I beat all the boys."

"You beat him too much. Beat them on the legs next time. The mother threatened to leave the boy here to see what you would do with him."

"She trusts her witchcraft," said Jo, blankly.

"Watch your words, Jo," said mother severely.

After that incident the herdboys grew very afraid of me and kept their animals well clear of our field. The mealies grew again undisturbed.

❋❋❋

We left with heavy hearts at the end of the holiday, knowing that there would be only mother to guard the crops. Every single day of the week, every week of the month, for two months she and the girls would go to the fields to guard the mealies.

We arrived in town late in the evening. The bus had been late. The trunk clanked on the bricks. I knocked on the door. We stood like policemen, waiting for the door to be opened. The streets were quiet now, insects whirled round the glowing yellow street lamps.

A shuffle inside and the door split open. Father stood in the doorway, tall and muscular and hairy without his shirt. His face was half-swollen with sleep, but he was smiling.

"Hello boys." He held out his hands. He was smiling, and we smiled back weakly, tired from the journey.

"You came alone?"

"Yes."

"Come in. Come in."

He carried the trunk in. "Heavy with books," he said.

He had moved the sofas and the small library. There were six new Reader's Digest magazines on the shelf. In the spare room the table was laid thick with books and papers. He had been doing the church accounts before he went to bed.

"I was getting tired of staying here alone," he smiled, scratching his head. "How were mother and the girls?"

"They were well and said how you are."

"The bus was very late. When did you leave the station?"

"Five o'clock."

"With school children coming back to town you can't expect any easy travelling."

"About five full buses passed us without stopping. We were thinking of going back home and postponing the journey. The last bus came and picked us up just in time."

"It's a booming countryside now. You can tell from the way people crowd the buses."

He scratched his armpits and hugged himself, looking blankly at the electric bulb, his smile easing off.

"Why did mother not come with you?"

"She couldn't come because of the cattle. Hardly a day passes without them coming to eat the mealies. Marufu's cattle ate every stick of maize at Christmas –"

"Yes, I remember. The letter you wrote. After that I suppose there was nothing in the fields."

"You wouldn't believe the mealies were eaten once if you saw them. They are green and some of them tasselling already."

"Don't tell me," he said as if really refusing to believe it. "I thought there would be nothing. It's all Jairos' fault. He gave us a good field, but the field is in the wrong place. No field can thrive a few paces away from the vlei where cattle are grazed. Jairos should have given us a field up in the west away from the grazing fields."

"But if we had a fence, father, everything would be all right. The soil is very good, especially that area around the thorn trees where the old graves were, and the old cattle pens. The mealies are very tall there. All we need is a fence."

"You are quite right about the fence but fences cost money. And with your school bills shooting up I can't spare a cent for the fence yet. That is the problem of having two homes, boys. I can't come home every weekend, let alone with rolls of wire. Your education gets top priority, boys, and that is why I think the fence can wait. That is why we can't buy cattle yet, and why we can't build ourselves a nice brick and zinc house. Wire and cattle and houses can wait but your education can't."

Yes, our education could not wait. But could our country home wait? We had put too much into it to bring it to a sudden standstill. Yes, our education was expensive, but mother would go to guard the field every morning, naked to the rain. She would act as a human fence to keep the animals away from the crops. I felt sad to see father going alone into the bedroom. He would be alone again when we left for our boarding schools. He would go to work everyday and come back to an empty house. To prepare his own meals. His sole companion would be the radio, but then he did not have money to spare for the battery. That was why he had looked blankly at the electric bulb and asked why mother had not come. At least mother had the girls to talk to. Perhaps mother should have come with us. Or was father simply falling out of touch? Twenty years in town is a long time. That was the trouble with two homes – they kept the family separated.

9

Mother

Later during the school-term as I lay snugly in my bed in the school
dormitory I thought of mother standing in the darkness and the rain
and saying in a tearful voice: "They have eaten everything here too.
Good God in the heavens, they have eaten every shoot." I thought,
too, of father scratching his armpits under the dull yellow globe and
asking, as he went miserably into the empty bedroom, why mother
had not come with us.

And I remembered my mother's heroic resilience. It all began with
a story she told us when we were children:

*Once upon a time a man had two dogs, a black one and white
one. One day the man had gone hunting without his dogs. A lion
stalked him, forcing him to climb up a tree. The sun was setting,
and he was far away from home. But the lion sat motionlessly
under the tree, waiting for the man to come down. The hunter
started singing, calling out to his dogs.*

'Machena my white dog
Come and fight for me
Come and fight for me
And you Matema, my black dog
Come and fight for me
Come and fight for me.'

*The faithful dogs had heard him and ran all the way from
home, beckoned by his voice. They grappled with and killed the*

lion, and the hunter came down from the tree to go home.

Whenever mother told us that story, I looked uneasily into the darkness and moved nearer to the fire. There was something ominous, about its atmosphere of desperation. I could feel the urgency: the setting sun, the darkness gathering on the vast uninhabited forest, and the solitary hunter clinging precariously to the thin, cracking branches of a tree, looking down fearfully on the lion below him. I could almost hear the sad echoes of his determined voice. It was a thick voice, half-crying like an old woman's. But the faithful dogs had come to his rescue.

There were other chilling stories too – like that of the girl who drowned in a well, again at dusk, and was captured by the maidens of the river, unknown to the people who drew water from the well, and whose efforts to find her were in vain.

Somehow I found a vague match between mother and some of the heroes of her stories, with whom her life shared a sense of mystery, pathos and resilience.

In a photograph taken of my mother when she was thirteen she wore a simple brown dress and a scout belt. She was already a young woman, with a budding chest and legs that a man would turn to look at. She had been born on a farm, and her father was the farm foreman. He was a farmer, growing potatoes and keeping many cows. Traders came from far with their lorries to buy his potatoes and his rich milk. He was a young man, and smart, with trim hair and a dark moustache. His wife was also a farmer – growing peanuts and raising chickens. She was a smart woman who loathed to see black specks in milk, or cracks in the walls of her huts. Later on she had lost her voice and talked continuously in a hoarse whisper.

My grandfather had died at an early age, when my mother was still only nine or ten years old. The last months of his life were months of illness and comas. Hospitals had failed to cure him. He had asked to be taken to his village to die in his compound. His wife had not given up hope. Many medicine men were invited from far away places to cure him but again these failed. On the day he died his wife and children had gone away to the river with a witchdoctor to perform the rites to drive away the spirits which we believed to be vieing for his life. Only my mother had been left behind to look after the sick man.

The darkness started creeping over him in the afternoon. He asked for porridge but could not eat.

"Look into my eye, daughter," he said to my mother. "There is a chip of wood in my eye which I want you to remove."

My mother had held the two thin eyelids apart and searched for the chip. She saw nothing.

"Remove the chip and I will give you all the wealth and wisdom you want. I will protect your homestead. You will not bury any of your children. Your crops will do well and your cows will give birth to females. Your chickens will hatch all their eggs. Your enemies will not harm you. Find that chip, my daughter, and I will give you everything you want in life."

She looked and looked under the red skin and the thin cornea but she saw nothing. The eyelids froze under her fingers. He passed away peacefully and my young mother thought he had gone to sleep. The family soon returned from the river and the alarm was raised.

They buried him on the following morning, on an antheap, and framed his grave with four blocks of granite. For a whole year after his death there was the property to be distributed among the dead man's brothers and his wife.

He left a family of five children. The first was a girl of marrying age, the second and third were young men, my mother was fourth and the last was a boy of nine. Shortly afterwards the eldest girl got married and went off to live with her husband. The two young men too, packed their bags and went off, to seek their fortunes in the towns.

The family dispersed but the homestead did not crumble. Under the stern hand of my grandmother, the remaining herd of cattle grew steadily and the fields were tilled. There were potatoes and milk and vegetables at all times of the year. A lorry came every May to take her maize to the market.

My mother and her brother went to school. My unenthusiastic young uncle soon left school and followed his brothers to the towns. My mother was a bright pupil and in her eighth year at school she was made head girl and placed in charge of the domestic science room.

She was a reserved girl and in her spare time she would shut herself up in her room to knit and sew. In the planting season she worked hard, yoking the oxen and holding the plough while her mother dropped seeds into the furrows.

She had few friends. The only time she had gone to the village concert was one dark spring night. She went with her two friends. The concert ended very late. On their way back home after the concert they passed by a deserted homestead. Here the grass grew inside the falling huts. Suddenly, two lights burst out in each of the ruined huts, as if the huts were on fire. But the huts did not burn. The three girls saw the lights and ran, losing their shoes in the dark and cutting their feet on the sharp tree-stumps.

After that, my mother was nervous of the night.

But their crops were in danger, at night, from the wild pigs which often came to eat the green mealies. They could destroy a whole field in only one night. So during the crucial month before harvesting my mother and her mother would go out in the middle of the night to chase away the pigs. I can almost see their two figures moving in the dark, the wind playing with their clothes, their skirts ruffling in the grass as they passed the sleeping compounds where an occasional cock would crow. They were determined farmers.

Soon enough young men began to look twice at my budding mother. She was a girl of medium build, with soft dark hair, good legs and a generous bosom. Sweet-tongued young gallants tried their luck on her, snatching short bits of conversation with her at the pump or on her way to the fields.

She was not rude to the men, but she did not lavish any futile words on them. But one man seemed to have captured her interest. He was a tall man, perhaps eight or nine years older than she was. He dressed formally in the fashion of the time – balloon black trousers ironed out to the last crease, crisp white cotton shirts, stringy black ties and black shoes. He worked in town and came every Sunday to see her. Together they would go to church. He held the umbrella and she carried the bibles and the books.

He was a well behaved man. He scorned beer and smoking and dicing. He was not afraid of his mother-in-law, as was customary of the lover-boys of the time. To hide behind the bush, gesticulating and calling to his girl, was not his idea of decent behaviour. He was bold and straightforward enough to go to his prospective mother-in law to let her know that he loved her daughter and planned to marry her. He loathed elopement.

As the tall Southerner from the town continued to visit his sister, my young uncle naturally started asking questions.

"Who is this tall man who comes here every week-end? Who does he want?" My mother did not have to answer these questions. Her mother defended her gallantly.

"Don't be a fool, Ruben," she rebuked my young uncle. "Do you think your sister will remain a girl forever? Do you want her to grow old and withered and unattractive before a man can look at her? Will you marry her then, yourself? Shame on you. The days are gone when brothers threw hot water at their sister's lovers."

That poured hot water over my young uncle and when the tall man came again Ruben behaved in a more agreeable manner. Before the courtship was completed my mother's people decided to emigrate. There was a small farewell party with rice and chicken. The lobola was demanded and paid quickly. The day of departure came. The emigrants went off on a battered yellow bus. My mother waved frantically at the bus and cried. But she had decided to remain behind with her husband and stay with him she did.

He took her first to his mother in the country. She worked hard, going to the well and cooking and washing and weeding. She was a strong energetic woman and the old woman was much impressed by her.

After three months he came and took her to the town. They lived together in a small neat house with four rooms, the wood stove, the electric lights, the Marylyn radio and a little garden with flower beds and choumoellier. They lived very happily together and soon the children and the problems they brought with them were on their way.

10

Changes

Yona would not be going home with us that April. "But father, can't I go for the week-end at least?"

No, he couldn't. He would stay behind and try to get a vacation job at a factory. He would also keep father company.

We went home without Yona. He came with us to the bus, however, to help carry the things. He hated cooking and washing and I wondered if he would enjoy the holiday. Perhaps he would get a job.

"Why didn't Yona come?" said mother. It must have been her second question. "Oh my son. When will I see him?"

"Let him work," said Tendai, "so that he can buy us sweets and dresses."

"You guarded the mealies very well, mother," I complimented, looking around. Her gumboots were torn with the roots and walking, so that her toes were showing. She had grass in her hair.

"We have just finished doing the nuts," she explained, "there weren't many nuts this year."

"How many bags?"

"Not many. The mice attacked the crop in February. We got only seventeen bags in the end."

I had thought it would be worse than that.

The girls came running towards us with a water-melon.

"Give the melon to the boys," said mother.

"The boys from the town don't know melons," said Tendai.

We roasted some mealies and went home. In the evening Mrs Pendi came to see us and brought her children. Emma was twelve now, and growing up. Sam was still too short for his age.

"Why didn't my friend Yona come?" she asked.

We talked and laughed into the night. Then we sang two verses of an old hymn. Mrs Pendi sang the alto. She had a rich voice. Afterwards she gave a long and elaborate prayer and we went to bed feeling happy. The dew was heavy on the grass in the morning. We spent the early part of the morning sitting round the fire, so that our eyes felt dizzy when we came out into the sun.

Jairos was coming along the path.

His appearance shocked me. Even from far he looked shrunken-up. His legs were as thin as stamping sticks in his trousers. He had lost weight.

His step was stiff, as if he was dragging painful joints. His head looked straight ahead, eyes glued on something ahead. His mouth moved slightly, as if he was talking to himself.

He stopped at the Pendi's gate. He threw the gate open and the gate gave a loud clank. He went past Mrs Pendi's kitchen towards the toilet. He went into the lavatory and came out a minute later, adjusting his wet, falling trousers. He blew his nose with his fingers and wiped the fingers on his coat. His nose blew like a horn. The sound brought Mrs Pendi out of the kitchen. She came out clutching her baby and stood ominously confronting him. He walked straight towards the gate, hardly noticing her.

"Hey you, Jairos," she shouted. "Didn't my husband tell you not to come and mess up my toilet?"

He hardly listened to her. He waved his hand vaguely in the air, perhaps not at her.

She charged him with more words, putting the baby down to point and gesticulate.

" You come here every day to mess up my toilet. Why don't you build your own? You only come when my husband is away, because when he is here he won't let you through the gate. Hey Jairos –"

She took a step forward but he was already at the gate. He did not shut the gate. He turned in at our gate and came towards us, eyes fixed on the ground, mouth moving, fingers twisting.

"Your mo… mo… mother… is she in?" he stammered.

"No," said Shuvai mechanically. "She has gone to the fields."

"Aaah!" exclaimed Jairos, disapprovingly, refusing to believe it. His desperate lips opened to show a grey tongue. He saw mother at the fire and went in to sit on the chair.

"Good morning, headman Jairos," said mother.

He looked into the fire and did not reply. The skull of his head showed clearly under his pale brown skin. His buttonless shirt was open, and you could count his ribs as easily as a plucked bird's. His feet, strapped up in black sandals, were cracked and thin and dusty. His mouth kept making little hissing noises.

He suddenly broke his long blank stare and looked up.

"Let me have *maheu*," he said, with a bewildered look. He drank it without pausing to take a breath. Afterwards he sat chewing the grains, swallowing, raking his cheeks with his tongue, and spitting into the fire.

He rose to go without a word.

The kids in the next compound saw him coming and a small boy shouted. "Go away, Jairos."

Jairos fumbled to unfasten the gate.

"It's locked, Jairos," said the boy insolently. "Go away."

"Open!" shouted Jairos. "You son of a whore!"

The kids laughed and went into the house.

Jairos gave up and went away. I asked mother what was wrong with him.

"Didn't I tell you?" exclaimed mother, surprised. "Jairos was ill for a long time after you left. Something seems to have gone wrong with his mind. People think he's mad."

※※※

We learnt from mother that when it started, Jairos had come home one evening and stood outside his compound looking at his huts. The light of the young sharp-horned moon was dim. Blueish smoke drifted from his huts into the night sky.

"I am headman Jairos," burst out Jairos. "I stand here just outside my own homestead. I see grey smoke. The smoke comes out of my huts. I don't want to go home. I see monsters in my huts. I don't want to go home because I see monsters in my hut."

His voice rose to a pitch. There was a strange new note of fear in it.

"Ernest! Ernest! Ernest! Come and take me, Ernest. They want to take me, Ernest! Help me!"

His voice echoed in the darkness and there was silence in the village. "Help me, Ernest!" he shouted again desperately. Suddenly he was surrounded by people and Simon's voice was heard among the agitated voices of women.

"Come on, brother Jairos. Let's go home."

"I won't go home!" he shouted, breaking loose.

"Here is trouble in my family," wailed Lulu's mother.

"He will be all right," said Simon. "Hold his hand."

He quietened suddenly like a mute child and they led him home. But next morning he wasn't there. For two weeks no one knew where he was. He came suddenly, at the end of two weeks. He came back looking twenty years older, and very thin. For five whole minutes he wouldn't blink. He crouched near the fire and stared into the flames with his sunken red eyes. He refused to eat porridge. His wife wept for a very long time and Lulu ran away from home.

Now Simon, Jairos's brother, was the acting headman.

He came to our compound one morning and sat on a stool in the sunshine. He wore a yellow shirt formerly white and balloon grey trousers which failed to disguise his small limbs.

"Wamambo," he said in salutation, clapping his hands.

"Good morning, Mpofu," said mother from the kitchen.

I brought a chair but Simon declined it, saying he was all right on the stool.

"Did you sleep well, Wamambo??" he asked us.

"Yes, we did," we replied. "How did you sleep?"

"My wife did not sleep at all. She is suffering from backache. She was in bed all afternoon. I told my daughter to make porridge for her but it didn't help. I went to Chiutsi and he gave me a herb. If the herb doesn't work I will take her to the hospital and let the doctors cut open her back to see what is wrong."

"What a pity," said mother, coming out with a mat. "Her backache still troubles her. Maybe you should take her to the hospital right away. Doctors do help."

"Hospitals are good, Masiziva, very good. But they want money and I don't have that. It's only people like you with husbands working in the towns who can afford to pay the doctors."

"We are no better, Mpofu," laughed mother. "This army of ours drains every cent from us when they go to school. You wouldn't believe how much we pay for their education. My only consolation is to live here in the country where I can spend a week without parting with a coin. I pity my husband in town who parts not with coins, but bank notes, everyday."

"Money is a problem, Masiziva," said Simon, picking his nose. "Have your sons nearly finished school?"

"Far from it," laughed mother. "Maybe another six or seven years before Yona finishes."

"Six years, Masiziva!" exclaimed Simon, genuinely alarmed. "Your sons will grow old while they are still at school. Let them find work now. They can read and write. They finished their grades long ago, didn't they? They have enough education now. One of them can even teach in our village school. The others can work as office clerks in the District Commissioner's office."

"No, Mpofu. We want them to have a good education. We don't care if it takes years to do that. Life will be very hard in the future and we might as well suffer now trying to make things better for them."

"You are lucky your sons are doing well, Masiziva. My brother's daughter Lulu was intelligent. She could read and write anything but after her father fell ill she could not go to school anymore."

"A pity," said mother. Secondary school and University were beyond Simon's imagination. Education ended at writing and reading letters.

"The purpose of my coming, Masiziva," said Simon eventually, "is to let you know of the changes which will soon be taking place in our village. You probably heard that the running of the village will sometime in the future be handed to local councils. The council will control five villages, namely ours, Matuvi's, Mponda's, Rushwaya's and Joachim's. The council will collect the cattle taxes and give out dip tickets. Any man who wants to have his field extended or to have a new plot will have to see the council. The council will decide everything. It plans to build new townships to encourage businesses, maize mills and stores. Eventually they plan to build a dam, which would be most useful to the cattle in the dry season. People would fish in the dam too."

He picked his short beard and continued: "Last week all village headmen were called to a meeting at the chief's kraal. The chief explained everything to us. From now on all fields will be ten acres each. All the fields on the steep slopes will have countour ridges to stop the soil from washing down to the river. Those fields on the more gentle slopes will have grass strips. The agricultural demonstrators decided, too, that the cattle are slowly destroying the stream by stamping on its banks. From now all cattle will go to graze in Mbumbuzi Forest. In the dry season the vlei area immediately around the stream will be fenced off to protect the gardens. The demonstrators will be coming soon to peg the fields. Tell your boys to sharpen sticks for the peggers..."

The peggers came after only a week, to lay out the grass strips. They were two ordinary-looking men with short trousers and farmer-shoes. One man criss-crossed the field with a painted pole, while the other man viewed the field surface through a kind of plain-table, and measured the depressions against the marked, painted pole. The man with the plain-table knocked the pegs into the ground to mark the grass strip areas.

"Who made such crude sticks?" he asked despisingly. He was huge and hairy and munched salted nuts all the time.

"What a waste of land," exclaimed mother, surveying the wide grass strips.

"The strips will conserve the soil, lady," explained the peggers.

"Wait till you see the mice which will breed in the grass," smiled mother. "They will destroy all the crops."

The peggers folded their instruments and quietly went to peg more fields. We were fortunate in not having got contour ridges. Everywhere other people went about with picks and shovels, chopping the earth into neat trenches and ridges of soft brown sand. People complained about the new council.

The construction of contour ridges and grass strips went on smoothly but the fencing off of the stream did not get started. Perhaps headman Simon had forgotten about it already.

〰〰〰

Back in town Yona been working for three weeks in a factory. "What do you do?" I asked him hesitantly, fearing that he worked with picks and shovels, sweating all day at the furnaces.

"I do a clerical job," he explained. "I help in the welfare department, keeping records of the overalls, gloves and boots given out to the workers, for instance."

"Is it exciting?"said Shuvai.

"Yes. People can be very interesting, especially Mr Rufoyo, the chief clerk. He lives in Zata Street – you should know him. He has been loafing recently because he has had me to do his work for him. He can be away from his office for hours going to the time-office, to the toilet or even to town."

"What is the time-office?"

"That's where people line up to have their work cards punched when they go into the factory and when they come out. Mr Rufoyo will be very sad when I leave the factory tomorrow. He has the shortest memory you can imagine. He keeps forgetting whether my name is Yona Wamambo or John Mbona. And right now he isn't sure if I am doing Form five or Form two! He seems to have a hangover every morning – he even brings beer to work sometimes!"

"It must be exciting," said Shuvai, "but where is that bag of sweets you promised us?"

Yona laughed guiltily. He looked so grown up in his black coat and blue tie. His hair was was combed better than usual, but was somewhat dishevelled after a day of headscratching at work. He went into the sitting room and pulled the string to light the electric bulb. He put the radio on and twisted the knob quickly to a shortwave station.

"Elton John's new record 'Daniel'," he told us.

90

"You tune in to LM a lot?"

"Sometimes it doesn't catch the waves and the music fades out."

"Headman Jairos has gone mad, didn't you hear?" said Jo. He couldn't wait.

"What?"

"Yes, he went mad," I explained. "He came home shouting all sorts of things one evening. He disappeared for two weeks and came back looking very ill. People said he had been working himself to death chopping down trees in Mbumbuzi Forest for no reason at all."

"That's unbelievable."

"He spends days walking up and down the village, systematically asking for food. He refuses to eat the food his wife gives him."

Yona opened a plastic packet and fished out a handful of nuts.

"How many bags this year?" he asked, munching.

"Thirty-one," said Shuva, "We have already sold the bags."

Yona munched away at the nuts, pushing them one by one through the corners of his mouth. He tapped his feet to the radio and plucked his ribs with his fingers. He loved music. Dirty plates were heaped on the stove. Shuvai touched the stove and Yona laughed.

"I didn't have time to wash the dishes this morning," he explained. "I was late for work. Now that you've come things will be easier."

"We did a lot of work this holiday," said Jo. "The peggers came last week. The council is now going to run everything."

Father leaned his bicycle against the wall outside. He came in with a big black trunk. Jo had damaged his old one. His schoolmates would call this new big one a coffin.

Father put the trunk down in surprise and smiled.

"We were thinking you would be late for school," he said. "You did well to come today so that you can get ready for your trains. How was everyone at home?"

In the spare room the table was strewn with envelopes, writing pads and various papers. He had been budgeting.

He went into the sitting room, tuned the radio for the news and slumped on the sofa. Shuvai started washing the dishes. Jo and I went in to give father the money we had made from the sale of the nuts.

11

Boyce

The dark night was pregnant with the promise of a storm. All round there was a warm stillness, and not a cricket could be heard. The dust road ran like a groove between the dark pressing flanks of trees. The bus had clattered away.

Jo and I lifted the heavy black trunk and Shuvai carried the blankets. The path was dark. Leaves brushed our legs. Perhaps it was two in the morning.

We moved quickly in the darkness. The trunk creaked and cut our fingers. We kept stopping to change sides and I imagined how much easier things would have been if Yona had been here to help. We went down the slope. The forest thinned out and the vlei came into view. The vlei was like a grey carpet. The grass was very still. The crop of reeds flanking the stream was aglow with the fireflies. The path widened, and the sand deepened and gleamed in the darkness. I knew this was where the herdboys played, weaving their cattle whips, rolling on their backs on the sand and catching locusts, while the cattle grazed in the vlei.

But now there was no sound. Even the frogs were quiet. If the fireflies could make a sound we could perhaps have heard faint murmurings. We went down to the bottom of the vlei and the cold blast hit us. I could feel the crisp frozen air around me. The soft damp ground trembled under our feet.

We searched for the stepping stones. Shuvai found them and went across. A bolt of lightning streaked down from the sky, showing the bewildered purple clouds, momentarily clothing everything in artificial white light. I saw our images in the water. Jo slipped and lost his grip on the trunk. The trunk clanked as it hit a stone, jerking my hand.

"You —" I turned on him fiercely. Somewhere in the reeds a frog attempted to croak. The other frogs did not join in and it shut up. We left the chilly grey vlei and went up into the warm dark trees.

The white walls of the mission primary school glimmered through the black trees. A dog bayed weakly at us from the dark. New huts had been built. We marched past the kraals where the cattle stamped and a cowbell clanked. There was a strong sharp smell of cowdung, of the dust, and human refuse. At night these smells seem to sink into the grass.

We almost ran into the water pump in the darkness, but a pool of water round it warned us off. Here the grass was soft and green where women washed their clothes and puff adders lay in the grass waiting.

Our three huts loomed ahead and the sand threw off a pale grey light. A dog broke into a sharp bark, his thick, strong voice crashing into the night. I fumbled with the chain of the gate. The dog came down to us, growling. Even in the dark I could make out his huge shape. I suddenly remembered the letter mother had written.

"Simba! Simba! Hello Simba! Come Simba!"

He stopped barking and came crashing into us, squealing with delight. The bedroom door cracked open and mother came out with a light.

"Oh, my children!"

She was leaner. Vimbai, Tendai and Rita lay on the floor. I went to Rita and shook her violently. She turned, opening her eyes, and uttered an exclamation of surprise. Her little body was warm as I lifted her from the blankets.

"You walked all the way from the station!" mother exclaimed, looking at her watch. "It's three o'clock now. Were you not afraid of the dark?"

"Shuvai was," said Jo.

"What about you? You dropped the trunk with fear when the lightning flashed and Godi scolded you."

"I don't like the vlei at night," I said.

"I know it gets scary with the fireflies and the frogs," said mother. "So my Yona is not coming again."

"He is starting work tomorrow at the factory."

"Oh, my son. Anyway, let him work. He must help his father."

"I smell the rain," said Shuvai.

"It rained yesterday but it was very hot today."

The door of the hut opened and a boy came and crouched at the door.

"Come in, Boyce," said mother.

I had almost forgotten the name. Boyce was a tall boy, a young man in fact. He was slim and strong limbed. His hair was long and kempt, although now there were threads of blankets in it. His face was swollen with sleep but I could make out the sharp features, the fine set of teeth and the light brown complexion. Pimples were swelling on the sides of his face and I knew he was about two years older than me. He wore a white shirt and green shorts.

"These are all my children, Boyce," said mother. "Would you believe it?"

Boyce laughed politely and shook hands with us.

"Boyce came to live with us and to help us," explained mother. "He has been here since October. He comes from Matuvi's line. I don't think you have met him before."

His face looked to me strangely familiar.

"His mother is Masibanda, the tall lady who usually passes along singing and stops to ask if I have any *mhunga* to sell."

One April night there had been a beer party in the Pendi's compound. Masibanda had drunk and sung exceedingly loudly. The grass near the kraals had caught fire and the fire had roared towards the Pendis' big house. Men had run off to put the fire out. Boyce's mother had protested, shouting: "Let the fire burn and come to the house. I want to warm myself. I say let the fire burn. . . ."

"Shut up," the men had told her, but she had gone on shouting.

Boyce was tall and slim like his mother.

"Boyce is an expert with oxen. You will see how he handles the oxen. He makes them run with the plough."

"Whose oxen, mother?"

"Didn't I tell you. I bought us two oxen from Matudu."

"You are wonderful, mother, you are wonderful. I never thought you could do that. I thought you were joking."

"But I didn't see any kraal outside."

"The cattle still stay at Matudu's kraal. You can go and see them first thing tomorrow morning before Matudu's boys take them out to the pastures."

Out in the dark the lightning flashed. Boyce put his head out of the hut and announced that the rain was coming.

"You had better go off to sleep or you will get wet," said mother. "Boyce is a nice young man and I am sure you will live very happily together. See you tomorrow."

We went out. It was so dark that Jo almost ran into the wall of our hut. The storm was peeling off in the north, buzzing confidently towards us. The air was very still and I could smell the rain. In the dark Simba grunted and curled up under the grain hut. Boyce lit the lamp. The hut was very warm. I suppose the walls had been heating up all day. The floor was newly swept and polished with cowdung. Boyce's mats and blankets were on the floor. He had tied a rope across the hut and his clothes hung from the rope – two pairs of shorts, a faded blue T-shirt and a brown shirt. He did not have a suitcase. We spread our blankets beside his and went to sleep. Boyce let the lamp burn for a few minutes and then blew it out. I could see his smile and his handsome teeth as he pulled the lamp to his mouth to extinguish it. The moment the lamp went out the rain came down.

It washed down steadily, soaking everything. The ground trembled to the thunder. I caught the wet smell of the grass and the sand but I knew we were safe from the rain.

It was nice to come home.

Perhaps I slept for only five hours. When I woke up the sun was shining through the slit in the doorway. I could see the raindrops glistening on the grass. Boyce was out and Jo was jumping into his clothes.

"What's the hurry?" I asked. "You look as if you want to tear your clothes."

"I am going to see the cattle."

"You seem to think the cattle will run away. Take your time."

He went out and a minute later I could hear him playing with Simba and greeting Mrs Pendi. I lay for another half hour, enjoying the warmth of the blankets and the sounds of the morning. When I went out the sun was high. The sky was clear. I looked out and saw several rooftops through the trees. Blue smoke was oozing through the damp grey grass and filtering into the air. The tilled brown acres appeared like neat cuttings against the soft summer green of grass and tree foliage. I looked out to the north and caught a glimpse of the vlei. In the north I could see the Mbumbuzi Forest, a solid chunk of green defying the green and brown of the village clearings. Half a dozen naked giant trees etched on its horizon, waiting to be cut down by the lightning, to be claimed by the women and the ants.

Our compound area had been tilled and the mealies were sprouting. Next to the gate sweet potato runners were inching across the path into the bush. The mango trees were big now, and drooping with green mangoes. The grass was dull green silver, the dew drying in the sun.

Simba was a fine dog.

He was something between an Alsatian and a hound — tall and strong, cream coat shiny, canines sharp and white. He left Jo and came to me, thrashing me with his tail, licking my knees, leaping to lick my face. I struggled to keep him down.

"Hallo Godi," Mrs Pendi called out from the fence. I pushed Simba away and went to meet her. She laughed, hardly waiting for me to get to her.

"What!" she exclaimed. "You are still growing tall. You've put on another two inches since last holiday. Where do you think you are going? You want to touch the sky? You won't be able to pass through the doors without bending your back if you continue growing tall like that. You've put on weight too. Look at your cheeks, as fat as tennis balls. What were they giving you at boarding school?"

"Beans and porridge," I laughed. I took the baby from her, lifting him high over the barbed wire. He was a strong little boy, with curly black hair and steady brown eyes. He scrutinised my face closely.

"Sam will be happy now he has a brother. Hurrah for the boys," I said.

"The next one will be a girl, to spite you," she laughed. She was darker now, and more slim. Her skin had not been burnt by the sun, but tanned gently. She no longer used skin lightening creams as she had done when I first saw her. That was when she was fat and comfortable and decried everything. She still talked and laughed and scolded her children but she no longer chased them all over the compound. The country was taming her.

Her children came to say hello. Her daughter was growing into a young lady. Sam was not growing as fast as his sister. The other two girls could run and talk now. I remembered one of the girls had been a very tiresome infant indeed but now she was growing up into a little beauty.

I put the little boy over the fence and took home the mangoes Mrs Pendi gave me. Boyce had returned. He was younger than I had thought, although he was still older than me.

"I went to see Mandlovu," he said, sniffing and rubbing his hands at the fire. The dew had washed his ankles. "She was waking up when I got there. I told her I had come for your money. She said she didn't have anything because she had not brewed any beer for weeks. But she said she would brew beer next week, if she happens to get *mumera*."

"Mandlovu is a crook," said mother. "I know all her tricks. If she sees me at the pump she runs away quickly because she knows I will ask for my money. Two dresses taken a year ago, and not a dollar paid. I will wait for two weeks and if she doesn't bring anything I will get hold of everyone of her chickens. If that doesn't satisfy me I will sell her goats to get my money."

"You will grab her chickens, mother! " said Rita, evidently thrilled.

"Did she not throw a beer party last Sunday, Boyce?" asked mother.

"I think she did," replied Boyce.

"And she says she did not have *mumera*. What happened to it all?"

"You don't know her," said Boyce. "Mandlovu! She's the laziest woman in the village. She cannot even grow enough maize to feed her chickens. This year she reaped absolutely nothing. Her husband was ploughing Deruka fields for money and tilled only one acre for her. But Mandlovu didn't even bother to weed that one acre. She drinks too much."

"What do they eat then?"

"They rely on their cattle. Her husband inherited a huge herd from his father. Every year he sells about two cattle to get money to buy maize. But this year he bought only two bags of *mhunga* and spent the rest of the money on beer."

"I should not have trusted her with those dresses," said mother, biting her mango.

"Is one of the dresses blue with a white collar?" asked Boyce.

"Yes."

"And is the other dress a brown one with black belts?"

"Yes."

"She wears those dresses alternatively, they are almost in shreds now and very dirty too. I bet the next time she washes them will be for Christmas."

We roared with laughter.

"And did you see Mai Dori, your brother's wife?"

"Yes, I did, but she said she didn't…"

"I knew she would tell such stories," cut in mother with a smile, "Tell your brother I am coming for his chickens next. The only woman who pays her debts in this whole village is Ndoga's wife."

"And Mrs Matudu," I added.

"Mrs Matudu!" exclaimed mother. "You don't know her. She takes two years to pay for a skirt. But wait till you see her pressing her own debtors. Now she is saying if we don't hurry up and finish the payments for cattle we might have to leave a calf with her as interest when we take our cattle. Whoever paid the full sum for cattle in this village in two months, let alone in two years?"

That reminded Jo of the cattle. He jumped up to say he was going to see the cattle.

"Wait till you have your breakfast," mother told him.

We went with Boyce after breakfast.

"Where does your mother live, Boyce?" I asked as we went to Matudu's home.

"In Mativi's compound. You pass two big compounds after leaving the headman's and you come to my mother's. There is only one small hut and one small grain hut. My father died when I was still a young boy and at that time we lived in another village. Eventually my sisters got married and my brothers went away to work in the mines. My mother and I moved into this village and there was no need to build many huts because there were only two of us and I was away working most of the time."

"Have you worked before, Boyce?"

"Yes, I first worked as a mill-operator. I spent all day grinding people's grain in the mill."

"Did you enjoy working?"

"Very much. There were two of us, me and another boy. We lived in a room at the back of the mill. The owner of the mill lived in town and came only on weekends to bring the diesel and to collect the money. He was a nice man. Sometimes he brought us meat and bananas and gave us a few shillings above our pay. I worked for about three months, then the rains fell and I had to go home to help my mother. But I didn't like to sit at home and ask for money, so after the harvesting I got myself another job. It was with a Deruka family in Goto's line. The Deruka man's name was Mugova. He was a very rich man. He owned two ploughs, two barrows and a tractor. He grew groundnuts and cotton and sunflowers in two huge fields. In the ploughing season we woke up at two in the morning and went to plough the fields."

"It must have been very hard work."

"Yes. We worked hard all year round. In winter we carried manure to the fields. You know how heavy manure is. One day the oxen hit a tree and the full cart tilted backwards, lifting the smaller ox off its feet. Mugova's son Richard broke the yoke with his axe to free the oxen.

The cart overturned and thew all the manure onto the grass. Mugova was really angry with me although Richard and I had only done it to save the ox."

Mugova was one of the illustrious agricultural demonstrators. He had built himself a fine white brick and zinc house and had fenced off his huge fields in the fertile land near the vlei. Here the soil was black and crumbly, so damp that worms burrowed it all year round. He kept his soil drugged with manure and fertilisers, so that even in bad years his mealies grew tall, and his acres went white with cotton balls. He was one of those Derukas who enslaved the soil, overworked and underpaid their servants, and sent out huge herds of cattle to tax the humble meadows. In such homesteads milk, eggs, meat, vegetables, rice and green mealies were available at most times of the year but human sweat oozed all year round.

We approached Matudu's compound. It was a sprawling compound built on a steep slope. Of the five huts, only the kitchen was well built, with a high wall and an even roof. Matudu built better huts for the Derukas than he built for himself. A giant tree towered over the roofs, one of its branches struck off by lightning. The slope was so steep that the rain had torn the earth in places, dragging fine white sand to the edge of forest. Coming down the slopes people found themselves running involuntarily. Two sides of the tilled clearing had been fenced off by two low strands of barbed wire which had succeeded in keeping out only the cattle because goats had invaded the plot to nibble the mealies.

We proceeded along the path where water from the girls' buckets had made cakes on the sandy path. Everywhere chickens were scratching in the green thorns and the lean brown hounds stared passively at us. We crouched outside the big hut. There were nutshells on the ground and the flies buzzed everywhere.

Matudu's daughter pushed her face out of the doorway and greeted us. She was as dark girl, about sixteen, with a big crop of plaited hair, and white grains in the corners of her eyes. There was sand on her knees. She had been kneeling near the door, grinding peanut butter on a huge flat stone. "We have come to see the cattle," said Boyce familiarly.

She went on grinding the butter.

"Are Jerome and Bvaku back from the maize mill?" asked Boyce, standing up.

"No," ' replied the girl. "They went late."

"And where is everybody else?"

"Mother and the girls have gone to pick *mazhanje* and father is chopping logs near the kraal."

"In that case I will see you at some other time when your father is away," said Boyce half seriously and the girl chuckled.

"Are the cattle still in?"

"Yes."

We half walked, half ran down the slope to the kraal. It was a big kraal of thick white poles planted close together. There were forty or fifty cattle in the kraal, all stamping their feet and swishing their tails to keep the flies away. Matudu was felling a tree some distance away. The tree fell, squeaking like a giant mouse, and thrashed the ground with its branches. Suddenly there was a gap in the forest where the tree had stood.

Matudu victoriously threw his axe on his shoulder and approached us, smiling.

"Wamambo!" he said, then added with a frown of mock anger. "Why is it that you never come to see me? You only want to greet me when you meet me drunk on the paths, and then I don't know anything,afterwards."

"But we only came yesterday," I protested laughingly. "And we have come to see you today. How are you?"

He clicked his tongue in a mock curse, half swung his fist at Boyce and put his axe down. He was a short man, thick-set, very dark and so red-eyed that children cried when he held them. His head was small and round, with short greying hair and a stubby white beard. His arms were rather too big and muscular for his small body, fingers shaped like clubs and nails black with dirt. Rivulets of sweat were trickling down his face, soaking his khaki shirt and even creeping to his brown shorts. He kept flicking his pink tongue over his lips.

"I am well, Wamambo," he replied eventually. "How was your father?"

"He was well."

"Why didn't he send tobacco, even old newspapers for my cigarettes?"

"Headman Simon took all the newspapers we brought."

"Oho! You give everything to headman Simon, forgetting me. Did Simon build your huts? Did he till your fields? Or did he sell you your oxen?"

"We will remember you next time."

"Next time! What if I die before next time? Don't you know I can become a ghost and torment you?"

Boyce burst out laughing and Matudu turned to him slowly, grinning, and said: "Shut your cave, Boyce."

"Oh, shut up, old man," returned Boyce good-humouredly.

"We have come to see the cattle," I said.

"Come to see the cattle. I see, and yet you never give me any tobacco. Your ox fell ill in spring. His foot swelled like a ball. He couldn't walk. I said to your mother, 'Let us cut the swelling to let the pus out.' She said, 'No.' But I knew the ox might die so I cut him on my own. I tied him by the horns to this tree. I roped his belly and pulled him to the ground, all alone. I squeezed his boil."

"You did well."

"For two weeks he couldn't go to the dip."

"Which are the oxen?"

"They are not both oxen. You see that cow sitting in the mud near the white log?"

"The one with the white face and red tail?"

"And that strong brown ox with sharp horns, standing near the black bull?"

"Yes."

"Those are your cattle."

I threw a stick at the white faced cow. She rose to her feet, stretching her dung-matted flanks and stiffening her tail.

She was a fairly old cow, and perhaps had calved half a dozen times. She threw her crying brown balls of eyes at me and turned away quickly, lumbering out of the corner. There was a slight turmoil in the kraal. The sleek brown ox took his time moving. He tossed his sharp horns aggressively at the timid wrinkle-faced white cow, but then his horns landed in front of the black bull. He stepped backwards, hardly blinking.

"How old is the cow?"

"She is old," said Matudu, putting his arms on the white logs. "She is old but she is still calving. She has had five calves, but any time now we expect her to have another one."

"Milk," said Jo happily.

Boyce smiled at Jo's happiness. Boyce had seen the birth of scores of calves. We looked at the cattle for a few more minutes and then went home.

There was yellow rice and tall green mealies in the vlei gardens. Simba spotted a flock of goats nibbling green tendrils near a garden. He stood alert and his ears bristled, his half forgotten hunting instincts roused. Next minute he was thrashing through the bushes towards the flock. The foolish goats nibbled on, only sensing Simba when he was dangerously close. They scattered. Their movements excited him. He closed onto the scattering flock like a giant hound, running faster. We watched him breathlessly. Our desperate shouts could not stop the over-powering rush of his blood. He swung to the right, making for a pink-skinned kid at the end of the arc of fleeing goats. He gripped the poor scrambling creature, took it up by the legs and shook it like a cat shaking a mouse. He pushed his canines into the soft pink belly, thrashing the kid onto the ground, raising a cloud of dust around him.

I stopped for a stick as I ran and hit Simba once, twice, and he let go and ran off into the bushes, howling. I picked up the pink kid and shook it gently. There were deep bloodless prints of teeth in its belly. Its eyes were half closed already.

"What do we do now?" asked Boyce, his hands on his hips.

"Is it dead?" said a voice from behind me. He was a young man, tall as Boyce, wearing a thin black tie.

"I don't know," I said. He took the kid from me.

"Do you know who it belongs to?" I asked.

"Yes," replied the young man. "It belongs to my brother."

I told Boyce and Jo to go home and tell mother about it. I followed the young man to his compound up to the slope. Outside the hut a woman was washing plates. She stood up when she saw us.

"What happened?"

"A dog bit it," said the young man.

"Whose dog?" screamed the woman. The young man looked at me. Another boy came out of the hut and examined the kid.

"My only goat," he moaned.

"What kind of dog is that which hunts goats?" screamed the woman, looking straight at me. "Did he think it was a buck? Why did you let him do it? You thought he was doing a fine job, didn't you, getting some meat?"

My heart sank. I couldn't talk. I sat down under the eaves of the hut and let them vent their anger. The young man went off to call his father.

The father was a shrunken man, perhaps sixty or seventy, short, dark and almost toothless. His toes peeped out of his broken shoes. He greeted me politely and even asked my health. His wife brought him pumpkins. He invited me to eat with him but I declined.

"What!" he exclaimed with suprise. "You won't eat with me? Just because your dog killed my goat you refuse to eat with me. Don't you like pumpkins?"

I told him I did not feel like eating.

The woman overheard our conversation and came over with a wet pot in her hands. "How can he eat pumpkins?" she shouted. "He wanted meat. He is disappointed we caught him before he could carry the kill home to his mother."

"Is your dog from the town?" the old man asked me.

"No," replied the woman before I could open my mouth." "The dog was born and bred in this very village. That boy deliberately sent it after the kid. The dog has been taught to hunt goats."

"Couldn't you stop the dog?" asked the old man."

"How could he stop the dog?" screamed the old woman, throwing sand into her pot. "He wanted meat. He must pay for the kid. We want our kid alive and walking this minute. You can take the meat to your mother and bring a live kid to us."

I brushed off an angry tear. They had given me no time to explain.
"Where do you live?" the old man asked me.

He knew my father and mother, he said. He had known them in
town, before he came to build his home in the country. He asked me
more questions.

Mother shortly arrived. The old woman ran about getting her mats
to sit on. The two women conversed about the weather and the crops
and no mention of the goat was made while I was there. I later learnt
that the old man had decided to let the matter pass as an unfortunate
accident. He demanded no compensation.

After that we kept a keen eye on Simba, however. He knew his
scarlet sin and whenever he saw a flock of goats he folded his tail,
dropped his head and ran slowly on. But at home he was a fierce and
efficient dog. Many people were scared of him. Mother warned us not
to call him by name in public because if all the people knew his name
and called him by it, he would soften towards them.

❀❀❀

Boyce turned out to be an expert with the cattle as mother had said.
He knew what to do to keep the yoked pair running with the plough.
But he used his whip freely. Bellum's sleek brown skin seemed to
absorb the blows easily but Sigwe was less fortunate. The cracking
whip slashed her hide, smoking a little, and leaving red marks.

Sometimes the whip marks exposed her red flesh underneath.
Bellum was younger than Sigwe, and being the ox he was more
powerful than the cow. Sigwe often trudged slightly behind Bellum.
Boyce whipped her mercilessly, till mother said rather uneasily, "Let
her rest for a while, Boyce. She is a pregnant woman."

One day Sigwe stopped in the middle of a furrow. Boyce drove
her with his whip and shouts but she stood her ground like a wall.
Her belly heaved quickly and her crying eyes bulged over her white
face. Suddenly her knees folded, she slumped to the ground. The yoke
tilted, the leather cords tightening on her throat. She grunted.

I grabbed her horns and pressed the head down, trying to loosen
the cord with my other hand. Bellum moved.

"Watch out!" shouted Boyce.

Bellum tossed off the yoke and surged past me. The plough came after him for a moment, its blade flying through the air. I felt the sharp glittering point stabbing my ankle. I fell. There was a snapping sound as the yoke broke. Bellum freed himself.

"Are you hurt?" asked Boyce and Jo at the same time.

"Not badly," I said. I slapped Sigwe's back. "Sigwe, Sigwe." Her hide twitched and vibrated. Boyce took her stiff tail in his hands and twisted it like a woman wringing a towel. Sigwe moaned. Boyce did it again and again but Sigwe did not move.

"She must be dying," Boyce gingerly released her tail. "Go home and tell mother, Jo."

Sigwe thrashed the dust. I suppose the darkness was clouding over swollen eyes. Bellum saw her kick and he raised his head as if to catch a scent on the air. He came bounding towards us. Boyce and I jumped out of the way but he did not want us. He jumped right over Sigwe's sprawling body. The massive dark form rushing through the blackness must have totally alarmed Sigwe; she scrambled onto her feet and raised her head.

Jo came up and said, "Is she up? I saw Bellum jump over her."

"Is that what all animals do to their dying partners — jump over them?" I asked Boyce.

"It's the first time I have seen it happen," said Boyce, patting Sigwe's back. "Sigwe. You foolish cow. You wanted to die in my hands and get me into trouble."

"What did mother say, Jo?"

"She said Sigwe would rise to her feet in a while if we let her rest. She said we should take her to Matudu's kraal as soon as we get her to walk."

"She didn't think it was serious?"

"She was alarmed but she pretended it didn't matter."

"And you told her I was hurt?"

"I forgot…"

I threw sand onto the wound to stop the bleeding. I liked to think I was not seriously hurt but I knew I would limp for weeks.

106

We took the cattle to Matudu's kraal. Bellum rushed ahead and we followed very slowly with Sigwe. Matudu's wife was waiting at the kraal when we got there.

"What are you doing bringing the cattle in after dark?" she snapped.

"Sigwe is not feeling well."

"I told you not to take Sigwe. If you continue to drive her she will miscarry. Cattle are just like people, you know. Go and tell your mother that Matudu's wife says she should not yoke Sigwe." From the bushes came Matudu's hicupping, drunken drawl.

"It's their fault if their cow miscarries. It's their fault... I bet them it is."

Sigwe calved on Christmas eve. The calf was brown and white faced like her mother. Sigwe would not let anyone come near her calf. Her formerly meek eyes lost their humility and became dangerously alert. Boyce had trouble trying to milk her. Eventually he tied her by the horns to a tree and got hold of her teats. The sight of the frothing white milk excited me. I asked Boyce to let me try my hands on Sigwe. I washed my hands, crouched under Sigwe's belly with a jug between my thighs and pulled the teats determinedly. I must have got two spurts out when Sigwe decided to refuse me her milk. The soft pink teats slipped out of my already numb fingers. The hungry, wet-nosed calf broke out of Jo's hands to claim her mother's teats. Sigwe decided that was enough. I ended up with milk all over my clothes and a big nasty kick on the chest for my Christmas morning present!

※ ※ ※

For a whole week after Christmas the sky was overcast with storm clouds. It rained every day. The fat showers plunged endlessly from the thick grey ceiling of heaven. God had forgotten to close his taps.

We pressed on with our work in spite of the rain. At five in the morning when the sun should have been rising, the air was ominously still and warm under the grey blanket of clouds. For two or three hours in the morning we weeded the rain-soaked acres. Boyce set the pace, cutting and hacking the earth with his hoe, his slim legs wide apart, white shirt creeping up his back.

"Come on," he laughed spiritedly. "Let us do another lap." He was

107

a very hard worker, and even mother had trouble keeping to his pace.

Around ten o'clock the sky broke and the rain came down. It usually came after a sudden calm, pounding us. We took shelter in the trees, holding plastic sheets over our heads, but we always got wet in the end. In the vlei the herdboys raced their tinkling herds home before the rain plunged down, but there was always the danger of one or two stray cattle coming for our mealies so we did not leave the field till the vlei was well clear of any cattle.

We got home soaked to the skin and sat by the scalding fire while the rain splashed outside. Sitting wet at the fire is nice. You suck the salty water from your nose and feel your flesh glowing to the bone in the heat. You put your fingers in the hot flames while your clothes steam all over you. Eventually you drowse over the fire. You hate it when the rain stops outside and you have to go into the wet grass again. But the sun shines and you have to leave the fire and go out. You go into the wet sunny fields feeling hot and sleepy and drenched, and full of sadza and biltong and peanut butter gravy.

Sometimes when it did not rain Boyce went to spend the evening with his mother.

"My mother is getting married again," he complained. He wasn't very happy.

His step father was Chinda, a Southerner who had come to the village to work for the Deruka families. After three jobs Chinda had decided to spend his energies on himself and to build his own home. Exactly how Chinda had gained his mother's affections Boyce did not know. But on the night of the Pendi's beer party and the fire it was Chinda who had half carried and half dragged Boyce's drunken mother home.

"I know that as a son I am not supposed to make decisions for my mother," said Boyce, ruefully. "But I think it was a silly mistake on my mother's part to marry Chinda."

"Why Boyce?" inquired mother.

"Chinda is a lazy man," said Boyce. "He hasn't ploughed a single furrow since the rains fell. What does he think my mother will eat? My maternal uncle gave Chinda full permission to use his oxen but he never bothered even to use the oxen once. All he does is drink. You give him beer and he will drink like a fish till he forgets how to get home. I despise him!"

"Don't be too harsh on your step-father, Boyce."

"I will never call him father, not Chinda. He found shelter in my mother's compound when the headman Simon threatened to send him back to the south. And because he came to live with my mother, my brother and his wife had to go and live elsewhere. My mother's huts are falling to pieces and the fields are reverting to bush. How can Chinda call himself a man when he doesn't even own a chicken? If I were a man –"

"Oh, Boyce."

"If I were a man…"

"What would you do?"

"At least I would speak against mosquitoes like Chinda and protect my mother."

"Perhaps she was a fool to marry him, Boyce, but it is not your duty to expose your objections. You should respect your mother."

"The trouble with Chinda is that he drinks too much. I hate beer. It cripples a man. My brother drinks too. I don't think I will ever drink. I will devote my energies to building myself a home which people will admire. I will grow nuts and maize and cotton."

We met Chinda at the stream one day. He was fishing. He was a curious man, perhaps in his early fifties. You could not call him an old man because although his face and neck were beginning to crease, his body had the curious muscular energy of a teenager. He wore tattered blue overalls, through which his full-blooded hairless chest showed. Perhaps Boyce's mother had loved him because he had a healthy young body. But he was squint-eyed, with a mouthful of misplaced yellow teeth and a vigorous crop of ashy grey hair. He chewed a wet, cold, home-made cigarette. With his black fingers he handled the slimy worms as if he would eat them.

We came down onto him without warning, as he threw his fishing line into the river. His thin brown dog spotted us from the grass and growled.

"Shut your dog up, old man," Boyce said to Chinda. Chinda barked twice at the dog and greeted us warmly. Boyce did not return his greetings. He started unwinding his fishing line.

The fish did not bite well, but Boyce caught a big eel and several bream. Chinda sweated and coughed in the sun, catching nothing. There were only two little fish in his tin. After a few hours he stood up to go and Boyce asked scornfully in a half laughing voice.

"Have you caught enough fish for my mother?"

Chinda muttered something about the fish not liking the huge worms. Boyce gave him the two large bream.

"Make sure you deliver the fish to my mother," warned Boyce grudgingly. "Don't trade the fish for a mug of beer."

Chinda thanked him, and left us his worms. He collected his tins and hooks and went home.

"You're very cheeky to your step-father, Boyce," I said.

"He deserves it. He married my mother just because he wanted a woman to share his hut. Some people never grow old."

12

Lulu

While we were walking home one evening we saw a girl ahead of us on the path and Boyce said:

"I had a funny experience with her one night last year. Her elder sisters kept nudging me into lying with her. The sisters had both had illegitimate babies and were jealous of their young unspoilt sister, and they arranged for me to go into the grain hut with the girl. It was very dark in the hut and my head hit the roof. At first the girl refused to take her dress off but I tore it away from her body. But I couldn't do anything. It was too dark, so dark that I couldn't even see my own nose. The girl cried out."

I had never imagined Boyce could do such things, let alone talk about his sexual blunderings.

"Have you ever fondled a girl?" he asked me. I had been anticipating the question, so I laughed.

"I can get you a girl if you want," he continued without waiting for an answer.

"I do not want to be a father yet," I laughed.

"It's not always dangerous," said Boyce. "I can get you a girl who is too young to have a baby."

"A girl without any breasts and without a single curl of hair!" I laughed. "You might as well get me a little baby girl. But you must be careful, Boyce. Even nine-year-olds can fall pregnant. This girl must have had breasts when you tried her?"

"She was only budding, things I could hold between finger and thumb. I know she wanted to, but she was afraid of the pain. And I did not like the atmosphere of her mother's grain hut. Something kept scratching the walls. I think there were little men in the grain hut. I scrambled out and left the girl to find her own way out of her mother's frightful grain hut."

"How cruel of you."

That night after Jo was asleep I decided to tell Boyce about Lulu.

"I fell in love once, Boyce."

"Who was the girl?"

"Won't you laugh if I tell you?"

"No. Why should I laugh?"

"Lulu."

"Lulu... Lucia?"

"Yes, Headman Jairos' daughter."

"I know her. She is a beautiful girl. I almost proposed to her once, myself. Did she say yes?"

"I never told her. In fact we never talked about it. It all started when we went together to pick fruit in the forest. We swam in the river."

"Did you do it?"

"No. We both fell asleep on the bank. Mind you, were only eight years old at the time."

"That was a chance wasted," he chuckled. "What happened afterwards?"

"We have always been friends. We went swimming again two years ago."

"And did you do it then?" came the excited question.

"I put my arms round her breasts –"

"In the water, you fool! Did you think you were a fish?"

"I put my arms on her breasts and she screamed and said if I touched her again she would walk away and never talk to me again."

"Girls are always screaming. That's their way of saying yes. I hope you did not give up."

"I came out of the water, snatched her clothes and ran up the bank. She came after me crying."

112

"Naked?"

"Yes. I felt sorry for her, so I gave her back her clothes."

"You should never feel sorry for a girl when she cries. You shouldn't have given her back her clothes."

"We have been friends ever since. But her father went mad and she ran away from home. I haven't seen her since."

"You love her still?"

"No."

"So you want another girl?"

"No."

"Then you still love Lulu. Just tell her you admire her and things will be all right for you."

"You know where she is?"

"She is working in Goto township."

"All right, I still like her a lot."

"Good. We tell her this Sunday. You will have a good time."

"But where will mother think I have gone?"

"To Goto village to see how good the crops are over there. Come on, you are no longer a baby."

Sunday was a fine morning. Beyond the solid acres of dew-laden mealies the first early boys were taking their herds to the vlei. It was still too early for the frogs to croak.

In the village the smoke went up from the grey-roofed huts. Girls chattered at the water-pump, preparing for the day. On Sunday the village girls wash and oil their bodies, and put on their crisp Sunday dresses. The boys, too, scrub themselves, comb their hair and put on their baggy trousers. They go to the church to meet the girls. The Catholic service in the village church starts at eight o'clock, but eight is anytime from sunrise to noon. There is never any hurry.

Jo knew that Boyce and I were planning to go to Goto, so he took the opportunity of taking Boyce's much coveted fishing line and going off to the stream to catch fish. I knew he would enjoy it. He would make clay bulls for Rita, weave cattle whips, jostle the herdboys' bulls into fighting and bring back berries from the forest.

Goto township was half a morning's walk to the west of our village. Already the sun was hot and I could feel the heat of the sand through my thin canvas shoes. I knew it was going to be a long hot day.

"Do you think she'll be in the church, Boyce?"

"I hope so. By the time we get there the service will be half finished."

"The trouble with Catholics is they kneel too much."

We passed kraals where cattle stamped their feet and tossed their horns to keep off the flies. Here and there boys crouched in the mud, milking cows. Near some kraals we saw the familiar crumbling framework of grass and poles enclosing bulging mounds of earth. These were the homes of the dead, scattered all over the place, barely a stone's throw from the compound huts.

Some of the huts were elaborately built; roofs decorated by the alternating pattern of new grass interwoven with old grass, walls freshly painted and decorated. Some of the homesteads had square brick houses with zinc roofs. Scotch carts, water carts with drums and taps, ploughs, harrows, cotton spraying equipment. Everyone was waking up.

Not all the huts were elaborately built, of course. A significant proportion of the homesteads still had clumsily built huts and small grain huts. Here a few chickens scratched in the dirt and half naked children loitered under the eaves. Thin dogs eyed us indifferently, too hungry to bark.

We came upon a very fresh grave and I asked Boyce whose it was. It was a large grave, with a wide path leading to it from the nearby compound. The wooden frame had been carefully erected. But in time the frame would crumble and animals would eat the grass on its mound.

"Didn't you hear?" asked Boyce, surprised."

"We don't hear much," I admitted.

"It's the grave of an old man who lived here. His wife poisoned him."

"Why?"

"Because she wanted to inherit his wealth. The man owned a huge herd of cattle."

"But how do you know she killed him? How do you know he didn't die a natural death?"

"A natural death! You should have seen the old man when they buried him. His stomach was swollen like a bull's and the dogs sneezed when they came near his body. He was ill for only two days, and then he died."

"What proof have you that she killed him?"

"Everyone knows about it. She herself confessed in a frenzy that she had poisoned him. People believe she has evil spirits. On the day they buried him she wanted to go into the grave with him. They struggled to pull her away from the edge of the grave. She had the strength of ten men."

I looked at the grave, trying to imagine what the dead man who lay in it might have been. I could only smell the green smell of the grass and the berries. I thought of the rain percolating that mound of earth, dissolving first the flesh, and the framework of wood, leaving only the dust and the bones. Where would the spirit of the dead man go?

"Don't look too much at the grave," smiled Boyce.

"Why?"

"People may be suspicious."

"Who is the dead man's wife?"

"Mai Mapanga. She lives right here. Shhh…," cautioned Boyce, lowering his voice. "She is coming."

A woman came out of the hut and came down to the path.

"Walk slowly," whispered Boyce.

The woman caught up with us.

"Good morning, Mai Mapanga," said Boyce, stopping.

"Good morning, Boyce," she replied. Her voice was thick, for a woman's.

"Are you going to church?"

"Yes."

She wore a black mourning dress, a black headcloth, black beads and black bangles. She was lean, with long arms and bony legs. Her skin was light, set off against her black clothes. She was perhaps forty, with rusty yellow teeth, cracked black lips and quick brown small deep eyes.

"Are you Maziziva's son?" she said to me. I nodded.

"How are you my son?" She held out her hand. Her palm was not hard as I had expected, and the fingernails were short. I wondered if I should console her for the death of her husband but I decided at the last moment not to.

"How is your mother?" she asked, rubbing her breast vigorously as if something was moving in it. "Does your mother still have maize to sell?"

"Yes."

"Tell her Mai Mapanga wants three buckets. I will come on Thursday to get it. All my maize was finished at the burial of your old father here." She motioned to the grave.

"I am sorry," I said.

"Your father suffered my son, and death only came as a relief. You had better go on your way. You might miss the service. Pray for us."

"Goodbye."

She went to the grave, stooped to clear some dry twigs from the path and when we last saw her she was leaning on the wooden framework of the grave, staring at the mound.

"Did you hear the way she spoke?" asked Boyce after she had passed out of hearing range. "She thought death was a relief to her husband – as if she really wanted him to die. Don't be deceived by her voice."

"She's a shrewish woman," I said, but I wasn't sure.

※ ※ ※

In the village church the heat fell from the low zinc roof and pressed down on the people. The few windows in the whitewashed walls did not let in enough air. I could feel the hot air pooling round me in waves. In the front of the congregation the priest was performing the last rites of the service. He was probably Portuguese, perhaps twenty-four years of age with a dishevelled head of brown hair falling across his forehead. He had sharp features — a long narrow face, thin lips and a straight nose barely separating the corners of his deep blue eyes. There was a starved look and an air of melancholy about, him. He was small and lean and wore dirty faded jeans under his robes. He spoke the local dialect fairly fluently.

I knelt, and moved my lips mechanically. My eyes searched the two halves of the congregation; the young men and the drummers on the right and the bright sea of yellow, pink and blue blouses on the left.

"Have you seen her?" I whispered to Boyce.

He winked his eye and nodded slightly. A drop of sweat ran down across my ribs. My armpits were damp already.

Suddenly the service was over and people were streaming into the passage between the flat benches, shaking hands and greeting one another. We were caught up in the slow, steady drift towards the door. Eventually we found ourselves standing in the bright piercing sunlight near the mango trees.

I saw her. She was coming out of the church with another girl, just in front of the priest. They were talking and laughing and when she saw me her laughter broke off slowly. She stopped.

"Hello," we both said at the same time.

"How are you?" I held out my hand and she touched my fingers.

"You come to church often?" I ventured.

"If I can."

"And this girl is your friend?"

"Yes, we work together in the store."

The other girl had turned away and was talking to two boys. We walked slowly under the mango trees.

"Let's see your Bible," I said.

She laughed and gave it to me. Her name was written in red capitals on the first blank page. I ran the pages under my thumb.

"From where was the reading taken today?" I asked.

"You weren't listening."

"I came in late."

"You don't often come. Today is your first time?"

"Yes. I still go to that church of ours under the tree, with my mother and brothers and sisters and the other women."

I chewed a twig, and then a leaf. And then a bitter blade of grass.

"So where are you going now?" I said, spitting.

"To the store where I work."

"You work in a store. Which store?"

"That white one with a red roof. Chenge Store."

"How long have you been working there?"

"Nearly a year now. I started last year in February."

"I didn't know you were here."

"How did you find out?" I almost told her I had known by instinct.

"Boyce told me."

"Boyce… ?"

"Yes. He works for us now and he lives with us. We came to the church together and I think he has gone after some girls. Is it nice at the store?"

"It's not too bad, except on very busy days."

"Like Christmas?"

"Yes. We spent the whole day behind the counter, serving the customers. I was so exhausted that I went to sleep without eating anything."

"You don't come to the village to see your mother."

"It's the work. I work every day of the week. The only time when I am off is a half day on Sunday." "Like today?"

"No, today I have to be back early. My work mate asked if she could go home to see her sick mother."

"Where is your father?"

"I don't know. If he is not staying with my aunt in Matuvi's line then he must be somewhere else." "Does he ever come to see you?"

"He usually comes to ask for money."

"Does he still drink a lot?"

"No. He doesn't drink anymore. If he drinks he vomits so much that you would think he might vomit his guts."

"Your poor father."

"He will be all right. My uncle Simon is preparing a family beer party to cure him."

"You think it will work?"

"It might. And Mai Mapanga will address the family spirits."

"Who is Mai Mapanga?"

"My aunt. My father's sister."

"Mai Mapanga whose husband died a few days ago?"

"Yes."

I tried to relate Jairos' madness and the death of Mai Mapanga's husband but it did not make sense.

"Are you in a hurry, Lulu?"

"Yes, I am. No, I am not." She looked at me, her eyes half laughing. "I can only spare a few minutes."

"Can I come with you to the store?"

"You may."

"Won't I be a nuisance, hanging around the counter and obstructing the customers?"

"Yes, you will."

"In that case I will go home. And here is your Bible."

She held out her hand but I did not give her the Bible. I did not go home either. Instead I touched her fingers.

"You haven't changed much," I said.

"No. I have changed. I am a big girl now."

"You are always saying what a big girl you are. I don't believe it. You still look like that little girl I went fruit picking and swimming with."

She creased her forehead in seeming puzzlement.

"Have you forgotten that day when I ran off with your clothes and you cried?" I asked.

"That was silly. I will never forgive you for it."

"Then I will never be forgiven, because I came to take you for another swim."

"Ah."

"Why not?"

"I would drown. I can't swim. And besides, there is no river here for miles."

"If there was a river would you come?"

"No, I wouldn't. I would drown."

"I would save you from drowning."

"You can't swim. You would drown too, and then there'd be two corpses."

She was a big girl now, of course, and I knew precisely that she would not come swimming with me again. Or was she a little big girl, perhaps? But even if I had gone away for fifteen years I would still have remembered her calm brown eyes, her smooth light skin and slightly pouting lips shutting away the close, sharp teeth. I had often taken a secret delightful pleasure in imagining those sharp teeth of hers biting me. Perhaps if I had been more violent in the water she would have bitten me. I had not been violent enough, and now there was no way of telling what those two soft buds I had once touched now looked like. They were locked up inside the bra whose pink strings I saw and envied under the shoulders of her dress.

She did not see my eyes looking over her. She was looking down at the path, swinging her free hand slightly. I saw a necklace at her breast.

"Let's see your necklace," I said.

She pulled up the chain and put the stone in her palm. It was an opaque, bright green oval stone, not expensive but very attractive. I stood in front of her and took the stone between finger and thumb.

"Who gave you such a nice necklace?" I asked, stealing a secret glimpse into her dress.

"Someone."

"He must be very kind."

"Do necklaces always have to be given?"

"Usually."

"Then you are wrong. I bought it myself."

"You promised to knit me a white woollen hat, remember? You didn't, so I am keeping the necklace."

She smiled uneasily and grappled her hands with mine for the necklace.

"I shall keep the necklace," I said.

"No you shall not," she insisted, half seriously.

"Then here it is," I dangled the necklace in front of her. She dived for it with her hand but I snatched it back just in time and put it into my pocket.

"What's the good of keeping somebody's necklace without permission?" she said in that tone which always alarms ambitious lover-boys.

"At least I will enjoy keeping it."

"You are behaving in a very strange manner today."

"I want your permission to keep and wear the necklace."

"But it's mine."

"I know. I want us to share it."

"You can buy your own. They are not very expensive."

"No. I want yours."

"But it's just like all the others."

"I just want yours."

"You are taking advantage of your strength. You wouldn't have snatched the necklace from a boy of your age. You came to take my necklace by force."

"I didn't come to take your necklace by force."

"Then why did you follow me?"

"I came to look for someone."

"Then give me back my necklace and look for the person you want."

"I will only give you back your necklace if you help me to find the person I want. She lives somewhere around here. You should know her."

"What's her name."

"It begins with a 'J'."

"Joyce."

"No."

"Jenipher?"

"No."

"Then who is she? What does she do?"

"She works somewhere here."

"What does she look like?"

"Like you."

"There is no one here who looks like me. Maybe she is somebody I have never met."

"Never mind if we can't find her."

"It must he unimportant if you are prepared to give up the search."

"Suppose you are really the person I came to see?"

"Then who is she?"

"Suppose I really didn't come to see anyone –"

"Then what did you come to do?"

"Suppose you are really the person I came to see?"

"I don't understand you. You are going round in circles."

"I came to see you," I said. I stopped and looked into her face.

"You are seeing me now."

"Don't be silly," I said without a smile. "You very well know I am looking at you, but that's not what I came to do."

"I will be late at the store. I had better go."

I let her take two steps and she stopped. She plucked a twig from tree.

"You can't go before you hear what I came to say to you."

She didn't say anything. She looked past me and chewed the twig.

"I came to say that I want us to be friends," I said, my heart beating faster. I felt like an idiot so I continued. "I know we have always been friends and have always liked each other. But liking is not enough. I more than like you. I want you to feel the same towards me."

"I don't think that's possible," she said daringly, staring past me.

"Why not? Is there somebody else. Am I late?"

"No. I just don't like to talk about it."

"But just now you were claiming that you are a big girl now."

She rubbed her eyes.

"Won't you do something about it?" I asked hesitantly.

"Something like what?"

"Something to show me that you like me very much. Like letting me keep your necklace."

"You still insist on keeping my necklace."

"I am taking the necklace with me, with or without your permission."

"Ah," she said in a tone of resignation. "You are a nuisance."

"Promise me one thing," I said.

"What?"

"To think about what I said to you."

"You said so many things."

"About us being friends."

"There is nothing to think about."

"Then you have made your decision already?"

"There is nothing to decide."

"You don't have to keep me waiting if the answer is no. You think about it. I will ask you later." "Time won't change anything."

In the store where she worked boys leaned on the counters. Two of them were talking to Lulu's friend across the counter. The others looked inquisitively at us through the windows.

"Goodbye, Lulu."

"But you said you were coming into the store."

"I think I have to go now," I said dubiously. Perhaps my going away would give her something to think about. "Your customers are waiting for you."

"They are just hanging around to talk. They probably won't buy anything. Yes," she nodded, and added mischieviously, "and waiting for me."

"So you had better go in."

"When are you coming back?" she asked.

"Maybe next year."

"Good riddance."

"In that case I will come back this Thursday."

She nodded very slightly, put her teeth in her lower lip and went into the store. I turned round to look for Boyce. I had seen him behind us in the mango trees but now he was nowhere to be found.

I put Lulu's necklace into my palm to examine it. I stumbled into the path, trying hard to decide if I was more worried than happy.

❦❦❦

Thursday was a hot day and Chenge store was full. Young men idled under the eaves, enjoying the free day. Inside the store boys stood leaning on the counters, gazing at the shelves and tapping their feet to the gramaphone music. It was not a very big store. The whitewashed walls were cracking in places and in the midday heat one could hear the zinc roof cracking as if in protest. The unpolished cement floor was swept, but the swishing feet of the customers brought constant trails of fine sand which crunched under the feet.

Her hair was combed straight and I could just tell that she had applied something to her face. She wore a bright blue lace dress and as she darted from the counter to the shelves I caught a glimpse of her grey stockinged legs. Three fellows were talking to her across the counter. One of them, a short, dark, thickset man in green shorts was insisting that she should replay the record which had just finished playing. Lulu shook her head and smiled. The other girl at the counter was good naturedly paying half an ear to the sweet tongue of another aspiring young man. She recognised me and gave me a knowing smile. She whispered something to Lulu, who afterwards came over to greet me.

"You are not very busy today," I said.

"Not very," she replied, drumming the coarse wooden counter with her fingers.

A small girl quietly put three cents on the counter. Lulu took the money and put six brightly coloured sweets in the child's palm.

"How did you know she wanted sweets?" I asked, perhaps exaggerating my surprise a little.

"The girl buys six sweets every day."

The thickset fellow had stepped to the window and was saying something to his friends. Together they laughed. Fat artificial laughter. I didn't listen.

"Four pounds of sugar, please," I said to Lulu.

She ducked under the counter and put a packet of sugar on the table.

"I was joking," I laughed and she put the sugar back.

"So what did you decide?" I said at last, before a customer could claim her attention.

"Decide?"

"About us being friends."

"Oh, that!" she smiled, shaking her head slowly. "I didn't decide."

"Why?"

"I couldn't decide. There was nothing to decide."

"You probably need more time."

"No."

"Then what is it?"

"It's just that I don't feel like deciding."

"I suspect you don't even like me at all. Maybe I am boring you very much," I said, lowering my voice uneasily. The fellows had laughed again. I pushed my head forward as if to probe her. "You don't like me."

She nodded.

"Why didn't you say so in the first place?"

"I hadn't made a decision."

"But you said just now there was nothing to decide."

The fellows went out of the store and there was a sudden silence. My voice seemed very loud and I wished they had stayed to drown it with their laughing.

"You are deliberately making things hard for me," I protested, "by being so evasive."

"Am I?"

"Yes. I don't think it takes ages to make up your mind. If I had been in your position I would have said yes or no immediately after the proposal."

She laughed and I liked that.

"It's difficult to decide…," she said pretending to be helpless.

"No, it's not. You tell me now. I don't care if it's no."

"Suppose it is no?"

"Then I will walk out of this store and hang myself in the nearest tree I can find."

"The answer is no."

"Is it?" I said swallowing. She didn't smile.

"Will you tell me the reason why it is no?" I asked.

"There is no reason."

"You write the reason on a small piece of paper."

The other girl must have caught fragments of our conversation because I saw her trying hard not to laugh.

"Write the reason," I said hoarsely, "so that next time I approach a girl I will be aware of my disadvantages."

"You really want the reason?" she asked, looking into my eyes. I

125

nodded. She tore off a piece of white wrapping paper and, thinking again, crushed it and threw it away. She took a piece of coarse brown paper, laughed at her friend and wrote a few words, shielding the point of her pen with her left hand. It hurt me to see her putting me off so easily and lightly. She rolled the brown piece of paper and bound it with Sellotape. She bent over the counter and put the paper in my shirt pocket.

"I won't even read your piece of paper," I said unhappily. "I will throw it into the nearest dustbin I can find. Goodbye. Maybe I'll see you next Christmas."

"Next Christmas," protested the other girl across the counter.

"Maybe Lulu will be dead by that time?"

"It won't matter," I said from the doorway.

My eyes blinked in the shimmering heat outside the store. I was thirsty but I did not want to drink anything. I just wanted to get away from it all. I wanted to get away from the miserable shop and its laughing fellows and frivolous girls. I wanted to get away from the nerve-battering blast of the maize mill. I stumbled into a group of chattering girls going into the shop. I gave them a scornful look and walked slowly into the trees.

She was a girl too and just because she didn't chatter it didn't mean that she was different from the others. It was very cruel of her to say no like that and I would never go back. To say no like that, after all I had done for her, after all our friendship. It was mean of her. At least she could have used a clean white piece of paper and a decent envelope. I took the thing out of my pocket and unrolled it. It was like a cigarette stub. The paper was half soaked in oil and the ball point had slipped. I deciphered the message slowly.

'It's all right, I love you too' the message said.

I laughed aloud and creased my forehead in puzzled happiness. I read the message again and again and laughed. So she wanted me, too. It was very cute of her to mislead me like that; to drive me to the brink of despair, only to crown me in the end. I fingered the coarse little piece of paper and laughed, talking to myself. It was not such a coarse little scrap after all. The sun was not hot anymore. I suddenly didn't mind the noise of the mill, and if a group of chattering girls had passed me I would have embraced them. I couldn't contain my happiness. I wanted the trees and the sunshine to share the words with me. I plucked grass shoots out of the ground and thew them away to wilt in the sun. I drove the ants with twigs.

I suddenly remembered that she would be coming out for lunch so I hid behind a tree and waited for her. She came out after a long while. I sneaked up to her from behind and she gave a surprised start.

"I have come to punish you for saying no," I said, hardly suppressing a smile.

"You punish people for saying no?"

"Yes." I extended my hand awkwardly and smacked her face lightly with my fingers. She flinched slightly. It was a difficult joke.

"I didn't read your little message," I said.

"Then you punished me for nothing."

"I read it," I laughed and then asked needlessly, "Where are you going now?"

"For lunch."

"In your hut?"

"Yes."

It was a small neat hut just behind the store. She pushed the door in and I hesitated in the doorway. One half of the hut was occupied by a bed and the other by a small dressing table and two chairs. Her clothes hung from a rope above the bed. A small pot was frothing on a burning Primus stove, and I could smell beans cooking. The hut had a curious lovable blended smell of soap, perfume, burning paraffin, coffee and cooking beans.

"You shouldn't come in," she said, putting her hands on the doorpost.

"Even for a minute? I must come in," I pushed the door and put one foot in. I put my arms on her waist and the door creaked loudly. I put my other foot into the hut and she fell forward, her breasts crushing into my ribs. I could smell her hair and all the time my face was searching for hers. My mouth fell on hers and for one electric moment her tongue touched mine. I drew her lips into mine with a large sucking sound but her tongue slipped back into her mouth out of reach. Her head pulled backwards and our wet mouths separated with a pop. We stood pressed against each other for five still minutes, till she said, "You must go now."

I released her and she patted her creased dress. I felt an intense passion for her. While I was holding her I had been too busy trying to capture the moment. We didn't talk as she took me half way down to the path, but the moment I turned my back to her I started reliving every minute of our embrace.

13

Madoo

On the path behind the huts where the dew lay thick on the grass in the morning, Jairos made his morning rounds of the homesteads. He walked like a robot, very steadily, with downcast face, arms slightly extended outwards like burning hot rods. His dirty khaki clothes clung closely to the thin frame of his body, shielding his brown skin from the sun. There was a marked difference between his shielded and exposed skin. His head and arms were black with the sunburn and that dirt of months. The only sign of life in his face was his intensely fierce, deep red eyes and the red inner folds of his black mumbling lips. His teeth and tongue were grey.

The dew soaked his trousers to the knees and washed his cracked black feet. He was past caring. Only his endless quest for food linked him to the human world. Inside his clothes he was shut up in his own world. People shunned him. Children spat their insolence on him. Jairos himself reminded one of a dog. He mauled his food like a hungry dog, hissing as if the food burnt his mouth. He was red eyed and hungry as a tiger, and yet harmless as a puppy. At times he could be quite pathetic. We ran into him one cool April morning and he said abruptly, "Please catch me an eel. A big eel."

"We don't fish now," I'd explained, wondering if he knew what month it was.

"Catch me an eel," he'd insisted, his eyes sparkling desperately, globules of saliva shooting from his mouth. "Catch me a big fat eel from Mbumbuzi stream."

His pleading voice trailed off into his usual hissing whisper and he went away. He had forgotten about the fish already.

When the moon was full he got worse. He stood with an uplifted face, shouting obscure phrases and sometimes obscenities into the night. "Ernest. Ernest. Put my water on the fire. I am going to buy milk for my tea."

The address to the family spirit had perhaps failed to work.

☘ ☘ ☘

Simon tried his best as the new headman. He put duty before pleasure and he drank less. When people brought a case to him he paid close attention before passing his judgement. He always tried to be a fair judge. But rather like his brother Jairos, he suffered from too much passive optimism. His proposed projects to fence off the stream and to build a dam and a new dip tank never came off the ground. But perhaps it was not solely his fault. The villagers paid no attention to the new council, being too busy with their own work. The villagers were at least prepared to pay the funds but when it came to providing the labour few people were willing to divert their time and energies to a communal project whose benefits were not readily guaranteed.

The newcomers were too busy growing crops; while the locals were waiting for the Derukas to take the initiative.

From Jairos, Simon had inherited leadership of the village as well as its growing problems. A decade of the newcomers had led to the inevitable strain on the land. There was a scramble for fields. Now many families were fencing off their compound areas and building bigger kraals for their cattle. Worried farmers like Mutudu were already putting pressure on Simon to guarantee the availability of land for their teenage sons.

The procedures of the headman's court were not strictly stipulated and perhaps that was why problems almost always cropped up in passing judgement. One of the ironies of the jury itself was that it often consisted of every man who was not the complainant or the accused, making the possibility of prejudice inevitable. The largest court case so far had been caused by a Deruka by the name of Madoo.

He was a tall slouching man, with a mischieveous twisted beard and twinkling brown eyes. Perhaps he was thirty, but he looked much older because he dressed carelessly in greasy shirts and trousers cut off at the knees. Boyce had pointed out that there were only three definite occasions on which Madoo bothered to wash himself, namely at New Year, Easter and at Christmas.

Madoo was the son of a rich newcomer who had settled further north about a decade before our arrival. Having grown up in his father's compound, Madoo had decided to build his own home in Jairos' village. With him he brought his new wife and his small herd of cattle to settle in an old compound left by a trader. Perhaps Madoo had been too lazy to build his own huts, but the compound left by the trader had its attractions. It had two round huts and one big rectangular hut. Behind the huts there was a flourishing orchard of mango and peach trees. Madoo also inherited the thirty acres of field left by the trader.

The first time I got to know Madoo was one summer ploughing season. He was at once an industrious and lazy man. With his pretty young wife he ploughed and sowed his fields from dawn to dusk. You could say he was lazy because he ploughed in between the sprouting green tree stumps and the unfelled green bushes, and he never weeded his crops. His farming was not intensive enough to yield any profits. Rumour said that he even ploughed his fields on Thursday, a forbidden day for work. At one time Jairos had threatened to give one of Madoo's fields to a Deruka – Madoo had vociferously protested, with success.

Madoo's huts were dilapidated. Grass was falling from the roofs, and blocks of clay from the walls, exposing the gaping wooden pole. The grass grew tall right to the walls of his huts, unweeded. He had a fierce pack of lean dogs which kept people away from his compound and from the orchard.

People said he had just finished serving a prison sentence for stealing a roll of wire from the local farmer's co-operative. Soon after his return from prison, however, news went round that the striking new blue door on his but had been stolen from the neighbourhood, and that at a time when people's chickens and eggs were mysteriously disappearing from the fowl runs, there were roast chickens and three-legged pots of boiled eggs every night in Madoo's kitchen. And Mrs Pendi was prepared to swear that the new zinc tiles on Madoo's fowl run had been taken from her own tool shed.

But those were minor accusations and no one could actually prove Madoo's guilt. Though Madoo seemed a quiet man, he was quick to pick a quarrel even with his intimate friends. Mr Pendi had angrily levelled his gun at Madoo once, on the charge of entering his bedroom in their absence, and had Mrs Pendi not thrown herself between the two men that might well have been the end of poor Madoo. But Mr Pendi was not Madoo's sole enemy. His bitterest enemy was a fat, light-skinned giant by the name of Munyu. Munyu was a local, with a large family.

The two men had become enemies while playing cards for money. Munyu was convinced Madoo had won through cheating. He brought out a huge knife and tried to hack Madoo to pieces but again the fox had escaped unhurt. After that they became mortal enemies, bitter even to the extent of trying to poison each other and setting medicine traps on the path to cripple each other.

Madoo had a pretty young wife but that did not satisfy his active sexual instincts. At the village beer parties he was often seen in close conversation with the mother of the man who had married his own sister. She was a portly, elderly woman, with a face, however, much younger men could still look at. Her husband worked in town and was therefore away for months on end. When he was away she drank freely and jived to the gramophone at the beer parties, and Madoo was her close companion. He bought her beer and accompanied her home after the party.

Madoo always arrived home late after escorting his elderly lady home. He came home staggering drunk, too drunk to notice that his wife was crying as she suckled the young baby. But she was too tired to quarrel, and she knew that quarrelling would only dangerously raise his temper.

One night he did not come home. The cock crowed twice. She sat awake all the time, nestling the baby. Long after the last drumbeats of the beer party had faded out he had still not come. She quietly put the baby down and opened the door to look out. It was a dark night without a moon. Dark clouds had shut the stars from view. Only the tall grass and the dark crouching trees stared at her as she stepped out and shut the door softly behind her. In the east the distant clouds cracked with a rumbling flash. She hugged her petticoat and stepped into the path between the two seas of grass, probing the night with her eyes. She heard the slink of the dog behind her and scolded the creature off in a harsh whisper. She glided into the path among the trees. She saw the two graves at the side of the road and suddenly shivered, her naked feet going numb as they gripped the damp sand. But she pressed on, past the soft dewy grass and the gleaming black pool near the water pump, down into the soft damp dark valley, full of a thousand fireflies and the muffled croaking of the frogs. She crossed the chilly stream and went up to the sandy path.

Further up in the forest two dark figures, a man and a woman, were staggering along the path. The man had his arm around the woman's huge waist and her arms were thrown helplessly at her side. Somewhere in the night a donkey brayed, his ugly fatuous voice breaking the silence of the night. She started and he uttered a phrase of reassurance. Close behind them the young woman in the petticoat darted among the bushes, hiding the whiteness of her petticoat.

The portly woman in front suddenly seemed to crumble and droop to the ground. He held her by the shoulders. She started vomiting; the stuff gushed out of her as if something was pumping it out from below. Some of the vomit must have slapped his arms but he let her vomit for a while. Afterwards she walked more steadily and even mumbled a few words to him. She collapsed again at the next bend of the path and this time he let her fall down onto the soft, deep sand. He knelt down beside her, put her arms on his shoulders and tried to lift her from the ground. He failed and she laughed, a thin cackling laughter barely floating above the frothing beer inside her. He tried again and failed. Then he laughed too and fell onto her bulging stomach. She squealed like a puppy. He laughed drunkenly as he undid his trousers. A moment later she had stopped squealing and was hissing and gurgling like a choking child as he crushed her huge, plump body.

He was up on his feet first, fastening his trousers.

"Get up," he said, kicking her hips. She grunted and lay still. He pulled her arm and kicked her again. She cried out in protest. He dragged her, so that her feet ploughed the ground. Then she pulled her hand from him, cursing mildly, and staggered onto her feet.

The young woman wept in the bushes, and had the staggering pair been less drunk they would have heard the noise. They left the big path and took a smaller one. From the dark trees a dog growled. The man helped the woman to the dark door of the looming square hut. He pushed the door and eased her in. She fell onto the floor near the door, like a bundle of logs, and he came out. He did not go away but stood near the door, making himself a cigarette. He was no longer as drunk as he had seemed and with a sly cough he went into the hut again. A moment later he came out carrying something wide and heavy on his shoulders. He struggled through the narrow doorway. The figure in the bushes let him pass on ahead. He breathed quickly under the load on his shoulders. She darted behind him long enough to see what he carried and then let him go ahead. She took another path through the forest and ran home like a girl, crying.

By the time he had pushed the bed into his grain hut the east was growing purple, and when he went into the hut he found his wife already asleep from fatigue and crying.

They went to work in the fields as usual on the next morning, but he was surprised when she did not come back from home with lunch. After some time he set the oxen loose and went off to find her. He got the biggest surprise of his life when, on getting to his homestead, he found four men lifting the bed out of the grain hut.

"What is happening here?" he asked bewildered.

"You are in trouble, Madoo," said Simon laconically.

His young wife had shown the men the vomit on the path and the tortured marks where Madoo had defiled her marriage.

"Why did you do this to me, my wife?" he asked gently. She did not reply. She just stared at the ground.

He did not beat her after the men left. He was not even harsh to her. He begged her not to testify against him in court, promising to reform. People talked. Many were delighted by the ironic betrayal of the erroneous husband by his own wife. The less malicious sympathised with the disillusioned couple. Madoo promised to buy his wife a cow if she did not betray him. But he had wronged her right in front of her own eyes. He was her husband. He was the father of her child. She did not know what to do.

On the day of the trial she initially sat composedly in the midst of the thick gathering but when she was questioned she broke down into tears. She was young and easily confused. They could not get a single word out of her and two old women almost slapped her in the face for humiliating the court. But it was useless to question her. She had given the four men more than enough evidence with which to prosecute Madoo. The court broke off with grumbles from the men and loud protests from the women.

The elderly woman's husband, the man whose bed had been stolen through the licentiousness of his own wife, had taken a surprisingly calm attitude during the procedure. He never rebuked Madoo. He divorced his wife, sold his cattle, packed his bags and left the village. His son followed suit by divorcing Madoo's sister, his wife, leaving Madoo's marriage the only surviving one in the wreck.

And now, especially after the court case of Madoo, things had changed in the village. Jairos had had an easy time as headman, while the village was young and the forests wild and human wounds could heal as easily as new foliage grew on trees.

Now the forests were gone and people became restless. The owls did not hoot any more. The huge trees where they had perched for the night had been cut down for firewood, or had fallen down on their own. Ten years before, the owls had been part of the village, but now when an owl hooted people woke up, with throbbing hearts, to listen.

The snakes no longer came slithering across compound clearings attracted by firelight. They kept away from the tread of human feet. Village children shook the once respected fruit trees, battering their trunks with rocks to make them shed their fruit. Some children even collected green fruit to ripen at home and sell to the bus passengers on the road. Gone were the days when children believed that shaking fruit trees would get them lost in the forest and that walking with upturned axe-blades would anger the Gods into witholding the rain. It was the reign of the axe and the goats now; the axe which opened the forests to the ravishing plough, and the flocking goats that mushroomed in number, rarely killed for meat, but serving only to create hatred between neighbours.

14

Strife

And sadly, somewhere on the fringes of this decay, I remembered my father, who for many years had forsaken our home. Somewhere between the teens and the late twenties the history of my father was dead or lost. As a young boy he had been a bright and eager pupil, walking miles to school in the foot cracking cold or in the rain and the hunger to get his education. In his mid-twenties he had found a job as a salesman in a town. In between these two stages of his life was a gap which I could never fill.

I knew him as my mother's devoted husband and my determined father who had worked for two decades without taking a single holiday in order to give us a thorough education. He had been born and raised in the country, in the midst of smoky huts and cattle and millet. In his later married years his country past had urged him to build a home in the country. He had built that home with the care and concern of a bee, but he was too busy working for our education to observe the fruition of that home.

Each time we arrived in town from the country, at the end of the holidays, I felt a pang of alarm on seeing him coming out of the bedroom to meet us in his vest – red eyed with sleep and hairy chested. There was something sad about the way he blew the wood in the stove to make tea for us, something touchingly cold about our dusty, wifeless house. I knew each time he would ask quick questions about mother and the girls and the crops, before entering into the details of our school fees.

Our education was his burning obsession, and we spurred him on because we were brilliant scholars and potential graduates.

I knew that by the time he went to work in the morning, a hundred miles away mother was already out in the dew, in the fields. Father spent the day on his two feet, his workshirts slightly torn under the armpits, selling clothes all day. Mother spent the day in the fields weeding and pacing the fields in her tattered gumboots all day, defending her precious crops from the cattle and the goats, in blazing sunshine or in drenching rain. She was the human fence of our field.

I weighed my father and mother against each other and found myself sympathising with my mother. I could imagine the pain of standing on one's two feet all day, selling clothes, but I knew better the greater pain of wading in the soaking morning dew, or of weeding under the blazing, sweat-sucking sunlight, of standing under the rain-soaked trees trying to find shelter from the dismal driving rain, without a raincoat. But when I came to town and saw the lean, stretched, solitary figure of father in the double bed, and the empty space where mother should be, but was not for about half the year, I found myself questioning the justice of my sympathies.

It was by no means a question of my father's educational obsession versus mother's driving farming instincts. Mother was equally concerned with our education and she actually thought our country home might relieve expenses and help father to save money for our school fees. Later father had disagreed on the claim that it cost more to run two homes. They never quarrelled openly but I knew there was a slow secret steady burning between them that must be put out.

I knew from that night when mother had received a letter from him saying he would not be coming for Christmas that the silent war of principles had started between them. That was why she had decided to run our country home on her own, growing groundnuts, selling home-made clothes to the villagers and buying two cattle. We felt proud of her. I knew father, too, secretly praised her for the imaginative industry, but he was too carried away by his own principles to display his admiration.

I dreaded what would happen if the war of principles went on. We all wanted him back.

He came back very suddenly, like a prodigal, one January afternoon. He came stealthily upon us while we were weeding. Rita saw him and cried out and ran to him. He put his umbrella under his armpit, took her in his arms and came to greet us. His great big black gumboots laid flat the ridges of earth erected by the plough.

"You are doing a fine job," he said with a complimentary smile, pacing the acres of groundnuts we had just finished weeding.

"How long did it take you?" he asked. A month, mother told him. He paced the field again and again, and only came home after dark. He sat with us in the kitchen.

"Your firewood is wet," he said, screwing up his soft town eyes in the smoke. We ate sadza and fish and he asked if we caught the fish ourselves.

"Not this lot," I explained to him. "We bought it from the women who use nets and sacks."

"There is a lot of fish in the stream," he said invitingly in his exultant mood. I knew his mood when he talked about fat cattle and fertile soils and good crops.

"But we don't catch big fish anymore," I said. "The women clean the stream of all the productive fish with their nets and sacks."

"So what do you do for relish?" he asked hesitantly.

Vegetables from the garden, *madora* from the forest, milk from the cow, *nyovi* and mushrooms from the fields and fish, if we could get it, we told him. Mother did not answer any of his questions. We sang a chorus and he prayed. Afterwards we went to sleep. He went off with mother, swinging the flickering paraffin lamp at the mango trees to examine the fruit.

He was up early next morning, out in the dew to see the cattle his wife had bought, and to have a look at the garden. Before the sun was up he was in the fields before us, hacking at the weeds with his huge hoe. He refused to sit down to drink *maheu*, worked twice as hard as Boyce, sweating freely in the sun.

"You are leaving the weeds behind you," mother said jokingly, pointing out a single blade of grass which had survived his huge hoe. "You don't know how to weed."

We all laughed.

At noon we took a break and the girls went home to fetch lunch. Father went out into the bright noon heat and emerged from the forest an hour or so later carrying something in his shirt which he had stripped from his shoulders.

"What did you bring?" asked mother inquisitively as he put the bulging shirt down. "Are these not poisonous mushrooms you brought us?" she teased.

"These," he protested good humouredly, fingering his small treasure. "This is *nhedzi*, the best type of mushrooms, totally health-giving. You cook it with the lid off the pot to let it boil freely."

"But that drives the taste and the smell out," said mother critically.

"But that is the way it should be cooked," he insisted. "I will cook it for you tonight if you want."

"If you want us to change roles just say so plainly," said mother jokingly.

" I can cook it well enough," he laughed. "I used to cook it for myself when I was a schoolboy. I almost lived on mushrooms then."

I loved to hear these bits and pieces of this childhood.

Immediately after lunch he was up on his feet, attacking the hot sand and the weeds with his hoe. "You don't have to work in this baking heat," mother rebuked him. "You won't get very far."

"I will," he boasted, working even harder.

"It's up to you," said mother, "but we don't want you fainting in the heat and failing to go back to work tomorrow."

At sunset he let mother and the girls go home and remained with us, to show us the area he wanted earmarked for our fields when we grew up. The area was about thirty acres in extent, and along each border he cut down the bushes and laid them out in a rough line.

"Tell headman Simon tomorrow that I propose this area for your fields," he said in an imposing tone that made Boyce smile. He cut the bushes fiercely, with his teeth in his tongue and his feet wide apart.

We wanted to laugh. We could hardly suppress our laughter.

"What's wrong," he gasped, stretching his back. "Don't you want fields?"

We laughed at the way he kept extending the area outwards, at his pathetic little bushes which would serve very poorly as boundary-marks. We laughed at the determination which was blind to the gathering dusk and to the fact that he was assuming the role of the headman.

"Don't you want fields?" he asked with a rebuking smile. "Can't you see that there will be a shortage of farming land in the this village and that the snails will get nothing? It doesn't matter if we claim your fields now. We can fence the area off and chop the trees later. It doesn't matter if you are all going to be graduates and live in your nice big town houses. You can buy a tractor and get someone to plough your fields for you. You can use fertilisers and manure and plough five acres and make hundreds of bags out of that. You can never totally break away from the country."

That sobered up our laughter. We brushed our way through the bushes in half-familiar places on our way home in the dark. We came to the edge of an open field and stopped. There was a big gap in the forest, as if someone had cut off a rectangular patch of hair from an old man's head, leaving a gaping section of the scalp. It was a field of about twenty acres. I saw the dark open sky and the stars above it. On the floor of the field dying tree trunks lay stretched, their wilting grey branches reaching out lamely to the dark sky as if asking for life. Only the stumps of the trees shone in that dark expanse, like still sentinels watching over the decaying trees in the large open mortuary.

"It's a beautiful field," said father, surveying the darkness.

"Yes, it's a very big one," agreed Boyce. "Mugova chopped down the trees all alone in two weeks. He is a monster of a man."

"Mugova?" said father in a half puzzled tone.

"The man whose cattle destroyed our mealies last year," I explained.

"I remember now. He is a tall man with a grey beard, isn't he?"

"Yes."

"He worked very hard," said father, "but he didn't do a very decent job of it. He chopped the trees too high up on their trunks. The stumps are tall, too tall for the oxen and plough. And he should have cut the branches up to make them dry quickly for burning."

He led the way through the dark maze of stumps, tree trunks and branches. I thought I heard a slight snap as if a twig was falling from a stump. I saw the glow of a fire through the trees.

"Which route are we taking?" I asked.

"The shorter one, behind the village line," said father.

"Behind people's huts?" said Boyce in a low voice of resentment. "It's not good to walk behind people's compounds at night."

"Why not?" queried father amused.

"It's not safe," said Boyce.

"Why?"

"We can get bitten by the dogs on the back path."

"But we can equally get bitten on the front path."

"It's not wise to walk near the kraals at night."

"And the graves," I added.

"Are you afraid of ghosts?" asked father coming to the point.

"I would rather not take any risks," I said.

"What would you do if you found out that you had married the daughter of a witch? Never pay your mother-in-law a visit because you would be afraid of meeting her ghosts?"

"That would be a different case," I laughed.

"You believe in ghosts?" said father, suddenly turning serious.

"Don't you believe in God?"

I stopped laughing and even in the dark I felt my cheeks twitching uneasily. I had never expected the question, nor did I know how to answer it.

"I believe," I replied hesitantly, "but I would rather not take any risks."

I felt more uneasy at the long silence which followed.

"But don't you believe in ghosts, father," I asked, suddenly remembering a fragment of his youth. One night he had had to lie flat on his stomach at the side of the path to let a strange creature pass. A tall dark form, tall as a tree, like a man standing on very tall crutches.

An unearthly thing with long stiff strides. He never got enough control of his senses to scrutinise the thing. It would simply remain a thing for the rest of his life.

"Ghosts," said father loudly in the dark. "They do exist sometimes and they are the spirits of the dead people, people who have been disappointed with their evil lives. Sometimes they are simply evil spirits conjured and given shape by witches. But a ghost will not hurt an innocent soul."

"There are ghosts which beat even innocent people," disagreed Boyce.

"Believe me, son," father told him, "they won't hurt an innocent soul. Have you met anyone who was beaten by them so far?"

"A man was beaten here once, in this village," said Boyce. That had been two years after our arrival, but we had never paid much attention to the story. The victim was a tough, hard working man, and people said the things had been sent by a jealous neighbour to cripple him. He stumbled home with a broken jaw and his mother had screamed on seeing him.

"Let us walk along your dangerous path and see what happens," said father and we had to follow him.

In the vlei the frogs were now croaking and the fireflies were shining in the reeds. Already the chilly air was creeping up into the forest and I knew there would be buckets of dew in the morning, buckets — drums of useless beautiful dew scattered over hundreds, millions of acres of grass, sparkling in the sunshine. One could not drink the dew, or collect it in a bucket. But it nourished the crops and kept them cool through the hot mid-morning hours before the sun in the afternoon. And dew was good for the milk-cows which were early enough to catch it in the morning.

But now was not the time to think about foaming milk and sparkling dew. The dark silhouettes of the village huts and the cattle pens and the graves loomed before us. The smell of the village drenched us.

At night the sun leaves the village to itself and the darkness envelopes the landscape. The dark clumps of trees cluster together near mother earth as if in fear of the night; the stars seem too far up to give consolation from the darkness. The darkness itself seems to have its own particular smell. Sometimes it is warm like baking earth, sometimes chilly and murky like the mud in the streams. Sometimes the night just smells like mudworms. There are distinct pockets of smells and as you come up from the valley you can distinguish them. You leave the crisp chilly, murky, rotten water-lily, fishy, froggy smell of the stream wondering if you can smell the fireflies and as you go up into the forest you feel the warmth of the trees wrapping you like an oven. You can even pick out the scents of the individual fruit trees and flowers. As you leave the forest and approach the actual village huts you are suddenly confronted by the strong smell of humanity. You feel half reluctant to walk into it. You catch the warm earthy smell of the mud huts and the smoke and the moist heavy damp stink of the cowdung. Beneath that you may smell the ash and the dirt from the rubbish heaps.

That is the smell of humanity, and you wish you could draw in some scents and shut your nose to others. As you pass each compound you can tell what is cooking in the kitchen, and what the relish will be — mushrooms, fish, *nyovi*, peanut butter and maybe chicken. The smell of food is reassuring in the darkness. You pass your eyes over the cowpens and their stinking stamping cattle battling against the flies, and quickly over the frames of the graves. You may stop to wonder if the earthy, grassy green scent is the smell of the graves, or just that of the grass and the earth.

You can smell the dogs too. They dashed at us from the bushes, but Simba stood his ground and growled, so that the cowardly creatures turned back and fled, yelping.

"I see Simba is a formidable dog," said father, laughing.

"The most formidable in the village," boasted Boyce.

"People are fencing off and ploughing their compound areas," observed father.

"There is a very big scramble for land but unfortunately Jairos is no longer sane enough to answer for it," I said. "He packed this village with Derukas."

"How can you say that?" said father, alarmed. "Where would we be if Jairos had not 'packed' this village, as you decide to call his hospitality. You haven't seen a really crowded village. You have never been to the south. The pressure on the land there is three times what it is here. No one owns more than six acres of land. We are still quite well off here – I am surprised you are blaming Jairos, as if it is he who commanded the human race to multiply."

I felt hurt and so confused that I barely heard father announce triumphantly that we had arrived home unscathed by the proclaimed evils of the back paths.

15

Midu

After reaping the crops he had sown in April, Boyce suddenly announced that he wanted to go home to his mother. We found him gone when we came home for the December holidays.

"It was only an excuse," mother explained. "He really wanted to go away to town to look for a job." We were going to miss Boyce and we wished him well in his quest for a job.

"I don't know what I will do in October without a boy to help me with the ploughing," lamented mother.

"Boyce was such a nice boy, so industrious and cheerful. He thought he would hurt me by telling me that he was going to town, so he only said he was going back to his mother."

" You will get another boy before the rains, mother."

"That will be difficult. The young men are getting tired of the countryside and flocking to the towns. And besides, people are reluctant to part with their sons."

"Why, mother? Do they think they are underpaid?"

"There is more money in the towns. And people are realising that it pays to work for themselves. Things are not the same anymore."

I would particularly miss Boyce because he had been the judge and hearer of my adventures each time I went to Goto village to see Lulu.

"We must beat last year's sales," said mother. "We must work hard this summer."

In an industrious spirit, Jo and I woke up in the crisp early hours of dawn to yoke the oxen in Matudu's kraal. All morning we ploughed the green acres. Then came the weeding, the sunstroke, the lashing rain and the nibbling goats. And dew in the morning on the green when we went to guard the crops.

As if to add our pile of problems, Matudu decided that he had looked after our cattle long enough and, accordingly, he drove them to our place and left them unceremoniously inside our fence. Jo and I spent two days building a kraal of wooden logs for them, and until we found a small boy to look after them, Jo had to look after the cattle.

"So Matudu simply decided to dump the cattle here without warning," said Mrs Pendi at the fence, clutching her ailing baby.

"I knew he would do that sooner or later," said mother.

"My little boy has been coughing all night," explained Mrs Pendi, soothing the baby. "What a night we had! There was an owl hooting on the roof of my bedroom all night. We couldn't sleep. And this same morning a snake slithered into my fowl run and swallowed a live chicken. You haven't seen a snake like that, Masiziva."

"It's very strange," smiled mother.

"This village is not safe anymore. And what are the people coming to? How can Matudu just leave the cattle like that? Who will look after the cattle when your boys go back to school?"

"Godi will be remaining for a few weeks. You know fifth-formers start a bit later. But I suppose I should try to find a boy."

"Herdboys are so difficult to find these days, Masiziva. And apart from that they will disappoint you even if you get them to work for you. Take this boy Midu, who has been looking after my cattle. I cannot understand him."

"Why?"

"Doesn't he seem strange to you? His eyes, his voice."

"Well?"

"Don't be deceived by his boyish looks. He is quite an old one, that boy. Yet he behaves just like a toddler. You know that he has been working for over a year now but hasn't bought himself a single shirt. He prefers to spend all his earnings on sweets and biscuits."

"But you ought to buy clothes for him. He needs your guidance, being only a boy."

"No, Masiziva, Midu is an exception. You can't argue him into doing anything constructive."

"But he is only a boy," said mother. "You should never put all the cash into his hands. He doesn't know what to do with it. Give him enough to buy sweets and to keep him happy. Save the rest of his money to buy him clothes, or send the money off to his father."

"You don't know his parents, Masiziva. If you buy clothes they will complain that the clothes are not worth what you should pay the boy."

"But what can we do? When we take a boy to live with us we must make sure that the boy is at least properly dressed. We can rest with an easy conscience that way."

" You are right there, Masiziva. I could buy clothes for Midu or send his wages to his father. But when Midu's father entrusted the boy to us he said we should give all the money to the boy."

"Maybe that was just talk. He could turn out to be happy if he hears that you are buying clothes for his boy. If he comes now and finds his son half-naked he won't believe you are paying him anything."

"You are right there again," Mrs Pendi nodded quickly, the way people nod when they think they have had more than enough advice. "But Midu is a queer boy. Each time he goes to the dip he buys himself a loaf of bread and a tin of corned beef and he packs his stomach as if it's the end of the world."

"All young boys are gluttons at one stage of their lives," laughed mother.

While they were talking, Mai Mapanga and Jo came hurrying along the path. Mai Mapanga proceeded to the Pendi's gate and Jo came through ours.

"What happened, Jo?" Mrs Pendi demanded apprehensively, clutching her baby. "I thought you had gone to the mill with Midu."

"Something happened," said Jo hesitantly, "Midu had some kind of shock and he fainted."

"Shock! Fainted! How and where?"

"We had gone to Mai Mapanga's homestead to ask for a pump."

"Mai Mapanga's compound! To ask for a pump –"

"One tyre was almost flat –"

"I do not know what is wrong with Midu to go asking for things from stranger's homesteads. As if we had no pump here –"

"What happened?" interrupted mother.

"We sat on a log and Midu just fell on his face. He was breathing, but he had lost consciousness."

Mai Mapanga had by then gone through the gate and was hurrying to the fence where the group was standing. She was visibly panicking and had her dress been short enough one could perhaps have seen her knees knocking together. There was something wild and desperate in her step. She trembled and swayed like a person with a full bladder.

"What is this I hear about Midu fainting in your homestead?" snapped Mrs Pendi. Mai Mapanga's lips opened and flapped soundlessly. I suddenly remembered the day I had first seen her standing at her husband's grave. I remembered the dry black lips, the cracked yellow teeth and the soft palm. She still wore black mourning clothes.

"It just happened," she explained shakily. "Midu and this boy came to my homestead to ask for a pump. They sat on a log and even before I could return their greeting, your boy fell forward on his face and didn't move."

"Was he bitten by a snake or a scorpion?" demanded Mrs Pendi.

"I don't know, my daughter," replied Mai Mapanga, and I half expected Mrs Pendi would reject the salutation. "He just fell forward. Maybe it was from the heat and the fatigue."

"From the heat and the fatigue, you think," said Mrs Pendi angrily. "Since when did boys start fainting from heat and fatigue at six o'clock in the morning, and in other people's homesteads? You know what you did to my boy and you will tell me."

"But I did not do anything to him," protested Mai Mapanga.

"You will explain to my husband and the boy's father when they come this weekend." Mrs Pendi put the boy down and hurried away with Mai Mapanga. We followed.

Quite a crowd had assembled in Mai Mapanga's homestead. As we drew nearer I observed that it had formed a ring round the outstretched figure of Midu. Headman Simon was shaking something over Midu's body.

"He was lucky," said Simon quietly. "They didn't really beat him. They just blew their chilly breaths over him and clouded his mind for a moment."

Mrs Pendi pushed her way through the ring.

"Mai Mapanga will tell us what she did to my boy," she said as if she was going to cry.

"He will be all right," said Simon.

"Is he breathing?" asked Mrs Pendi.

"Do not touch him before the powder settles," cautioned Simon. "The powder will drive them away."

There was silence for about five minutes, in which only Midu's belly seemed to move. He lay on his back with his face turned to the sun. His mouth and eyes were open but there was an empty stare in his eyes.

Men brought medicine in small bottles, liquids thick and yellow as cooking oil, or brown as chocolate, powders like cocoa and jellies like mucus. Each brand of medicine was administered to Midu's body by its owner. Men muttered advice every now and then.

"We can put him by the fire now," said Simon. "It will drive the chill out of him."

A man pointed to a fire roaring in the middle of Mai Mapanga's homestead.

"I would rather take him home and put him near my own fire," said Mrs Pendi and people muttered in agreement.

Simon took Midu on his back like a baby, and someone held the dangling head in place to prevent it from straining the neck. The procession went slowly to Mrs Pendi's compound in a silence that was broken only by the hushed whispers exchanged by members of the crowd.

They laid him by the fire in Mrs Pendi's kitchen. Jairos staggered into the doorway of the crowded hut and stared at Midu and the medicines. There was alarm in his face as he whispered in a tone of question and statement, "The little men beat him —" He turned and went away, muttering to himself.

Midu lay by the fire for a while. At last he moved his legs and opened his eyes and sat up like a boy waking from sleep. He sneezed twice into the fire. They took him out behind the hut to empty his bladder. The sneezing and the passing of urine were good signs of recovery, said Simon. Midu sat blank-faced at the fire all day, long after the hut was empty. On the next day he was up and about, herding cattle as if nothing unusual had happened.

Three days afterwards Mrs Pendi accompanied her children to school. My family also packed and left, leaving only Midu and myself in the two compounds. We were to share each other's company in the evenings and sleep together.

I started feeling very lonely after they had left. I opened the kraal to let out the cattle. Bellum eyed me eagerly. Sigwe rose lazily from the ground and the calf came to sniff my hands and to lick the tips of my fingers with his small rasping tongue. I whipped the cattle grudgingly as I drove them to the pastures, punishing them in advance for the trouble I thought they would give me.

It was still very early when I got to the fields and there were no cattle yet in the vlei. It was still in the vlei and I wondered how long the dew would last before the herds of cattle came to scatter it with their hooves.

I let my cattle browse in the lush grass near the edge of the field and I sat in a commanding position from which I could keep my eye on the cattle as well as on the fields. I opened my novel and was absorbed in it till the tinkling bells warned me that the other herd-boys were coming. I was happy I had been first in the vlei and I somehow felt unhappy as the herds of cattle passed by and flooded into the yellow vlei. Bellum looked up and lowed, but his family was not there so he browsed on. All round me I could hear the cattle pulling the grass out of the ground and munching.

Towards noon two girls passed by the field and went down to the gardens in the vlei. They came back later carrying baskets of vegetables on their heads. I stood up to greet them.

"How are you?" said the older woman. She was not a girl and I

151

realised that she was possibly married. "Has your mother gone to town yet? I wanted to pay for the dress she sold me."

"You can leave the money with me if you like," I told her.

"I did not bring the money," she said, chewing a blade of grass, "but I can bring it tomorrow. So you remained behind to look after the cattle?"

"Yes," I replied. " And to guard the crops."

"Guard your mother's crops well," she said. "Your mother works very hard."

"Could you sell me a cabbage?" I asked, just as they were turning to go. I put my book down and went into the grass to meet them. They put their baskets down and I realised that the other girl was much younger than I had supposed. She was perhaps sixteen, with a big crop of dark plaited hair. Her breasts were showing like little horns inside her dress. Her knees were soiled, she had been kneeling in the mud. There was something sad in her wide face and slow, brown, wide apart eyes.

"You can have the cabbage for nothing," said the older woman, "because your mother is kind to us." She handed me a cabbage and said to the girl, "Give him two mealies, Jeni."

I took the mealies from the girl and thanked her. She made an effort to smile. They went away along the path and disappeared in the grass. I read again.

In the afternoon it rained. It had been hot all day. The storm had built up suddenly. A sudden chill swept in from the east. I stood contemplating the storm, shivering in my shirt, waiting for the last herds to leave the vlei. Then I rounded up my three cattle and frantically drove them home. The rain opened onto us before we got far, humming down onto us, enveloping us in the splashing white downpour. There was the warm steaming smell of the earth everywhere. A bolt of lightning split the grey sky, reaching down to touch the trees and for a moment I thought I had been hit. I shut the cattle in the kraal and went into the kitchen. Simba lay under the grain hut. He whined and wagged his tail when he saw me, sorry that he could not come to me in the rain. I realised with surprise that he had not been with me to the vlei in the morning.

In the kitchen I smashed the logs together and blew the fire into flames. I sat sleepily, leaning over the fire, knowing that I was safe from the lightning and the rain. By the time the storm abated the sun was setting. It was too late to take the cattle out again, so I went by myself to check the field for stray cattle.

I had finished feeding Simba and bathing myself when Midu came. It was dark; he loomed suddenly in the doorway, the lamplight vaguely defining his body against the background of the dark night.

"Hello, Midu," I said.

"Hello," he muttered. " I thought you were not around."

"There was no sound from your place. Did you come late?"

"No."

"Just after sunset?"

"Yes."

"Have you had supper?"

"No."

"I am sorry. I have just finished mine. I gave all the leftovers to Simba."

He sat on the floor near the fire, with his chin on his knees, surveying the hut slowly, blankly.

"So where were you herding your cattle today, Midu?"

"In Mbumbuzi Forest."

"You don't like the vlei?"

"I went with Matudu's sons to Mbumbuzi Forest."

"Is there a lot of grass there?"

"Yes."

"I was just about to go to bed. I wish I could get you something to eat. You didn't eat anything?"

"No."

"So you are going to bed hungry?"

"I ate mangoes."

"I see. But you ought to have a proper supper."

"I will cook something tomorrow."

"Shall we go to sleep then?" I asked. I lifted the lamp, went out of the kitchen and bolted the door. When I turned round I was surprised to see Midu's figure disappearing in the shadows.

"Where are you going, Midu?" I half shouted.

"To get my blankets," he said without stopping.

"We can share mine tonight," I said but he went on in the darkness. I wondered if I should go with him with a lamp. Somewhere in the night a baby cried. I heard Midu kicking open the door of his hut in the Pendi's compound. He did not even strike a match. I heard him close the door again and come back.

"You are not afraid of the dark?" I said to him, and in the lamplight I saw the cheeks moving as if to smile.

He spread his blankets next to mine and took off his clothes. He lay on his back, staring at the roof. "Won't you go to sleep?" he asked me.

"I want to read for a while," I told him, flipping the pages of my novel. "Do you want something to look at?"

I gave him a magazine full of pictures and he turned over to examine the book, moistening his thumb.

"Is this a train?" he asked me, pointing to a picture. I nodded.

"And is this the head of the train?"

"Yes."

"Does the head push or pull the train?"

"It pulls."

"I think I would enjoy a ride on a train."

"Why, have you never been on a train?"

"I haven't seen a train in my life. Maybe I will see one when father takes me to town next month."

"Is your father coming?"

"He might. Here is a girl with a big packet of sweets."

"A very big packet."

"They almost look like real sweets. I could tear them out of the page and eat them "

"Oh."

"They make me feel hungry. Who draws all these pictures?"

" A person. But a machine prints them on the paper."

"Oh, a machine."

154

The lamp burned between us. I could smell his thick dark curled hair. His hair wasn't combed. His skin was very smooth and light, but his eyes were too big. The eyelids were swollen. His lips were moist and thick and stayed open all the time. There was at once something young and old in his features. The smoothness of his skin put his age at eleven or twelve but the thick gaping lips and the slow dark brown eyes suggested fifteen or sixteen. There was something queer about his eyes, something stern and even aggressive. Even when he smiled his eyes seemed to disagree with the rest of his facial features. Yet at the same time he was little older than a boy. He had a clean body and slept naked like a baby. His arms were small and boyish, but the knuckles and the fingers had a swollen look. There was black earth under his fingernails. I wondered if he had been digging for mudworms. Perhaps he had been fishing.

"I have finished my book," he said, gathering the tattered pages into place. "You haven't finished yours yet."

"Mine is a novel. I have to read all the words."

"All the words? Every single word?"

"Yes, or I will not understand the story."

"But its more interesting to read pictures."

"You think so," I said. I stopped reading and put my book away. "When is the dip this week?"

"On Friday."

"I have never been to the dip."

"We wake up very early."

"Are you going to the dip?"

"Yes. Why do you ask?"

"I thought perhaps you were not all right, after that day when you fainted."

He lay on his back and stared at the roof. Outside the dark the Pendi's gate clicked. Midu jerked his head.

"It's that sick old man Jairos coming to mess the toilet," Midu said loudly. "I wish I was there to scold him off."

"What really happened, Midu?" I asked, brushing Jairos aside.

"When?"

"That day when you fainted in Mai Mapanga's compound."

"They hit me."

"What hit you?"

"Mai Mapanga's little men."

"You saw them?"

"I saw a bit of them."

"What were they like?"

"I can't easily describe them."

"You can try."

"I only saw them for a very short time. They were two very little black men, black as soot, and with backs bent like wire. They had very small feet."

"Did they make any sound?"

"They seemed to mutter and hiss."

"And they raised their hands and slapped you?"

"They did not slap me. I just saw them and fainted."

"You fainted just from seeing them?"

"Yes. And they blew their cold breaths over me. I saw them and felt cold and fainted."

"You don't remember anything else?"

"No. I only remember waking up lying near the fire and going out to pass urine."

"You are not afraid the little men will beat you again?"

"Again?" He seemed puzzled. He had never thought about it.

"Why do you think they beat you?"

"Maybe because I sat on their log."

I blew the light out and went to sleep. In the middle of the night I woke up and saw Midu's dark, upturned face. His mouth was open, but he did not make a sound. He slept very quietly like a baby. The blankets had rolled off his body and he lay on his back with his knees up in the air. I covered him with the blankets and felt a vague sensation on touching his dark, naked body. He did not move when I touched him. Outside in the dark Simba was growling ferociously.

When I woke up in the morning Midu had already gone. He had

folded his blankets and carelessly thrown them onto the floor. He had left the door half open and I could see that the sun was rising. I stretched my arms and yawned lazily, reluctant to get out of bed. I hated rising early.

Midu was picking mangoes when I saw him.

"You are up early," I said to him.

"You are up late," he replied across the fence. "The sun is up. The chickens came out ages ago."

Simba jumped at me and put his paws on my chest. I patted his head and pressed him off.

"Have you milked your cows?" I asked him.

"I shall. Have you milked Sigwe?"

"I shall." I laughed. I went to the pump to get water, washed the dishes and made a fire.

"You are cooking something sweet," said Midu across the fence. "Something fat and oily."

"Oil buns," I told him.

"Come and get some mangoes," said Midu. I went to the fence and he handed me a plate of mangoes.

"Thank you," I said. "They are so ripe."

"There was one very big one in this tree. It was almost ripe, but now I can't find it. I think Joki came and stole it."

"Who is Joki?"

"Munyu's last boy. He herds the cattle. He is a nuisance. He comes to play here and he steals things. He pays most of his visits at a mealtimes too."

"You should discourage your friends from coming to play here, Midu," I advised him. "Otherwise Mrs Pendi won't be very pleased to learn that you were bringing people here during her absence."

I went into the kitchen with the mangoes and saw Jairos coming. He followed me into the kitchen and grabbed a chair, his eyes flying.

"Please let me have a bun," he said desperately, his eyes glued on the pan on the fire.

"But they are not ready yet," I told him. "Will you have a mango?"

"I don't like mangoes. They make my teeth ache. I want a bun. A bun please, that brown one in the middle of the pan." He went to the

157

fire to point.

I eventually forked the dripping brown bun out of the pan and put it on the table. Jairos took the bun with unsteady hands, took one bite and put down again.

"Can I have some tea?"

"The water is only warm."

"It doesn't matter."

I poured the warm water into a cup and stirred tea leaves and sugar into it.

"What about milk?"

"There is no milk. I haven't milked the cow yet."

"You haven't milked the cow! Does the cow have no milk today?"

He took the tea, however.

"Where is your mother?" he demanded, munching.

"She is away in town."

"And your father?"

"He is in town, too."

"Tell him to send me tobacco and gin. He doesn't like me any more. He wants me to die."

He finished eating and took his dirty woollen hat to go.

"You have a shilling?" he asked, stopping in the doorway.

"No."

"Can I have a shilling?"

"No, you cannot. What do you want it for?"

"I want to give it at the funeral."

"At the funeral? Who died?"

"Jeni died. You didn't hear?"

"No."

"You don't have a shilling?"

"No."

"All right, I'll ask next door."

He went out humbly, holding his hat in his hands. He put his hat on and coughed and went away with his eyes turned to the ground. Midu came just after Jairos left. He found me having my tea. He sat on the stoep of the hut.

"I'm having breakfast," I told him.

"Yes."

" Would you like a cup of tea?"

"Yes."

I gave him a cup of tea and a bun.

"You fry well," he remarked, eating the bun.

"You still haven't milked your cows?"

"No."

"But you should. They say if a calf has too much milk it will have a running stomach."

"I will milk them."

"I have to take my cattle out now," I told him, picking up the cups.

"But it's still very early, in the morning."

"I have to guard our field," I told him. "There could be stray cattle eating the crops even now as we talk."

"But no one takes cattle to the vlei this early."

"There could be stray cattle."

"And there is the dew."

"It doesn't matter."

"So you graze your cattle near the field."

"Yes."

"All day?"

"Yes."

"I may see you in the afternoon."

I took the cattle to the vlei. I felt more tolerant towards them. They were only cattle, I told myself, and all they could do was munch grass. In the end they all ended up in the cooking pot. I looked at them and tried to imagine myself eating their meat. Sigwe was too thin and there was an air of melancholy about her slow sad eyes which would haunt me. Bellum was fat and sleek. I knew every inch of his body. I would prefer his meat because he was fat and there was an aggressive defiance about him which was challenging.

I sat reading under a tree. From somewhere in the village I heard voices but I could not tell whether they were singing or not. At noon I put my book down and ate sadza and sour milk. I stood up and looked out across the vlei.

The grass was tall and so still that you would think that someone had planted it. It was quite level and at the edges of the vlei the clump of trees locked the grass in like a crop. The grass obscured the stream at the bottom of the vlei so that all I could see was a portion of the steep dark bank which the water had cut in the heavy rainy season. Across the stream I could see the thin plain of grass and the thick forest beyond.

There were no cattle in the vlei yet. It was so quiet. I could not even hear the rustling of the grass. There was something about the grass. In the morning when the grass was glossy yellow with the dew I could stand for minutes looking out at the plain, wondering when the dew would dry up. Did I like the dew, I wondered. It was beautiful to look at, but then it made you wet and it could even give you a cold. But even after the dew dried I still wanted to look at the grass. I swept my eyes from one end of the vlei to the other, wondering what to do with it.

I could bring paints and brushes and paper out to the fields but then I had never been a good painter. I could never reproduce the glossiness of the grass. The view was too wide, and I would make too much fuss over the individual features. The forest looked thick and close from far off but I knew when you walked into it and started seeing individual trees and splashes of sunlight spilling in between the crowns of trees you realised how isolated the trees were.

I knew too that I could perhaps write about it, but words alone were not enough. Perhaps I wanted to take off my clothes, kick off my boots and wade through the grass into the blazing sunshine down to the shimmering stream. To be drunk with the sunshine and sensation, some kind of sentimental consummation perhaps. And then what? Exhilaration? Shame. . . ?

Two figures, Midu and another boy, came into the field, parting the tall grass with their hands and my dream fell in fragments around me.

"Hello," I said to them, as they sat near me under the tree, scrutinising my empty lunch box.

"You graze your cattle so near the crops," said Midu loudly. "One day they will eat your mealies."

"I keep a sharp eye on them," I said.

Joki, Midu's companion, dug in the dust with his toes.

He was a skinny boy with a face like a knife and dirty oversized clothes.

"What is the box for?" asked Midu, pointing.

"For putting things in," I replied.

"You bring your lunch out to the fields?"

"Yes. I can't go home and cook in the afternoon. What do you do for lunch?"

"I don't cook in the afternoon."

"But you don't cook in the morning either. You only eat mangoes. You never cook."

"I just do not feel like eating."

"If I gave you something to eat would you refuse?"

"Do you want to give me anything? Is there anything in the tin?"

"No, I ate everything. Are you fishing today?"

"I did not bring a fishing line."

"I don't have a hook," said Joki.

"Who is singing?" I asked, listening. "I have been hearing the sound all morning."

"Didn't you hear?" said Joki with surprise. "There is a funeral. Someone died."

"Jeni died," said Midu.

"Jeni?" I said incredulously.

"Majuru's daughter," said Midu.

"What does she look like? I mean what did she look like?"

"She was a big girl," said Joki.

"With tall dark plaited hair?"

"Yes."

"And long slim legs?"

"Yes."

"Where did she live?"

"In Matuvu's line."

"Does she ever go to the garden to get vegetables and mealies? Did she ever go to the garden...?"

"Yes," said Joki. "She usually went with her brother's wife."

"I saw a girl like that yesterday. It was her. She was with an older woman. The older woman addressed her as Jeni. They were coming up from the gardens and they gave me a cabbage and two mealies."

"That's her," said Joki.

"But she did not look ill yesterday."

"She died suddenly," said Midu, "of witchcraft."

"Mai Mapanga bewitched her —" interjected Joki.

"Her little men tortured her for many nights —"

"In fact Mai Mapanga and Jeni were enemies. Mai Mapanga hated Jeni because she worked hard —"

"Because Jeni worked so hard in the fields —"

"Mai Mapanga said 'Let me kill her and see who will work for her parents. She thinks she is a tractor and yet she is only a girl'. "

"And so Mai Mapanga started torturing her —"

"Jeni couldn't sleep at night. She woke up every morning complaining that someone had been sitting on her back all night."

"And yesterday when she came from the garden her foot started swelling —"

"Mai Mapanga had set a medicine trap on the path —"

"She felt pins moving in her breast —"

"Last night she did not sleep —"

"Early this morning she was dead."

"I thought the voices were singing," I said. "I remember headman Jairos asking me for a shilling this morning, to give at the funeral, he said. I thought he did not know what he was talking about. He even said Jeni's name."

"She was such a nice girl," said Midu.

"She gave me two cobs yesterday," I said. "I can't believe she has died."

"She was an industrious girl," said Midu. "I wonder why Mai Mapanga killed her."

"She was jealous of her. She will kill us all."

"I guess she will want to raise her spirit and turn it into one of her little men."

162

"When are they burying her?" I asked.

"On Monday."

"Why so late?"

"They want her body to decompose first, to make sure that the witches don't dig her grave to eat her flesh."

I looked out into the grass and saw the girl holding out two mealies to me. The tall grass covered her up to the breast. Her breasts looked like two horns under the blouse and the wind seemed to play with them. The mealies fell out of her hands and rolled in the grass and I was afraid to take them. Her whole body seemed to blacken and crumble like hard clay till only the eyes were left, large, dark wide-apart eyes looming in the grass. Her body lay rolled up in a blanket inside a hut. There were flies all round the hut. Outside the hut people wept and Mai Mapanga wept among them. She still wore her black mourning clothes. There was a strong stench all round the hut, and a narrow deep stickhole in the grave. There were tall weeds on the mound of the grave and Mai Mapanga stood knee-deep in the grass plucking the grass seeds into her basket in the rain...

No, it wasn't raining and there was no one in the grass. The sun was still shining and I asked Midu to stand up and look to see if my cattle were still grazing in the tall grass near the edge of the field.

⚘ ⚘ ⚘

On Sunday morning the sky was overcast with dark clouds. I woke up late. The village was soaked with the rain. Grey roofs were damp and dripping rain, some of the mud was falling from the walls exposing wooden poles like lipless teeth. I hated the ground when it was green with moss. I knew the rain would not come very early in the morning.

I asked Midu to take my cattle out to the pastures, promising to return early in the afternoon. I took my umbrella and raincoat and set off for Goto township to see Lulu. People were going into the church when I got there but I did not go into the church. I hung around in a nearby thicket idly stripping the bushes of their leaflets and feeding the leaflets into the wind.

I saw her after the service. She came out with books and said hello to me. I stood with my back to a tree, digging into the dust with my heels.

163

"You didn't come in for the service," she said.

"I did not. I didn't feel like coming in."

"You're a heathen," she laughed.

"Satan will have a nice big fork for me and a bag of coal in Hell."

"You make fun of that?"

"Sometimes I can't help it."

She wore a knee length dress and she had stretched her hair and combed it backwards. I could see the skin on her head under the hair. Just above her breast I could see her neck bones. She wore no necklace. I still wore hers and felt guilty at not having provided a substitute.

"So how is work at the store?" I asked.

" As usual."

"Boring?"

"Not boring. Just hard."

"I am staying alone these days."

"How alone?"

"All the others went to town, including mother. And would you believe it — I am looking after the cattle."

"So how come you are here?"

"Instinct."

"Go back and take your cattle out to the pastures. They are starving."

"Midu is taking care of them today. I came to take you out to the pastures. Hiya Lucia! Hey, come! You cow."

"I am not a cow and I am not coming to the pastures. I don't eat grass anyway."

"You can come over to our place now that I am living alone."

"To do what?"

"To see me. So where are you going now?"

"Where else? To my hut."

"Can I come with you?"

"No, you shall not."

She unbolted the door of her hut and ducked in, shutting the door in my face.

"But I want to come in," I protested.

"There is no place for you in here."

"I shall bang the door down."

"It's your fault if people see you and think you are crazy."

She opened the door slightly and peeped out. I pushed in and the door gave way. I knew as soon as I got in that she did not want me to go away because she put her arms around me. She put her palms on my cheeks and kissed me.

"I want to sit down," she said, pulling away from me and patting her dress. She sat on the bed and put her head on the pillow.

"You are ill?" I asked.

"Yes."

"What ails you?"

"Headache."

"Can I help you?" I bent forward.

"No you can not."

"Why not?" I asked, sitting on her bed.

"There is no place for you on my bed."

"In that case I am going away," I said, going to the door.

She kicked her shoes off and stretched her legs on the bed. Somehow she seemed to chide my boyish fantasy in the vlei.

I closed the door, came back to the bed and put my nose on the pillow.

"Is that all you want?" she said like a pail of cold water. I had nothing to say.

"You know the state my father is in. Our affair can never get anywhere."

I looked blankly at the pillow.

"You don't have to say anything," she said, "and you know you don't live in this village all the time?"

"What has come over you, Lulu?"

"I am no longer a child. I know it's hopeless. I can never dream of belonging to you. There is too much competition."

"What makes you say that?"

"You wouldn't marry me. A girl who works in a shop. You, with your education."

"But —"

"And there's my father."

"What has your father got to do with this?"

"Since he became ill I have been thinking. I have been thinking of my family. You know how poor we are. I should be helping them. I shouldn't be having affairs."

"But this is not an ordinary affair."

"It wouldn't be right for me to get too far into this."

"Who has been talking to you about this, Lulu?"

"I didn't have to be told, although my mother warned me. No. I am sorry. I would have loved us to continue. I have been working for a long time now and I think I have been growing up."

"And you want me simply to break it off and leave you?"

"Yes. But not because I want you to go. I just want to be alone to think out my problems and to be responsible."

"You can't even imagine how hard it is for me. . . ."

"You think your mother would be happy to have me in your home? If I had another father perhaps. Or if I was educated. Your mother likes but do you really think she would accept me? Don't answer." There was nothing I could say. She lay there quietly while I tried to absorb the shock of the truth. Later she handed me my raincoat and umbrella and took me to the path. She couldn't take me far because she said her head was aching and the storm was buzzing down towards us. I put on my raincoat and turned blindly away.

🔺🔺🔺

After shutting up the cattle that evening I went morosely to the kitchen and prepared myself a meal. I ate a little, and then took the paraffin lamp and went out to feed Simba. He was barking furiously in the dark near the trees, just beyond the fence. I called out twice and whistled to him before he stopped growling. He came very slowly, and kept bristling his ears and growling even as I fed him.

Afterwards I bathed on the grass in the lamplight. Midu had still not come when I finished bathing. I stood in the doorway of the kitchen looking at the Pendis' compound. Not a sound came from there, the big compound lay in silence. Not a hen clucked in the fowl run. Only

166

the huge zinc roof of the big house gleamed timidly in the darkness. He had still not come when I went to bed. I did not read. I just lay in the darkness, unthinking, vainly courting sleep.

In the morning I staggered into the sunshine. The green and the dew didn't thrill me. Simba ran up to greet me. He seemed glad that the night was over. I saw Midu just when I was going to take the cattle out.

"You didn't come last night," I said.

"I couldn't."

"You didn't sleep in your hut either."

"I went to sleep with Joki at their place."

"I knew you were away because it was so quiet. I was the only soul here."

"Were you afraid?"

"Not very. Except when Simba barked."

"He barked a lot?"

"Yes. At the fence near the trees, over there."

"What was he barking at?"

"I don't know. It was so dark. So why did you not come last night?"

"I can't tell you. I might scare you."

"Come on, I am not a baby."

"There was a strange light near our lavatory."

"A fire?"

"No. A light."

"Torchlight or lamplight?"

"A strange light. It seemed to hang in the air."

"Near the lavatory?"

"In the doorway."

"You are sure it was not Jairos' cigarette?"

"No, the fire was too big."

"He would not have gone there if there was a light."

"He is mad. He could."

"So you saw the light and you ran?"

"I saw the light and I ran, back to Joki's place where I had been. I slept there."

"Did the light go on and off?"

"No. It was on all the time."

"Was it big? Did it throw any shadows?"

"I can't remember very well. But it didn't throw any shadows. It just shone and its light obscured everything else."

"You are sure it was not my lamplight? I came out with the lamp to feed Simba."

"No, it wouldn't have been you. The light was right in the doorway of the lavatory. It made the lavatory look as if it was on fire. And I think you were asleep when I came. There was no light in your huts."

"I went to sleep early. So you think it was a — ghost?"

"I don't see what else it could have been. There was certainly no fire burning near the toilet."

"What would a ghost do in the lavatory? Wait for people?"

"Or maybe for jairos."

"But this is strange. Why should a ghost choose to appear now when there is only me and you in the two compounds? Why now, of all times?"

"That I don't know."

"You think maybe someone sent it?"

"It could be."

"But are you sure you were not imagining it? I was within view of the lavatory and I never saw a thing."

"You don't believe me, Godi. Why should I lie? I swear I saw it with my eyes." He raked his tongue with his index finger and made a cross on his forehead. He was not lying. He had seen something. He was a brave boy and not easily scared by the darkness.

He opened the kraal to take the cattle out. I knew he had not eaten anything. He did not even take any mangoes. He was away before me and later I realised that Simba had gone with him.

He came back in the evening, exhausted by hunger. I knew now why he was so skinny. But his flesh had a glow which seemed to survive his sustained and self-created bouts of starvation. Simba came back with him, limping.

"You took Simba with you," I said.

"I couldn't make him come back."

"He is limping. What happened?"

"Is he limping? I didn't notice. Where?"

"The hind leg. The right leg, as if something hit him."

"Maybe it's a sprain."

"Where did you graze the cattle today?"

"In the Mbumbuzi Forest."

"He did not chase anything?"

"No, I didn't see him chase anything."

"At least you ought to have noticed he was limping."

I took Simba's leg in my hands. He whined. There was no bruise, nothing to indicate how he had hurt himself. Afterwards I prepared my evening meal. Midu and I ate together and went to sleep.

In the morning Simba limped heavily. I took his leg up and was surprised to find a huge circle of pink flesh showing just beneath his stomach, as if his fur had been neatly plucked off. The skin had not been cut. I did not know what to do.

"Give him wild melon juice," Midu advised. "Bathe the rash with the juice and make him drink some of the juice."

I followed Midu's advice. I had heard of the cure before. That day Simba lay in the shade near me, not running about as he used to do.

In the evening Midu did not come. I spent the night alone. In the morning Simba's voice was hoarse. He limped very heavily. I wished I could help him. I only hoped that he would hang on till mother returned, then I could attend to him. He did not come with me to the fields.

I came back at sunset and found him dead. He lay on his side under the grain hut. I stood near the grain hut looking at him and felt angry and remorseful. I wanted to run up to Midu and force him into saying how Simba had received the injury. But I felt remorseful because I had not loved Simba as Jo had done. I felt remorseful because I had watched him die.

He was a huge dog and in death he was even bigger. His brown belly was swollen. I wondered if it was the air inside him, and why the air did not rush out through his open mouth. His tongue was already

169

stiff and ran out of his mouth at the side. His eyes were open, staring at me. There was no smell. I guessed he had died after noon. As I watched him a big green fly entered his mouth and buzzed inside. I knew he would smell.

I would have to bury him up the slope in front of the village line. If I put him behind the village line the wind might blow the smell up the compounds, and the rain might expose his bones.

I grimly tied his uninjured hind leg with a rope and tugged him up the slope, weaving through the crops of mealies. He was heavy and his body swept the sand like a bag, leaving a fine white trail on the ground. Twice I ran him over wooden stumps. Some of his fur remained twisted on the stumps. I pulled him under the fence of barbed wire and into the trees where he had been barking and growling a few days before. Already the darkness was falling.

I started digging with a shovel and felt my anger rising again.

The ground was hard. I wished I had a pick. I cut the roots with the edge of the shovel and scooped the earth out with my fingers. There wasn't enough earth to fill the shovel. I fumbled on in the pressing darkness. I felt the dark trees looming over me, staring at the strange company I was bringing into their midst.

I pulled Simba into his grave. His body slumped in clumsily, with hind feet out of the hole. I enlarged the hole and pressed his feet in. It did not take me long to fill the hole up with earth. I was glad of the darkness because had it been in the light I would have seen his brown fur turning to a dirty grey as the earth hit him. I picked up the shovel to go and noticed that the rope was still tied to his leg. I did not want to uncover his legs to untie the rope so I just chopped it off with the shovel. Perhaps later on people might spot the tattered shreds of rope locked round a piece of bone but they would never bother to dig the bone up.

I hurried out of the trees in the darkness. I felt angry and miserable. I could not eat. I did not want meat. I went to bed and lay staring at the roof, knowing that outside there was the darkness. There was the darkness but Simba was not there to bark anymore. He couldn't bark because there were clods of earth in his mouth.

"Where is Simba?" Midu asked the next morning.

I did not answer.

"What happened to Simba?"

"I don't know," I replied angrily.

Midu did not believe me. He saw the fine trail weaving through the mealies and I knew the whole village would know by sunset that Simba was dead.

✕✕✕

Mother and Rita returned after three weeks. They arrived without warning. It had been raining and I stood drying myself in the sunshine, whistling, when I heard their shouts. Rita ran up to me, laughing. I swept her up from the ground.

"You did well to come," I said.

"How are you? How was your long stay alone?"

"Not too bad, but I was beginning to feel lonely. Did Tendai start well?"

"Very well. They put her in the 'A' stream. You guarded the crops very well. Not a nibbled plant in sight. Your cattle look fat. You gained weight too."

I grinned.

"Anything happened while we were away?"

"Two women brought money."

"And how is everyone?"

"A girl died."

"What girl?"

"Jeni."

"How sad. And Midu kept you company at night?"

"Only the first few nights."

"It must have been lonely for you. But you had Simba."

"Simba died too."

171

16

Remoni

Remoni was a local young man with a good working record. He had worked for two or three Deruka families and had left very good records of his industry. I was very happy when mother wrote to say that Remoni had agreed to work for us. I looked forward to seeing him.

But he was not the person I had expected him to be, when I saw him. He was, a very short man, very dark and lean. He had gleaming red eyes and a mouth which was quite ready to smile — these features gave him his sly looks. His flesh had hardened into muscle. He wore a dirty yellow shirt and tight white shorts, went about without shoes, leaving the unmistakably small prints of his feet on the ground. There was something imposing in his person because when we asked his health he did not reply but very briefly asked ours, as if his health was a concern of him alone.

At the table he was very neat and well-mannered, but he threw his first piece of sadza into the fire. Later on I learnt that this was no mere habit of his. He believed that by throwing the first piece of sadza into the fire he was rendering himself immune to any possible poisoning by the food. If that first piece of sadza by accident fell to the floor before it reached the fire he would leave eating altogether, believing the accident a favourable omen from his guardian spirits warning him not to eat the food.

He kept one small suitcase, his mat and blankets, and two or three items of clothing on the line. I smelt ropes of oxhide in the sleeping hut and the vision of the iron chain and the *skeis* sent a secret shudder through my body. I had heard that he was a great night worker.

He woke up at three in the morning. The moon was shining brightly, through the doorway, and I felt very tired after the journey. He was gathering the chains and the *skeis*. Jo was already putting his clothes on. I rose hesitantly and put my clothes on, too.

"Wake mother up," said Remoni. There was no need to. She was up and out already. We went to yoke the cattle in the dark. Remoni did not even shout. He just slapped the cattle's faces and they moved into their positions. We took the path behind the village. Everywhere there was the moonlight. You would think it was just after sunset, except that there were no children playing under the eaves of the huts. There was dead silence, except when a cock flapped his wings and crowed, and dozens of others echoed the cry over the village.

We got to the fields and started ploughing. The grass was so tall that at first I could not see the furrows. Remoni held the plough and barked short orders to the cattle. He seemed to know by heart where every tree stump was in the grass. Once I tried my hands on the plough, and narrowly missed knocking my teeth out with the plough-handles when the plough hit a tree stump. Remoni laughed softly and took over, leaving Jo and me to drive the cattle. Mother came behind us dropping maize seeds in the furrows.

The moon sank just before sunrise and the day broke slowly on us. In the vlei the haze melted like wax till I could make out the waves in the grass and the individual trees. The sun broke out, flooding the vlei with orange. The forest did not look so dark and forbidding in the sunshine. I found myself chiding myself for feeling afraid in the dark. What was it about the darkness that made people afraid? Just because the sun left out part of the earth for while? But then the landscape did not change at night. Each tree remained in exactly the same place, each blade of grass swayed in the same place, it was the same reeds that bore the fireflies, the same frogs that croaked, the same footmarks remained on the paths. It was only the expectant imagination which saw distorted figures in mere tree stumps and heard the tread of secret feet in the mere movement of leaves.

173

Or perhaps it wasn't.

By the time the sun rose to the crowns of the trees and the other plough-boys came to the fields we had finished ploughing two acres. People stared at us as we went home, wondering how we could go back so early in the morning.

"That is the trick in ploughing," said Remoni, smiling. "Work at night and play during the day. That should surprise the lazy loafers. They see you leave the fields in the morning while the dew is still shining and they laugh. But when they go to spy on your fields and find the mealies tasselling they will be in for a big disappointment."

After breakfast I lay on a mat and tried to make up for the sleep I had lost in the morning. But Remoni would not let me rest.

"Won't you come and see what I did in the garden?" he asked in a tone which mocked my exhaustion. I put on my boots and went with him. I felt so tall besides him that I let him go ahead slightly. He walked in short, quick, stiff steps. His limbs were so stiff inside his shorts that the flesh of his thighs and calves did not tremble.

He had done wonders in the garden. Cabbages and choumoellier grew big and green as bushes. Onions, spinach, tomatoes, rice and budding mealies.

"Your mother planted too many mealies," he said.

"But it's a fine crop," I said, "and it's ripening too."

"It would have been even better if the plants had been more spaced out."

"You put on fertiliser?"

"No. Manure. Cowdung."

"You did a fine job."

He grinned.

"You repaired the fence too. There was a big gap here through which goats broke in to eat the vegetables."

I stood admiring the garden.

"Won't you take some vegetables home?" he asked.

"Mother didn't say anything, but we can take a cabbage just in case –"

He chose a big green cabbage and put it in my arms, closed the gate and went home. At the side of the path we came upon a tree heavily loaded with ripe berries. I put the cabbage down and ate the berries, holding the thorny branches up with my fingers.

"You eat those?" said Remoni, stopping ahead. "Those are bitter berries."

"I like them," I said, sucking. "Won't you have some yourself?"

"No. They are for kids. I only like to eat them when I am drunk, then they seem to taste like curry."

"You drink?"

"A little," he said, smiling quickly.

"Yesterday I was in trouble," he resumed shortly.

"What trouble?"

"The two sons of Munyu were after me with axes and knobkerries. That is why I am staying indoors all day today."

"Why were they after you?"

"They caught me in their sister's hut on Sunday night."

"What were you doing in a girl's hut at night?"

"What does a fellow do in a girl's hut at night?"

"So they caught you and then beat you?"

"No, I was too fast for them. The younger brother swung his axe at me but I was already out of the way. The axe hit the doorway and broke it into two."

"But why take such risks?"

"I enjoy it. I can't spend two nights without going into a girl's hut. There is not a single girl's hut whose interior I do not know in this village. I have always wanted to know all the girls, too. Every one of them. I want to know how they hold a man and how they cry."

"You are not afraid?"

"Of getting caught and beaten?"

"Besides that… of making the girls pregnant."

"It's up to the girl," he laughed, shaking his small head. "I usually deal with the wide-awake ones who know how to go about it."

"But it's still dangerous."

"Not these days anymore. There is not a girl who doesn't know about pills."

"Pills from the hospital?"

175

"No. From Mai Joki. She has got a whole basket full of them and she sells them by the cup."

"Mai Joki! Where on earth would she get the pills?"

"Her brother works in a clinic. He gets them for her."

"But she could get into trouble. It's illegal."

"Why should she get into trouble? She is helping young girls not to fall pregnant."

"She is helping to corrupt them too."

"I don't think so. Pills do not drive a girl into trading with her body."

"But there are those who refrain from it because of fear of pregnancy. The availability of pills will drive them into doing it."

"Maybe."

"So what do you give your girls?"

"Me!" He put his hands on his hips and stopped laughing. "Me give a girl anything! Not me! I am too smart for them. I flatter them into doing it. I don't spend my earnings on those girls. I don't work for them."

"But there are always other dangers."

"Like what?"

"The girls who sting."

"Oh that! I am too smart for those too."

"You keep away from them? But how do you know if they sting or not?"

"I don't have to keep away from them."

"You go to the clinic afterwards?"

"I don't waste my time going to the clinic. I know the simple remedy for the girl who stings. The moment I finish with her I go out of her hut and urinate. It washes out everything. And I wash immediately afterwards, of course."

I looked at his tense, dark-skinned thighs, his bulging, tight-fitting shorts and his moist dark, laughing lips. There was a bold aching sensuousness in his diminutive features which many girls would no doubt find attractive. A sudden thought struck me, perhaps disease was eating him away very slowly.

"The only trouble with me," he said with a sudden, surprising frankness, "is I can't have children."

"You have a wife?"

"Yes, I have been married for nine months now, and my wife has failed to conceive."

"Where is your wife now?"

"In Goto village."

"With her parents?"

"No, in my compound."

"You have your own place?"

"Two huts and a ten acre field. If I was not working now I would have built myself a big zinc and brick house. The trouble with me is I have worked too long for other people. Had I stayed in my own compound I would have produced fine crops, and raised cattle and sent my children to school. I don't want them to look for other people to read and write their letters for them when they grow up."

"I didn't know that you were married."

"You are not the only one," he laughed. "I know I am a pleasure-boy but when I decide to work hard and do something I on really do it. My wife doesn't go about naked. We never buy maize. We never beg. We can look after ourselves."

"So when do you go to see her?"

"During the weekends."

"I'll tell her you plan to enter every girl's hut in the village," I threatened.

"She knows I do."

"How does she take it?"

"Sometimes she fumes. But she is only a woman."

"I hope you don't beat her."

"Double-crossing, yes. Wife-beating, no. I think it's below a man's dignity to beat his wife."

We reached home and found a man waiting in the kitchen. His bicycle was on the wall. Remoni briefly shook hands with him and left.

"Call Remoni," mother told Jo. "Tell him the man came to see him."

Jo came back to say Remoni wanted to know why the man wanted to see him.

177

"It's about the money I lent him," said the man. Remoni said he had nothing whatsoever to do with the man, but on mother's insistence he came to the kitchen.

"I want my money, Remoni," said the man.

"I told you I don't have it, old man."

"You have been saying that for the past eighteen months. It's month-end now and I want my money this minute, Remoni."

"But I told you I don't have it," said Remoni angrily.

"Just now you said you had nothing to do with me. It proves that you don't care."

"But what do you expect me to do, old man? Tear myself into dollars?"

"Eighteen months is a long time, Remoni."

"Come next month."

"I don't trust you, Remoni. You don't care. I think your employers should hold back your wages till you pay me." He looked at mother with an appealing eye.

"I don't think I should come into this," said mother.

"But I don't trust Remoni," the man protested. "He is a cheat."

"Come next month," insisted Remoni.

"All right. I will come next month. But if you don't give me my money then —"

"What?" interjected Remoni, smirking. "You will go to the witchdoctor?"

"No."

"You will hack me to pieces with an axe?"

"No."

"You can do anything you want, old man. If you go to a witchdoctor that poison he gives you will turn on you and destroy you. I am immune to witchcraft. My grandfather was a great medicine man." He bared his chest to show razor slashes. "This medicine will protect me. Even the little men of the night flee from me. Your axe will bounce lightly from me and hack you, its owner, to pieces."

"I will leave you to your own imagination," said the man with a dignified air. He rose to go, putting on his most solemn looks. He mounted his bicycle and rode off without saying another word.

"Give him his money, Remoni," said mother, after the man had gone.

"He is an idiot! " laughed Remoni. "To spend eighteen months pressing me for a miserable shilling or two he lent me while were playing cards."

"You should pay him back all the same," said mother, seriously.

"No, I won't," grinned Remoni. "I will teach him to be clever next time. Let him go to the witchdoctor, let him send his Little men. Or let him go to the devil. Like I said, I am immune to witch craft. And besides, he won't dare."

🀄🀄🀄

After breakfast Remoni usually went away, sometimes to drink. When he drank he came back in the afternoon, full to the nose. But he controlled himself amazingly and only the slow twinkle of his eyes told me he was drunk. At sunset he would yoke the cattle, even when he was drunk.

"But it's going to rain," I would protest. I hated going to the fields at night.

"It might not rain," mother would say.

"It will not rain," said Remoni.

The rain did not come and Remoni drove the cattle into a neat gallop, so that whoever handled the plough had to hold fast and keep a keen eye for tree stumps. After sunset he built a roaring fire in the middle of the field. The flames lit the whole field and threw long red rays over the vlei. I knew somebody in the village might catch a glimpse of the fire through the trees and think it was something else.

"The fire will drive the ghosts away," explained Remoni.

At one point Jo whistled loudly at the cattle and Remoni chided him laughingly.

"Don't whistle at night."

"Why?"

"They will take your voice."

We ploughed on into the late hours of the night. Everywhere there

179

was a crouching stillness, save for the shrill of the crickets. Even the frogs did not croak. We left the field after midnight, tired to the bones.

On Sundays Remoni put on his best suit. It wasn't exactly a suit. The faded grey trousers were a shade lighter than the jacket, which was too big for him. He wore a white shirt, a red tie and thick khaki stockings that only fitted into the shoes because his feet were very small. One day a boy had come to take his tie from Remoni and from that day we had concluded that most of Remoni's clothes were borrowed from his friends. His own belongings were not numerous enough to fill a very small suitcase, although he evidently enjoyed referring to his things specifically as his 'property' .

He always claimed he was broke, although he could afford to get drunk three or four times a week. Then he came and sat on a chair at the fire and opened the pots to see if there was meat cooking. He hated vegetables.

He was one of those people who do a dozen different jobs in a few years. He had been on the roads, in the dips, and in the tsetse fly teams. He talked enthusiastically about the road and dip-building as if he was one of the shareholders in the building companies. You could pity him for expending his personal energies on projects that were so vastly remote from his personal comfort. Yet you could admire him for his selfless devotion to work that did not directly improve his way of life. He enjoyed work. The benefits of his industry were not even enough to foot the expense of his licentious life but how somehow he kept himself alive and breathing.

You could believe most of his personal accounts but it was easy to see through his exaggerations and self-glamorisations. He was always the hero who fought the lion, hauled stuck lorries out of the mud, and killed the pythons in the forest. It was he who always escaped from the jaws of the hippopotamus and the tusks of the elephant. You could listen to his accounts with curious enthusiasm, delighting in his imaginative originality, but secretly rebuking him for his exaggerations.

He had had his first job at the early age of ten. That was a herdboy to a huge herd of cattle. The herd was so large that three boys in all looked after it, but even then a few cattle managed to stray away every day. There were always buckets of milk from the cows. The boys got tired of drinking milk and longed for meat. They eventually conspired to kill a calf once in a while and keep the meat, drying it in a tree. Remoni and his mates ate till their teeth ached. The owner of the cattle assumed that the missing calves were dead or lost, till the day he caught the boys roasting meat in the forest. There followed much thrashing and weeping and all the boys lost their jobs.

At fourteen Remoni found his second job as a labourer to an agricultural demonstrator. That was when he got the opportunity to learn about fertilisers and gardening. He was held in very high esteem by his employer till the day he was caught with his employer's daughter. It was a very dark night. The two were in the mealies. They had taken off their clothes. The demonstrator saw a white shirt and pink blouse hanging on a mealie stalk. He could hear the mealies rustling and the sounds of his own daughter. He crept in dazed anger towards them. He stood like a statue, watching them. The girl did not get pregnant, but within minutes of the discovery Remoni was out of the compound with his small suitcase. The demonstrator had not even gathered enough strength to strike him.

Remoni spent the night in the bushes near the kraals. Early in the morning he was on the road to town to seek his fortune. He trudged at the roadside with his suitcase. Towards sunset when the heat and hunger had exhausted him, a car stopped to pick him up.

The car dropped him in the outskirts of the town. He clutched his suitcase and stared around him. He loitered on the pavements for a while, till hunger drove him into a café where he bought a bun. The café closed early in the evening and he had to go out. There was only one other place where he could go and that was the beer hall. But there he sat feeling very lonely in the midst of all the noise and the shouting. No one offered him a mug. The beer was expensive. Even the girls did not excite him. They threw their painted dark eyes at him, mini skirts dancing over stockinged legs, busts shaking under see-through blouses. Lipstick and wigs and high-heeled shoes scared him. He preferred the village girls. They were much less sophisticated.

Later the beerhall closed and he went out to sleep under a hedge. He woke up early the next morning to the bell of the milkman. The sun was shining and he was very unhappy.

The glare of glass and metal hurt his eyes and the smell of petrol fumes upset him. While he was wandering in the market-place he ran into a man who was recruiting volunteers for the tsetse teams. He volunteered and after two days he was on the back of a crowded tractor, snaking along the thin track of road, going further north to the villages where he had worked as a boy.

The roads and dips and wild elephants were still to come.

❦❦❦

Sometimes he came home very late in the night. Sometimes we did not hear him come. Frequently he whistled. He banged the door when he entered, and simply fell on top of his blankets, leaving the door slightly ajar. Sometimes he stripped himself so that in the morning he was completely naked on top of his blankets.

One night he came very late. It was after midnight. I woke up to the tread of his feet. Something thrashed in the bushes and moments later he burst in, breathlessly. I could almost hear the beating of his heart.

"They chased me all the way from the stream," he gasped. In the starlight coming through the doorway his face had a strange expression.

"What?" I said, rubbing my eyes.

"The things of the night chased me. The water in the stream was red as blood. I saw my image in it. Then I heard them coming at me from the reeds. I ran like a rat. They chased me right up to the water pump and only turned back at the gate."

"You saw them?"

"They looked like flying black rags. They squeaked like giant mice."

"You haven't bolted the door," I said.

"It won't make a difference, they won't come in."

"What are you doing?"

"Putting my charm in the hut. It will keep them away."

He lay on his back with his clothes on. He did not snore.

The incident did not stop him roving about at night. But from

182

that night he always wore his charm. It was a charcoal block, heavy, chipped and oily. He wore it on his breast. Nothing would hurt him as long as he wore it, he boasted.

After the ploughing came the weeding. Remoni hated weeding and openly indicated his feelings. It was woman's work, he said. Men worked with oxen and ploughs, not with hoes.

"So what work will you do in place of weeding?" mother asked him in a tone of resentment. In the ploughing weeks he had been her superior but now she was his.

Father did not receive Remoni's decision not to participate in the weeding with pleasure. Employees never decided which types of work pleased them and which did not, he complained.

"You will clear the field of the thorn trees and the bushes and the stumps," father told him sternly, when he visited us at Christmas. "And you will repair the compound and the garden fence. You will also fetch truck loads of firewood from Mbumbuzi Forest."

Remoni listened quietly, staring into the fire with the suggestion of a smirk on his lips. Later he stood with his axe on his shoulder, contemplating the girth of the trees that he was to fell. There were four thorn trees with very thick trunks and thorny branches.

"But the trees will crush the mealies," he protested lamely.

"It doesn't matter," said mother. "It will only be a few mealies."

He chopped slowly at the smallest of the trees. Every now and then he stopped to rest and to pick the chips out of the wedge with his fingers. The tree fell slowly, its trunk groaning and squeaking as the fibres of its heart snapped. It thrashed the dust, laying flat a small patch of mealies.

"I am going to sharpen my axe," said Remoni, going down to the village. It was about nine o'clock in the morning. He did not come back. He did not come home in the evening either.

We found him in the field the following morning, chopping the second tree. He did not talk to us. He left again after felling the tree.

He yoked the cattle at sunset and fetched home a cartload of firewood. The wood wasn't dry. The lichen on it was still green and you could strip ropes out of its bark. He was very silent and polite in the evening.

"So when are you going to repair the fences?" mother asked him quietly.

"As soon as I finish felling the trees," he replied.

"But you can't ever hope to do much taking one whole day to fell one tree, and working only half the morning."

"But after chopping the trees I go to chop firewood."

"Damp firewood."

"What can I do? Have you not heard that people are no longer allowed to chop firewood in Mbumbuzi Forest? Matudu had his axes confiscated by the forest-keeper last week. And besides that the cart couldn't stand the trips into Mbumbuzi. The wheels need new axles and bolts."

"But we have got to do the best we can with what we have, Remoni. I sent for spanners. Why did you not repair it?"

"I couldn't find the time."

"You obviously can't find time if you decide to spend half the working day on holiday."

"I will repair the garden fence tomorrow," he announced and left. He came home in the morning to say that his cousin had died in Goto village.

"So when are you coming back?" mother asked him.

"It depends on how it goes," he replied calmly. "A lot of our relatives are coming from far-off places to attend the funeral and it's difficult to expect an early return.

He put on his suit and went away whistling. He came back after ten days, wearing other clothes. "How was it?" asked mother.

"It was a big funeral."

"What did he die of?"

"A swollen belly. Someone poisoned him. He died after only two days. There will be trouble in the family sharing out his property. There will be trouble from the deceased. They did not bury him the right way. They put his head in the eastern end of the grave."

"How could they make such a mistake?"

"They were careless. They only realised the mistake after they had covered his grave up."

"They are courting trouble."

He sat at the table eating a mealie.

"How is the weeding going?" he asked.

"We finished with the groundnuts. You took so long to come back."

"It was a big funeral."

"Ten days?"

"But I couldn't leave before it was over."

"If we had to spend the rest of our lives attending to our dead, life would come to a standstill, wouldn't it?"

"I didn't spend a lifetime. I spent only ten days mourning my cousin."

"The rituals were over in three days."

"Three days! Maybe you Derukas can forget your dead after only three days. We locals mourn for as long as we feel like doing so. We think funerals are important."

"No wonder a lot of your people starve half their lifetimes. Never mind, what your customs are, or what you claim they are, I have got full evidence that you spent the past week in various places, and not at the funeral."

"Who told you?"

"Never mind who told me."

"Why shouldn't I travel about? Am I chained to one place like an animal?"

"No, you are not chained. And you are not an animal. But we all have to observe regulations of work. If my husband had to leave his job, as you did, without giving good reason, we'd all be starving now and there would be not a cent for your wages. My husband also works, you know."

"But I had a sound reason. A funeral —"

"The funeral took only three days, Remoni, and you can't deny that. You spent the past week on an unauthorised holiday. And besides, you had been doing nothing before you left for the funeral."

"Doing nothing?"

"Yes."

"I chopped down the thorn trees."

"If someone asked you to give an account of the work you did since Christmas you would be ashamed of yourself, Remoni."

"I chopped the trees and the firewood."

"Two trees and one cartload of firewood. Nothing more. And you worked half-days only. You worked two hours in the morning and went off for the rest of the day without telling anyone. Can you deny it?"

"But if I can do a day's work in two hours there is nothing to stop me spending the day in whatever way I like."

"You call chopping down a tree a day's work! My son Jo could do that in an hour."

"Then why did you not let him do it?"

"You refused to do the weeding, didn't you? You can't refuse the alternative. And you can't work half-days. You can't do as you like."

He put down the mealie he was eating and stared into the fire. I could see the veins sticking out in his neck. There were drops of perspiration on his forehead. Mother looked away from him, out into the night.

"You have a grudge against me, haven't you?" he said eventually.

"What!" exclaimed mother, her eyes darting back to him.

"You heard me," he replied loudly. "I said that you've a grudge against me."

"Why on earth should I have a grudge against you?"

"Since I started working here, there's not a single day that you left me alone."

"I must be deaf or you are speaking a different language," said mother, flaring her nostrils. "Talk about a grudge! And not a single day when I left you alone! What exactly do you mean, Remoni?" "Exactly what I say. You've been pushing me about. You treated me like an ox."

"You ungrateful boy!" shouted mother, angrily. "Your ingratitude shocks me! All along I've been treating you like an equal, barely knowing you could harbour such ill feelings towards me. I never knew you could be such a snake-in-the-grass, Remoni, and for no reason, too."

"I have reason enough."

"What reason? Tell me."

"I don't have to tell you, you know."

"You have got to tell me. My conscience demands it."

"You and your husband. You piled lots of work on me. Lots of useless work. Just to spite me – to keep me working like a machine, to make sure I sweated for every little cent you paid me."

"What do you mean by useless work?"

"You want me to tell you? What do you call chopping those thorn trees? Why did you not call back the man who cleared the field to come and complete his work? The trees had been standing in the field for years, waiting for Remoni, I suppose."

"The trees had to be chopped down Remoni, at one time or other. You refused to do the weeding and we had no option but to give you other work. Mark my words – you refused. Refused. Who ever heard of workers refusing to do their work and getting away with it? I did not say a word against your refusal. Did you want me to shut up for ever and leave you without any work to do? Tell me honestly."

"But the thorn trees –"

"I know they hurt. But you know they harmed the crops. Are you satisfied on that one?"

"I have other reasons," he said trying hard not to budge.

"What?"

"You don't respect me."

"What do you mean?"

"You called me a boy just now."

"How many times have I called you 'boy' before? Think honestly and tell me. I called you boy just now because you were reasoning like a boy. You showed an ingratitude which only boys can show."

"You are treating me like a boy even now."

"Because you choose to behave like a boy, Remoni. You want to pick a quarrel with me but you can't find sound excuses. I decided from the first day you came to live here that I could be nice to you and treat you like my own son. I speak from the conscience of my heart. It only hurts me to see you hurling my kindness back into my face."

"You make yourself out to be a very kind person."

"What do you want from me, Remoni? I can't stand your insults anymore."

"Nor can I yours."

"In what way was I unkind to you? Haven't I paid you twice as much as what you would normally be earning? Haven't I lent you money, never to claim it when I realised you were always in debt? Didn't I pay your wife's medical fees when she was in hospital? Didn't my husband give you clothes? Have I ever quarrelled with you before, Remoni?" He stared into the fire, battling not to let his anger melt.

"You are always praising yourself."

"You are a fool, Remoni," shouted mother, losing her patience. "A stupid fool. I wasted my time on you. Had I known what an ungrateful boy you are I would never have taken you."

He stared blankly into the fire. He had never imagined she could be so bold. "I wasted my time too," he said eventually. "I should never have come to work for you. I will leave you and see what your little compound will come to."

"You think your leaving will be an earthquake to me. That is why I said you are a boy, though you have beard on your face. Were you here to help when I built the huts? Did you till my first field? Did you contribute a cent to buy my cattle? Now how long have you been working for me? Is it not only three months? Yet you seem to think your going away will unroof my huts and crumble my walls and send the clay back to the claypits, and the poles back to the forest. No Remoni. Ten men like you would not wreck me."

I expected him to spring from his chair and strike her. I wondered what would happen if that happened. Jo and I might try to stop him, or even fight him. He was short and small. But he did not rise. He sat staring into the fire, hardly comprehending her attack. She attacked him relentlessly, with a lack of mercy that surprised me. "You were nothing when you came here, Remoni. And you are still nothing. People like you are born to own nothing of their own."

"I have my own property," he bleated lamely, falling for the trap.

"What property? You call that little suitcase property? Have you got a cow, or a goat, or a chicken, or even a rat you can call your own?"

"I have got my compound and my wife."

"Talk about your compound and your wife! Isn't it your wife who built the huts before you married her? Even the soot on the roof of the huts belongs to her, and her alone. And isn't it your father-in-law who supports your wife, while you spend your time filling yourself with beer and wasting yourself on the scum of the village girls? I pity your wife. She is a bold and resolute girl. A beautiful girl. Sometimes I am happy you couldn't give her a child."

"My affairs are none of your concern," he blurted angrily.

"You are right. Your affairs are none of my concern. I made them my concern to show you what a poor little creature you are. I was soft with you and then I realised I was wasting my patience on you. I replied to your verbal insults accordingly."

"I stop working for you tonight," he announced unceremoniously. "On Monday I am going to town to look for work."

"I wish you good luck in your quest. I hope you will keep your job if you find one –"

"Tomorrow I am coming to get my wages."

"You are coming to get what?"

"My wages."

"You got your wages for December."

"I mean, for the days I worked this month."

"But you were away on your ten-day leave. You are not getting anything for those days."

"Why?"

"Because you spent the days on an unauthorised holiday."

He grinned suddenly, and waved his hands at his ears.

"I will get that money from you. Even if it means going to the bottom of hell."

"In that case you can get your wages from the devil himself. You can go to the grave of your grandfather to get the strongest medicine he can give you and I shall not part with a cent you don't deserve. After all witchcraft has never worked on innocent people."

"You will give me my money," he said, rising. He went out into the dark and moments later we heard him digging behind our sleeping hut.

"What is he doing?"

"Probably digging up the medicine that he put behind the hut," said mother.

"He believed the things of the night were after him," I explained.

We didn't hear him pack. There was very little to pack. We only heard the squeak of his small suitcase and the click of the gate. And the quiet shuffle of his feet as he went into the night.

17

Lights

I stood at the side of the path hesitating. The thin brown dogs eyed me apprehensively. I decided they would not bite me. I proceeded slowly along the path. Behind the huts the smell of urine met my nostrils. A girl stood in front of the hut stamping mealies in a wooden mortar. Her dress kept moving up her thighs as she raised the pestle, shaking her breasts. She only saw me when I was within a few paces of her.

"Good morning'," I said, realising that she was only budding into a woman. There were balls of blanket wool on her plaited hair and white smudges on her mouth. I caught the scent of her body as I passed her. It was the smell of sleep — the smell of blankets and perspiration and virginity, I decided.

She returned my greeting briefly, her pestle still poised in midair. There were groundnut shells and dry mealie leaves on the ground. The girl was still looking at me when I turned to look back. She pounded away at her mortar uneasily.

I went into the next homestead, already regretting that I had taken a path which went right between the huts. A woman in black came out of a decorated square mud hut escorting a little boy who had just come out of the blankets. I recognised the woman as Mai Mapanga.

"Good morning," I said, sitting on my ankles. It is rude manners to stand while talking to elders. "Oh, it's you. Good morning, my son," she said in a loud voice. "I had almost forgotten you. How is your mother, Masiziva?"

"She's fine."

"You finished harvesting the mealies?"

"Not yet. We only came last week."

"You are still at school?" she said, opening her mouth in surprise. "In what grade are you now?"

"I finished with the grades," I said smiling.

"Work hard and become a teacher. The fathers in the mission school want teachers."

She wiped the boy's nose with a cloth. The boy was a strong stout fellow with a face like a bull's. Her grandson, I thought.

"I am looking for Gandanga's huts," I said, inviting her to direct me.

"Did your mother send you to collect money from him? He took two dresses from her for his wife."

"Yes."

"How much does he owe your mother?"

"I am not sure how much."

"He sold a cow two weeks ago. He should still have some money on him. That's his hut there," she said, pointing. "The one with the red door. He should be waking up now."

There were five huts in a rough circle. In the centre a group of men sat round a huge fire, talking. A few cobs were sputtering near the red-hot coals. I crouched near the assembly, waiting to be noticed.

"Her little grandson says he saw Jeni in her hut this morning," a man was saying. "The boy also says he saw a child's hand in one of her cooking pots."

"This village is turning into a nasty place," said another man, turning his cob in the fire.

"Women have to throw away the water and any left over food at night –"

"She walks at night. They say she rides on the backs of men. They caught her at the graves once —"

"She didn't have a thread on her skin."

"She claims she is only a somnambulist."

"She is the worm that has corrupted this village."

"Old Jairos refused to have her sent away from the village —"

"She being his sister of course."

"No headman can really have the power to expel villagers —"

"Many people are witches or medicine-users to some degree but witchcraft is her profession. She lives on it."

"There is also that old lady up the slope who steals the green out of people's crops by medicine."

"And the little men at night who are beating people. No one knows who sends them."

"They might be just evil spirits of long dead people who enjoy scaring people –"

"They are the spirits of our own relatives, raised and enslaved by the witches, to torment us. Haven't you seen the stickholes in the fresh graves?"

"And the plastic bags of blood and medicine which seemed to fall from the sky –"

"Only the witchfinder can sniff the witches out and beat the witchcraft out of them."

"Yes, only Chikanga, the witchfinder."

"Yes, Chikanga."

"But even witchfinders can be overcame by the power of some witches–"

"And they can be bribed."

"Not Chikanga, the famous witchfinder from the south. He lived with the maids of the river, eating mud and fish for three years. He sniffed out every hut and he beat the witches till they howled for mercy."

"At least he frightened them for a while."

"He burnt all their herbs and potions."

"But witchfinders demand bags of money."

"A goat from each man –"

"It doesn't matter. Better give away a goat than die. Better call the witchfinder."

"Yes – Chikanga."

"Chikanga from the south."

Gandanga came out of his hut. He was a huge man, and very muscular. I recognised him instantly, although I had never seen him before. Gandanga was his nickname, appropriate to his physique. He glanced uninterestedly at me and went to join the group at the fire.

"The young man came to see you, Gandanga," a man told him.

"Which young man?" said Gandanga. He raised his head and saw me. He came over and stood in front of me, his hands in his pockets.

"My mother sent me to –" I began.

"Collect her money?" he interrupted. "I don't have it."

"She –"

"I don't have it," he said firmly, imposingly, looking at the ground. "I sold a cow last week but I lent the money to a person who went on a long journey, and the person won't be returning for a long while."

I looked up at him knowing it was useless to say anything else.

"Tell her I don't have it," he said with finality, turning to go back to the fire. I got up and went home.

⚱⚱⚱

That night Jo and I sat waiting for our bath water to get hot. We had made a big fire outside the huts, in the centre of the compound clearing. Jo lay on his back near the fire, half asleep, while I sat with my hands on my toes, staring into the fire.

It was a dark night. There were no clouds and the stars seemed too remote. I looked to the north where the land sloped downwards to the stream and up again on the denuded slopes. In the south I could see the dark crust of Mbumbuzi Forest, distinct from the grey sky. In the west I could see the line of trees bordering the fields, and the grey starlight falling between the tree trunks. That was where I had buried Simba. The grass had sprouted on his grave.

The fire threw faint beams on the walls of the huts. There was silence everywhere, but it was the sort of silence you could actually detect with your ears; the low-toned shrill of the night itself, as if some sounds were being muffled. Somewhere up the village children had earlier sung and played but their voices had died away quietly.

I smashed the logs together and watched them blaze into red-hot coals. The bucket of water cried and cracked in the heat.

I took my eyes away from the flames. For a moment the landscape was one exploding heap of darkness. The crowns of trees stared down at me. I looked up at the twinkling stars. The milky way was falling to the south. A piece of star shot down from the sky and plunged down to the trees, burning itself out.

The Pendis' gate clicked.

Jairos ploughed his way in the darkness, making his usual hissing noises. He stopped in the middle of the clearing, turned, and came to the fence. He was a moving shape in the darkness and I recognised him because it was only he who moved like that.

"Godi!" he shouted, his voice strangely sane in the night. "Give me a stick of fire, please. I want to light my cigarette."

I took a stick of fire and went to the fence. I could see his eyes gleaming in the darkness. He snatched the stick over the fence and put it to his mouth, as I turned to go back to our fire.

He steadied his hand but the red point of fire shook visibly. He cursed, put the stick down and rolled his cigarette again. He was about to pick the stick up again when he stopped. He stood still, looking to the west and gasped.

I raised my head and looked to the west. Out of the fields a man was walking with a paraffin lamp. The light was very bright orange and concentrated to a small ball. It did not throw any beams and shadows. It seemed to cut right across the tree trunks, as if the trees and the open dark air were made of one substance. It moved very steadily, darting from one direction to the next, now fast, now slow. It came down from the fields, cutting through the darkness as if making towards Simba's grave. Somewhere near the fence it went out.

Jairos gasped again, threw the stick down and went away, his cigarette lighted. Jo woke up. I put my fingers gingerly into the water.

"Is the water hot now?" he asked.

"Obviously," I replied cuttingly.

He raised his head and saw the light. I followed his eyes. The light was shining again, this time moving steadily into the forest till it seemed to sink into the dark solid horizon. I was not even afraid. I could not tell how far away the light was. As long as I saw the light I was not afraid but after it went out I peered uneasily into the darkness, searching for it everywhere, expecting it to burst into view anywhere without warning.

I saw Jo looking into the darkness too. We did not talk about it. I fumbled for the soap and the towels.

I knew now that the light was not a paraffin lamp.

ele ele ele

We did not tell mother about it. We did not even talk about it ourselves. On several nights I would stand in the doorway of the hut staring into the fields, searching for the light among the trees. If the moon was shining the light seldom showed. Sometimes for days I saw nothing and sometimes there were two or three lights moving at random.

Mother never confessed to having seen anything, although I suspected she probably kept her secret observations to herself, fearing to scare us if she told us. But whenever we talked about witchcraft she repeated her unshakable belief that witchcraft never worked on those who did not believe in it.

"Only those people with charms to keep off spirits will indeed see the spirits. I have never used any charms to keep off spirits in my homestead yet I have never seen anything unusual. Other people talk about owls on roof tops, strange footsteps on the sand, strange residues on plates and pots in the morning, things I have yet to see. Ghosts and spirits are there but do not work at random. They work on people who believe in them."

I listened to her, wondering if I should let her beliefs reassure me. Perhaps she too had her secret fears. Why should the things hit Midu if they only attacked superstitious people? He was only a boy.

How naive I had been to believe that there were no ghosts or witches in the village! Perhaps at one time they had never been there, that was perhaps the time when we made trips to the bus station in the middle of the night. Perhaps there had been less sightings because the village population was then still small. It took years before the true personalities of the villagers fully emerged.

It did not matter who caused the nocturnal disturbances. Witchcraft did not choose between the locals and the Derukas. The hard fact was that something was happening in the village. One could not disbelieve everything.

❀ ❀ ❀

The news that the witchfinder was coming to "sniff out" the village steadily gained ground. He was well known throughout the country. I wondered if I should take his coming as a consolation.

"I saw him once," mother explained, "but it was only for a short time. You would never believe that he is a witchfinder. He is a very affluent man. He wears expensive suits, drives his own Combi and employs several girls to help him. People say he lived with the mermaids under the great river. They taught him everything from rain-making to witch-finding."

Headman Simon went round the village collecting contributions to hire Chikanga to clean out the village.

"Are children supposed to come too?" mother asked.

"Only the older children," said Simon. That included me and left out Jo.

There was varied response to Simon's call for contributions.

"Chikanga is charging too much."

"Chikanga could be bribed."

"Chikanga will create hatred between families."

But Chikanga was coming.

18

Chikanga

The chief's compound was a big one as polygamists' compounds usually are. There were twelve huts and twelve granaries for his twelve wives. By midmorning, when we arrived, tired from the twelve mile walk in the heat, the place was already swarming with people. Men and women sat together, men on stools and women on mats. There was a buzzing chatter which increased in volume with the passage of time and the growing anticipation of Chikanga.

Around noon a sudden hush descended on the gathering. All heads were twisted to the road as a battered looking Combi squeaked to a halt just behind the gathering. A wiry brown man in a black suit jumped energetically out of the driver's cabin and walked towards the crowd. Six young girls climbed out of the back of the van and followed the man to the centre of the gathering.

In the crowd faces grinned and faces wilted. People sprang up to see, others jeered those who rose, and shouted them down. A woman ululated. The wavering crowd gradually gathered into a loud clapping of hands.

Chikanga picked his way through the seated crowd like a master-farmer walking through a crop of mealies. He turned his snaky head from side to side assessing the crowd like a farmer making a preliminary survey of the true crops and the weeds.

The crowd edged outwards to open a space for him in the centre. He sat like a king, with his pretty teenage girls flanking him on mats.

198

He looked a very ordinary man. You could almost think he had sly looks. The only hints of his profession were the inches of black and red bangles on his wrists and the necklace on his breast. The necklace was a piece of wood shaped like a nut. It was brown and shiny and oily.

He sat on his high stool arranging his gourds and calabashes. He took off his shirt and rubbed his chest with oil. He took off his shoes, rolled his trousers to the knees and oiled his legs as well. His girls rubbed oil on their faces and arms.

The girls finished oiling themselves, rose up and made their way through the seated crowd. They disappeared into a clump of trees and emerged later with thick green sticks. The crowd gasped and whistled on seeing and guessing the purpose of the sticks.

"You brought building poles, not whips, girls," said a woman.

"Your poles will kill people, not discipline them," added a man, and the crowd laughed.

"Witches!" burst out Chikanga, gesticulating violently as he jumped from his stool, instantly stilling the crowds. "Sorcerers! Magicians! Eaters of human flesh! Today we will beat your witchcraft out of you. We will burn all your herbs and poisons and make you eat some of them. We will beat every finger of your skin till the whips are torn to shreds. Today we will teach you to live without the smell of human blood in your nostrils. We will teach you to shun your craft. Girls, my tools."

The girls lifted his things from the suitcase – among them a huge looking-glass, a bottle of water and a calabash with a black cork. The crowd started murmuring again.

"Do I hear voices?" said Chikanga authoritatively, scanning the people on his flanks. "Do I hear murmurings of fear? You don't have to display your fear now."

The crowd shut up. Faces gazed in fear at him, lips half open with frozen words.

"This is the mirror in which I will see into the characters of people," he explained, raising his instruments. "This is my water. Each one of you will touch the bottle. Whoever touches my bottle and turns the water red is a deadly killer, an eater of human flesh. Whoever turns the water brown or grey is a mild offender, but a dangerous person all the same. Whoever touches the bottle and leaves my water as it is, is as innocent as a baby. Before I start, let me make it clear to those people with black hearts that any attempts to injure me or my girls will only harm the offenders themselves. I shall sniff out all the twists of poison and roots hidden even in the most remote corners of the village. The offenders themselves will be beaten thoroughly before they are sent to the hut of the witches for cleansing. Anyone who tries to use medicines again after today will die of a strange sickness. The chief has given me the names of all the villagers so no one can escape. I shall begin."

The first woman to be called was from Goto village. She rose slowly and stood beside Chikanga.

"Touch my water," he told her. She put her finger on the bottle. "Touch it with all your fingers," shouted Chikanga. "What is it you have under your other fingernails that makes them shun the bottle?" The woman put all her fingers on the bottle. I could see her fingers shaking. Her eyes were glued to the bottle.

"I can see into your character," said Chikanga, looking into his mirror. "You are not an evil person. You are not a witch and you have never tasted the human flesh. You don't walk at night and you don't spin stickholes in fresh graves. You are not evil. But your spirit is weak to the forces of evil."

The woman trembled. The water had not changed its colour.

"Your spirit is weak. Strengthen it. My calabash tells me you don't have a child. Is that true or not? Answer me."

"It is true, my king. I have no child," replied the woman, trembling.

"You don't have a child because you refused to inherit the witchcraft of your dead grandmother. You disappointed her. She punished you by shutting your womb forever. For years now you have been visiting village doctors to ask why you have no child. Is that true or not?"

"It is true, my lord."

"You were unwise to refuse to bring home your grandmother from the grave. But you were wise to refuse her witchcraft. Your wisdom is greater than your folly." He raised the bottle up to the sun and looked through it. "You did not change the colour of my water. I dismiss you."

There was a split second of silence before the crowds burst into fervid ululation and congratulatory grunts. The woman's face broke into a disbelieving smile. She cupped her hands and ululated, sketching a short, impromptu dance with her legs. The crowd laughed at her joy.

The next person was a young man, newly married. He put his fingers on the bottle before Chikanga told him to do so.

"What!" exclaimed Chikanga, flaring his nostrils. "Have I told you to touch my water yet? You want to elude me with speed. My mirror tells me you steal other people's crops by magic. You are young, yet you are lazy. You never make use of the first rains. You prefer to transfer the greenness of other people's crops to your own poor ones. Fortunately your herbs have never worked. But had you found the effective herbs you would have ruined your neighbours. You are guilty of the will to swindle your neighbours by magic. Look! You changed the colour of my water."

There were gasps of surprise when Chikanga raised his bottle. We did not have to strain our eyes to see the muddy grey tint in the water.

"Grey water. Where do you keep your herbs?"

"I know no herbs," replied the young man.

"You lie too. You lie to Chikanga. You keep your herb in your sleeping hut, don't you? Brown powder in a piece of cloth. Your wife thinks it's the herb for pnuemonia. Have I lied?"

The young man lowered his eyes and crushed his knuckles uneasily. He mumbled something.

"Tell the gathering where you keep your herbs. Loudly," said Chikanga.

"In my sleeping hut," shouted the young man, looking up only long enough to say so.

"And you spray the powder over your neighbours' green fields?"

"Yes."

There was a loud clicking of angry tongues from the crowd.

"When do you work?" pursued Chikanga.

"At night," replied the young man, shamelessly.

"You are a lazy fool. Go home and eat every grain of your herb. Every grain of it, I say. It's your fault if the herb cuts your bowels. And tell the crowd you will never do it again."

"I will never do it again," shouted the young man, not daring to look up. He took a step backwards as if he wanted to go back to his place in the crowd.

"A! A!" shouted Chikanga. "Where are you going? Who said it's over? Have I dismissed you? You haven't received your punishment yet. Teach him, my girls."

The pretty young girls rose from the mats with their green sticks. They surrounded the young man. He inched backwards uneasily, his fingers twitching at his side, face torn between a grin and a grimace. The girls thrashed him quickly. I could hear the crunching sound of thick green sticks against his bones. They beat him till he screamed like a child, and left him moaning on the dust.

"Up!" commanded Chikanga. He scrambled onto his unsteady feet, fingering his badly bruised face.

"To the hut of the guilty," Chikanga beckoned.

The young man limped away painfully. No one helped him. Chikanga put fresh water in his bottle.

Two other people from Goto village were found guilty and were beaten and sent to the hut of the guilty.

Mother came fifth in our village.

"My mirror tells me many things about you," Chikanga told her. I looked at my mother. My mind ran unconsciously to her folk-story of the belated hunter with the black and white dogs. For the first time in my life I felt really anxious for her.

"You are an unusual woman," Chikanga told her. "Have you ever wondered why the little men never hit any of your children? They came very close to your compound on several occasions. Once they even beat a nextdoor boy, did they not? They chased a man who worked for you right to your gates. Have you ever wondered why none of your children got bitten by snakes, or poisoned by mushrooms, or died of strange diseases? I see a deadly snake that came to your homestead years ago. An ugly black snake with a mane and black scales. It smells. The snake was meant to bite one of your children. I also see two cursed birds, that lodged in a tree near your fence. Did the rainmaker not send for the birds and order them to be destroyed? You were lucky. Had the matter been pursued you would have been accused of stopping the rain from falling because the birds lodged right next to your compound. You could have been sent away from the village. But you were not banished. You lived among enemies, some of whom have been working, since you planted the first pole of your hut, to bring harm to you. Yet you are safe. You have reaped fair crops in lean years. You even sell maize to your fellow villagers. Do you believe it's your wisdom which has kept you safe and well-off? Answer me."

"No," replied mother.

"Then what is it? Do you own little men to weed your fields and ward off strangers at night?"

"No."

"Do you use herbs to steal other people's crops?"

"No."

"Then what do you use?"

"Nothing."

"Yes. You use nothing. There is not a twist of herbs in your huts, no nails in your trees to keep the lightning away, not even a single root to protect your homestead. Perhaps you do not know it but the spirit of your father protects you. Tell me. What was your father's death wish? Did he not ask you to do something for him?"

"He asked me to remove a speck in his eye."

"You did not find that speck. But that was an indication of the favour he bore for you. Never fool yourself that your own wisdom has kept you safe. No one is safe from witchcraft and medicine, even the innocent. You may go to church but you must never foresake your deceased father. Never, never, ever. I don't have to hold my bottle of water up to see if you have changed its colour. My mirror alone has spoken for you. I congratulate you and dismiss you."

She smiled, turned and went back to her place. There was loud ululation for her. I stood up and waved my fists in the air.

Munyu came next and was beaten and sent away for plotting to cripple Madoo by magic. Madoo himself very narrowy escaped the whips but was very sharply rebuked for being a bad neighbour and a loose-tongued brawler. Charamba and his wife were both thrashed and sent away for first-rate witchcraft. Both of them admitted to having mutually poisoned to death their neighbour's son.

Makepesi came after them. He took off his cap and put it under his armpit. Chikanga uttered a long whistle and shook his head reflectively over his mirror.

"Who taught you to love the smell of human blood, my son?" he asked him. "You still have your mother's milk on your nose, yet you are the son of the devil himself. Have you ever spent a single full night in your sleep hut? I doubt. Even the owls of the night know you. You are the living cousin of the ghosts whose lights shine in the night and blind the eyes of the innocent. How many stickholes have you spun in the graves? How much hair have you cut from the heads of people while they slept? Tell me, son, where do you keep the horn of your witchcraft?"

Makepesi stared at the ground, his fist on his chin.

"You cut the hair from the head of your own sister's son, to use for your potions. What did you do to Jairos? Did you set a trap for him on the path or did you send your little men to beat him? Did you poison his mug of beer? Tell us why you did what you did to Jairos."

"He gave my field to a newcomer," said Makepesi, momentarily raising his head.

"And you thought that was enough reason to turn him insane? You turned him into an animal. Have you ever listened to his hiss and to his mutterings. Why did you not kill him, instead of turning him into an animal?"

Makepesi did not move his eyes. He clasped his cap waiting for the girls to beat him. The girls cut him down with their sticks. He did not utter a sound. He lay still on the ground, taking their blows without any protest, like a person who knew very well why he was being punished.

Mai Mapanga came towards sunset, after dozens of people had

been sent to the hut to bath in Chikanga's water. She still wore a black mourning dress. Her husband had not been dead for a year yet. She approached Chikanga very slowly, her eyes encircling him desperately. Chikanga's mirror fell from his hand. A bright beam of sunlight shot from it like an exploding bullet. There was dead silence and the black figure of Mai Mapanga stood trembling, staring at the mirror in the dust.

"Her evil overpowers my mirror," said Chikanga, stooping to pick the mirror up. "Even I am afraid of your powers. If you touch my water you will turn it to blood. Put your fingers on my bottle."

"I will not," whispered Mai Mapanga. Those who heard her, laughed.

"Why will you not touch my bottle? You very well know that you will turn the water into blood."

"No, I will not."

"Then touch my bottle like everybody else."

"I won't be made a fool in front of everyone," she said boldly, loudly.

"You are too evil to be regarded as a mere fool. Touch my bottle."

He took her fingers and touched the bottle with them. She tried to pull away but the water had turned already to red. An opaque, flowing mass of red. Everyone saw it. Mai Mapanga threw her head back and cried. Chikanga dropped her hand and she stumbled backwards. She put her face in her palms, covering her eyes and cried.

"You ate human flesh."

"I didn't know it was human flesh," she protested in a hoarse, sobbing voice. "One side of it was goat's meat and the other was a type of meat I didn't know."

"Then why did you eat the flesh?"

"I didn't know."

"You knew. It was the flesh of your own sister's son. He didn't have his tongue when they buried him. You had eaten it."

"No."

"You woke up in the night to dig him up. You ate his heart and his liver."

"No, I didn't."

"Yes, you did. Your hunger for human flesh did not subside. You killed your husband too. You poisoned him. You fed your little men on human flesh and they grew fat on it. As long as you kept your little men fed there was no trouble. But there were never enough corpses, and then trouble started. They refused to do your errands and threatened to eat you. You had to act fast. So you poisoned your husband. He died after only two days. When he died you wanted to eat his flesh too. But your little men beat you to his corpse. You found only bare bones when you dug him up –"

"He died a natural death–"

"A natural death you call it? With his stomach swollen like that. And after only two days. The stinging hunger drove you into despair. You did worse things. You chose poor Jeni, that pretty, hardworking daughter of your neighbour. Her flesh was young and soft. You drove worms into her breasts; it did not take her long to die. But they let her body decompose before they buried it. For days they lived with the stench of her body. For three days after they buried her they guarded her grave. They starved you. Your little men pressed you for meat but you could not give them anything. You had failed."

She cried.

"I pity you," pursued Chikanga. "I pity you very much. Your own little men you raised from the graves are driving you insane, and threatening to kill your grandson. You taught them to eat human flesh. They loved it, but now you can't supply them with flesh anymore. I pity you because you are your little men's next victim. They will tear you like cats tearing a bird and people won't even find your skull. Your bones will be scattered all over the forest. . . "

"No!" cried Mai Mapanga, her eyes wild with fear.

"Where do you keep your little men, Mai Mapanga?" he asked softly. "Bring them out and we will thrash them like we thrash corn. Where do you keep them? In your grainhut? In your sleeping hut?"

She cried and people did not laugh. They clicked their tongues softly and shook their heads.

"Tell us, Mai Mapanga," said Chikanga.

"In a sack in my grainhut," she sobbed, and then cried even more loudly, wringing her hands.

"We will destroy them, Mai Mapanga. I am glad you now realise that witchcraft does not pay. Witchcraft is the cub that grows up to tear the limbs of his master. I will help you to destroy them for ever."

She screamed when she saw the girls coming for her with the green sticks. She darted this way and that with her arms spread out like a bat. They closed on her, cutting her down mercilessly, tearing her black dress to expose her withered black breasts. She howled like a dog and yet fell down lightly like a bat. People thought she was dead.

"People like her don't die," said Chikanga. "She has just fainted. Take her away."

The girls took her by the limbs and carried her to the hut of the witches. Her eyes were open and solid as brown marble. There was white froth on her lips.

19

Rain

Six months after Chikanga had passed his judgement on the village and gathered and burnt all the herb, potions and sacks in a bonfire, the rains came.

People came out to till their fields again. They bought fertiliser and seed from the Grain Marketing Board and turned the crisp green weeds into the brown earth.

The sky seemed to promise the village a fresh start, but the rains came with lightning, and several trees were hit in the forest. With the rain, too, came overcast days and mouldy earth.

Jairos was caught many times on the paths by the storm, and drenched. In his terrible quest, he never stayed indoors long enough to dry his clothes at the fire. Even at night, we could hear his sandals swooshing on the wet sand. His weather-beaten body could not take it any more. Skin started peeling off his face and legs, and he grew surprisingly silent, so that when he came to our hut, he sat quietly at the fire, not even asking for food. There was a strange new sobriety in his eyes.

Two weeks before Christmas he fell violently ill. He was taken to the hospital, but the doctors were baffled. They knew that the rain had sparked off the illness, but what it was, they never understood. All they could say was that his body had been breaking down over the years. He died after only a week in hospital and there was no one to bring him home. For a week he lay in the mortuary. Eventually, an ambulance brought his body home.

There was loud weeping in the village. I could hear Lulu's voice weeping above that of her aunt, Mai Mapanga. "The Derukas have killed our father. He died giving them land. Now they can have his body as well."

Makepesi cried with the others. "You have come, Jairos," he remarked laconically, "I was expecting you."

They buried him in the pouring rain on the day before Christmas. He had delayed the Christmas preparations. They did not even have a coffin for him. They just wrapped him, small and bony as an unfeathered chick, in a blanket and put him down to rest.

When they laid him in the grave Lulu rolled on the wet sand. Her mother and Mai Mapanga pulled her up and struggled with her. She wore a black dress, and her head was shaven in sorrow. There were deep shadows over her eyes but her face had a haunting kind of beauty which frightened me. As they led her away I thought of the day when I had made Jairos a cup of cold tea and forked a bun out of the pan and told him I had no shilling for him to give at the funeral. With a shudder I realised that all along Lulu had been deeply caught in the web of sorrow.

As they shovelled the glistening wet sand over him, the rain intensified. Everywhere the trees and the grass were dripping rain. A drop of water snaked down my back and I tried to curl my sandalled toes away from the mouldy green earth. One more shovel of wet sand, and Jairos was gone. He had come and gone. Like Cheru and Boyce and Remoni and Lulu. No one, nothing, came and stayed. Each had promised a fresh start but the many callings of life had torn them away from us. All that remained were the memories, and now the anxiety and the fear.

The gathering had just begun to disperse but now people stood half-frozen in their steps, staring at the newly erected mound of the grave. A strange silence had descended in the rain. I edged back towards the crowd. Men and women hunched their shoulders against the rain, lips open, pink tongues softly sucking in droplets of rain.

There was something on the mound of the grave, a plastic bag with something red in it that no one dared to touch or describe. One by one they turned, in mute surprise, to go home to prepare for Christmas. And I too turned and went home in the rain.

Printed in the United States
By Bookmasters